WEED  WINE
MAGIC

WEED WINE MAGIC

A Freaky California Cannabis Country Chiller

STEVE CORBETT

Cover art by James Callahan for Camp Rattler Media
Cover model: Kristin Callahan

ISBN 978-1-936936-17-5
Copyright ©2025 by Steve Corbett

Again, as always, for Stephanie

 ## SCORPIONS ROCK

DEEP into Sonoran Desert sand beyond the Nogales border I'm belting out lyrics to my favorite Mexican death metal song "Chain Saw Taco" when a sizzling white-hot rocket-propelled grenade launches out of nowhere, slamming into the trunk of my flat-black 1963 Lincoln Continental complete with suicide doors.

Shearing the back half of the customized lowrider with fire-fueled impact scalding enough to melt the skull-shaped silver door handles, the blast blows me and Tripper south of the disorder, sending us airborne from my ride's blood red leather bucket seats. We hit the ground stunned but rolling hard, rising and running for cover like ninja movie action heroes.

My pet scorpion, Regalo, skitters through brown ground dirt, leaving an agitated trail no attacker in his right mind wants to follow. Tripper and I are bad enough when we're angry, but a scorpion with a chip on its stinger will tear you up.

Unarmed I take cover behind a rickety Tecate billboard. Sliding like a flashy Los Angeles Dodgers third base stealer, Tripper dives face forward into the shadow of the beer advertisement. I could definitely use a drink.

"That RPG should have turned us into carnitas," I whisper through dusty grit in my front teeth.

"Little meats" wrapped in soft flour tortillas is the best English translation I know for my favorite comfort food. Violence makes me hungry. Assassins want to turn us into rare grilled meat, but other than my sainted mother, who knows we're heading to honeymoon in Culiacàn, Mexico? Who knows I got a job waiting as a crusading newspaper columnist? Who knows I'm coming to spread truth and light on the frontier? Who knows I'm on a mission to take down the cartels?

Loud buzzing noise in the distance catches my attention, popping like high-powered electric lines exploding and going haywire. The droning din moves closer paired with a tornado-shaped dark cloud that accompanies a high-intensity whine screaming, whirring and stinging in my ears even from far away.

"You hear that?" I say.

"You see that?" Tripper says.

The funnel cloud gets closer, thicker, blacker, hovering over the potholed dirt and asphalt intersection by the dilapidated cantina where a 2024 $106,000 black Ford F-150 Raptor R pickup complete with emerald green cash-colored painted flames on the doors and roof, tinted bulletproof windows and bulletproof body armor sits idling, shuddering like a wild beast in heat.

Two round soccer ball size rubber globes meant to resemble testicles hang from the transmission beneath the truck, dangling like giant bull's balls meant to bounce with each bump in the road.

I catch a glimpse of the driver, my Uncle Arturo, who leads a crew of renegade soldiers who recently broke from the powerful Sinaloa cartel that fights to control all of Mexico.

Arturo wants more.

Arturo always wants more.

One cool commando jogs to the passenger side of the Ford Raptor and covers Uncle Arturo, the eldest brother of my mother, Zita, and new boss of the breakaway cartel he created to totally control the drug trade based in drunken machismo, deadly recklessness and the promise of an early grave.

Arturo carries a 24-carat gold plated AK-47. Around his neck Arturo wears a square 24-carat medallion about the size of a playing card emblazoned with the stern image of the Mexican Robin Hood and underground saint Jesús Malverde. Arturo's boots are hand-tooled, fresh leather crafted from brown human skin, the tanned bounty of a once great personal rival who recently stopped kicking.

"Shit," I say.

"You know him?" Tripper says.

"Satan," I say.

Three heavily armed bandits dressed in the same digital pattern camouflage the Mexican Marines use - black, rust and olive green pixelated shapes on a pale green background - leap from a tan tarp-covered truck. Bug-eyed and flushed, probably hopped up on methamphetamine, they randomly open fire in all directions.

I look to the swarming darkness that begins to descend and see them - bees, thousands of bees flying in a tightly-knit cyclone of terror. At first I think of hornets and wasps, as written in the Popul Voh, the creation storybook of the Kiche Maya people my mother told me about when I was young and she related tales from her mother's Maya family history. When the enemy appeared in ancient times Maya warriors filled gourds with hornets they threw into the midst of the attackers. The hornets exploded from the gourds and bombarded the invaders. The Maya won.

Bees cover Arturo like a full fur coat from the top of his head to the tips of his flesh-covered boots, undulating in a living, moving pelt that wraps him in thickening layers of honey bees, tens of thousands of honey bees now expanding their reach to his men.

Screams wail like air raid sirens. Guns drop in the dust. Arms flap until no more flaps exist in frozen muscles stung into immobility. Bodies twitch in red dirt as nerves flicker like crimson cemetery candles caught in the wind on a stormy morning.

As quickly as they came the bees lift off, taking to the sky where they fly higher and higher toward the sun until they disappear as if they never descended from the heavens to make short work of their victims on the ground. Skin bubbles with blisters so swollen the professional executioners' hands, wrists, fingers and faces look like balloon figures ready to burst and take to the sky for a holiday parade.

"The bees should have died," I say. "Honey bees lose their stingers and their innards when they strike. They always die."

"No lack of guts in that gang," Tripper says.

"They're all female," I say. "Only female honey bees sting."

"You go girls," Tripper says.

"Sick," I say with a grin.

"Looks like your mom casting another nasty witchcraft spell to save her little boy," Tripper says. "Or global warming ransacking the poor bees' systems they don't know they're bees anymore."

"Or both," I say. "Big brother Arturo served as my mother's protector when they were young."

"But you're her only son, Jesús. She must have known Arturo turned on you. Now she protects you."

"So does Jesús Malverde," I say.

Tripper nods, not yet knowing the deadly significance of my coming out as the sacred Mexican legend's great-grandson, sole heir to the legendary myth, the great robber saint who protects the peasants, the sick, the poor and others in need. For whatever his reasons Malverde sometimes protects the cartel masters, too.

Even I'm not sure how competing bosses throughout Mexico will accept me taking back Malverde's name after they hijacked his image to justify narco-trafficker evil. I doubt they will do as I urge them to do, to turn their evil ways into something better than a classic rock Santana song to be played at drunken fiestas to celebrate another grisly murder of a competing drug gang boss.

I am not the Mexican American Robin Hood. I must remain my own man, a man of the people who can only do so much to change the world, but a man who, nevertheless, must try.

"I'm really too old for this shit," I say.

Tripper grins.

"How old are you, 45?"

"Like the caliber pistol?"

"No," she says. "Like my favorite malt liquor."

Trying to lighten up and catch my breath watching five failed terminators litter the ground, I give Tripper a rare sweet look. She picks up on my sugary vibe. I'm good under pressure and like to tease. Tripper doesn't play.

Reading my mind she says, "I know what you're thinking. Don't you dare call me honey."

"Run for the truck," I say.

Regalo is already moving into the Raptor. After sniffing around, angry in the way only cannibal, night-fighter scorpions understand, the ancient arachnid stops briefly to urinate on Arturo's bloated remains. This debasement seems only proper, only fitting, for the punishment fits the crime.

The keys dangle from the ignition as we roar deeper into Mexico from the fresh border carnage followed by a bird gliding on brisk winds from the southwest.

"Falco mexicanus," the prairie falcon, rides the air currents with dignity and ease. Desolate plains and desert wilderness appeal to his comfort level, preferring to take it easy in his quest for survival although he enjoys the occasional close-to-the-ground attack, flying in fast and low, taking his quarry by surprise. Sometimes he climbs high into the sky and plummets like a dive-bomber. Sometimes he hunts song birds in midair, abruptly stifling their melodious tunes as he snags them by the throat.

Arturo, the runaway drug savior now curled stung and dying in a fetal position on the ground, had no clue. Before the bee attack, Arturo, fashionable in a sleek purple double-breasted linen business suit, removed his Italian Arnette sunglasses, cleaned them with the end of his yellow silk necktie decorated with tiny blue agave cacti and replaced them snug over his eyes. Pulling a silver case from his pocket, he removed a fat rolled joint and clamped the doobie between his teeth. Lighting a match to the reefer tip he inhaled deeply and tossed the match aside. Before the stick hit the ground the bees hit his face and body.

Still barely alive and jerking with involuntary spasms, Arturo senses a falling shadow as the falcon swoops. Landing on his prey's head as the body wriggles in the dirt, the bird snags Arturo's left eyeball on a jagged claw tip. Real raptor rapture in motion results in calculated instinctive frenzy. Now the bird digs in, dislodging both eyeballs as the creature shakes the victim's head from side to side in a steely grip. Blood spurts from a deep open wound in Arturo's throat where the falcon bites deep and hard, tearing flesh and leaving its mark.

A prairie falcon attack on a human is rare but occasionally happens. Maybe chemically polluted air caused confusion in the bird's brain. Maybe he mistook the louse for a fat mouse. Perhaps the bird was driven by a higher spiritual power beyond his control. Lifting off, the falcon carries Arturo's eyeballs aloft. Mucus drips from the small globs until sunshine swallows any and all traces of the attacker.

The bird follows Jesús and Tripper as they flee in the sleek pickup truck, disappearing into the bright horizon as a small silver peace sign hanging from the falcon's neck by a thin silver chain sparkles spectacularly in the sun.

DUNE FEAST

FURRY and furious, moving through cold blue dawn, a silver male coyote shimmers almost invisible against the rugged California Central Coast landscape of majestic brown Oceano dunes. By his side the black female coyote moves as the darkest shadow, nimble and primitive. Three gray coyote cubs trail their parents, young hunters becoming increasingly more aware of their surroundings, bouncing on soft paw pads, playing and nipping at each other's heels as they make their way through tan sand mountains.

The predator family long ago left the pack. Now they descend as a tight team, mother and father in front, pups flanked to both sides. Eighteen hours earlier the family last dined on a skinny gray fox Alpha Dad, a better hunter especially when starving, chased down and killed.

Alpha Mom dug in first, tearing the carrion flesh before leading her pups to their reward. Sparkling dark blood dripping from her white teeth showed the simple savage reality of the hunt, the kill and the feast. Before eating the fox remains, the family's last meal had occurred two days earlier when they dined on two American bullfrogs, a Southern Alligator Lizard and a nest full of tiny snowy plover eggs. Since then nothing had crossed their path to kill and devour.

Alpha Dad carries his nose high, with a raw primordial edge pulsing through tightening veins, geared toward catching the smallest scent floating on warm wind that will lead him to his prey. Alpha Mom seems edgier, her steady gait more agitated than usual. Cubs usually take living for granted, until they don't. Today they seem sullen, hungrier than usual.

Alpha Dad's ears rise.

Alpha Mom moves closer to the pups, her gold eyes focused on their every move. But even the young stop when the human singing voice comes from near the sea, intermingled with soft sounds of morning ocean waves lapping the shore. The coyotes slow their pace. The alpha pair recognizes the danger and opportunity that rarely come at the same time, but when they do, how the nexus can warn of death.

Above all, her family must survive.

Nosing the cubs closer together, Alpha Mom covers the rear. Alpha Dad runs ahead to the highest sand dune overlooking the beach. The pitch grows louder in his ears, agitating and tempting him to move before he is ready. Just before a fine pink dawn breaks the woman hangs wash from a line she strung between two scratched and dented campers pulled by two even more beat-up SUVs, one flying a "Don't Tread On Me" flag, the other a Civil War-era Confederate Stars and Bars battle banner.

Still wired from a long night snorting a half dozen short white lines of homemade methamphetamine, the woman's oily, ratty hair hangs below her bony freckled shoulders as she rolls up the sleeves of the orange and black flannel shirt she wears over a flimsy black nightgown and scuffed brown work boots into which she's shoved splay-toed dirty bare feet. Hanging threadbare bikini briefs from the makeshift clothesline, she spits a few times into the sand as if she's trying to remove a bad taste and a worse memory from her mouth that now holds a lit Spittle filter cigarette, the brand she's smoked for 12 years ever since she was 12.

Coyotes do not normally attack humans, usually shying away from major confrontation that's often more trouble than it's worth. Attacking a human is far different from attacking a fawn that stumbled away from its mother between the broccoli fields and the tree line leading to the dunes. Coyotes sense the lethal human potential. But sometimes hunger, sickness, or protective instinct drives even a young coyote to take uncertainty by the throat and try to bring it down.

Alpha Dad had mostly digested the rabid fox the family shared for dinner and needed more meat. By now his brain misfired on poison, sending mixed signals that caused him to stop every mile or so and vomit along the dry riverbank. Alpha Mom also retched from eating the rabid fox. The pups were not yet worse for the wear, attacking and eating a small Ringneck snake they rousted from the underbrush as they kept their eyes on their parents and the chance for another meal.

Laying back his ears, Alpha Dad begins to stalk about 100 yards out, getting as close as he can before breaking from cover and closing the distance on his quarry. Killing usually comes easy because the vulnerable rarely fight back. Rodents and small game mostly just die. Humans can go either way or both, fighting viciously before giving up and succumbing to the realization that death's grip is moments away and the best way to ease the pain and fly to the afterlife is on the wings of calm peace. Serenity is difficult to attain with your throat opened up, but regular churchgoers swear faith works wonders. Silent pups sense a payday as Alpha Dad stands ready to move, to race to the target and strike. The family advances slowly.

Singing country song lyrics about a trailer park girl feeling shame because she's built like an outhouse, Abigale feels a cool breeze raise thin ends of her ginger locks, sending wispy strands across her flat broken but healed nose. In the middle of attaching a wooden clothespin to a faded leopard-spotted thong, she quickly brushes hair from her eyes. Now she senses the threat. After surviving and escaping Bakersfield and its perilous working-class whiteness, she possesses premonition-like intuition that has saved her in the past. Judging from the coyote's speed, she knows she can't make the rusted camper door.

Alpha Dad has her just where he wants her. The impact of his body slamming at full speed into hers knocks the woman face forward into the sand. Tan flesh on the back of her left thigh goes first, opened above the knee with the sharpest teeth, clenching and locking with jaws powerful enough to bite through a cat backbone in about seven chomps. The animal hits her hardest on his first chaw, cutting through muscle and flesh, gnawing through hamstrings. Crushing through fatty tissue on the second bite, he tears more flesh, shaking his head from side to side, chewing and biting and chewing some more.

Alpha Mom pulls up strong and stable on the other side of the thin woman's body as she screams and tries to rise. Alpha Dad hits her rear right leg, ripping tendons, hitting gristle, relentless in his carnivorous longing. Losing blood fast, panic takes over and shock sets in as the woman knows she has nowhere to go. The frenzied alpha pair strikes her buttocks, shredding nerves in her waist. Blood flies in focused fury when both beasts destroy smooth flesh and move on to another chunk of meat.

Dragging and shaking her body about 10 feet, Alpha Dad digs in again, this time tearing into the left shoulder and pulling at his prey. Alpha Mom's nose violently burrows into the abdomen as the creature snaps its jaws, jerking at a thick piece of today's fleshy feast. Berserk pups descend from the left and right, clumsily running into each other but awkwardly getting the job done, helping to mangle nature's target whose corpse lies hot and steaming in the rising morning sand. Imitating their predator parents, three small but mighty coyotes fight and whimper among themselves as they eat their fill and eventually lose interest and appetite.

Passing out before passing away, the once carefree dune camper lay mutilated, a sliver of her cheap wedding band drenched in blood catching a ray of California sunshine, offering a last ray of life in this raw western part of the American scream. Licking his paws, Alpha Dad reclines by the body and yawns. Alpha Mom playfully chases the pups, warmly moving away from the carcass of their latest kill.

Inside the camper parked by the beach, awakening oblivious to the carnage, Adam Haggard wheezes through thick cottonmouth.

"Abbie?" he says. "Abigale?"

Rolling from his humid, sweaty sprawl on dirty brown sand-speckled sheets, Adam grabs a warm can of Pabst Blue Ribbon from a 6-pack he left overnight on the floor. Standing naked and moving to the camper door with the dexterity of a slug, he scratches his behind, pushes open the door with the palm of his left hand and immediately spots the animals.

Up and running, Alpha Dad sprints to the sand dune mountain. The pups follow. Alpha Mom looks to her mate, back to her pups, and then at Adam who screams like he's got a sharp chicken wing bone stuck in his throat when he sees Abigale's mangled remains. Alpha Mom throws back her head and howls as Alpha Dad joins in as excited cubs let rip with shrill howls in a savage symphony.

High atop a distant dune, wearing a homemade burlap loincloth and a faded camouflage headband, 76-year-old Mel Moyle squats, tugs on his footlong white beard and pays close attention to the music only he can hear and see as notes emerge bouncing from the coyotes' mouths, climbing into the sky, brilliant colored sheet music dancing among swirling clouds that hang low in a haunted sky.

Mel lights a Hoocha Weed joint, the most powerful cannabis strain in the world that he grows in the secret plot he tends near a small dune lake. He closes his eyes and inhales magic mist from the pure pot he grows with the ease of an Iowa farmer planting corn. Throwing back his head, he exhales.

Taking another deep breath, Mel Moyle howls.

YOU CAN CALL ME BUD

WEALTHY white heir to his father's cigarette company fortune, Arthur von Spittle II went wading nude one day in the water by the Pismo Beach pier. Declaring a new life on California's Central Coast, he screamed, "Hallelujah, brothers and sisters, I am a born again stoner boner, standing erect amid the chaos of America's petrified forest of the mind."

Shocked women from the Santa Maria Avocado Club on a Sunday outing stood stunned, digging pudgy toes into the sand trying to ignore the shocking outburst of skin and male private parts. Three hammered teenage surfers nodded approvingly, recognizing the stratospherically high level of consciousness this evangelical weedhead had experienced.

"Whoa, stoner boner, man," said the kid with the tattoo of a cross-eyed pit bull smoking a bong inked across his back.

With the ease of a cannabis-infused hummingbird, this naked 21st Century marijuana messiah escaped in a flash before police arrived. Nobody saw anything to tell the cops even though a number of the snooty club women took discreet videos they posted on social media as soon as they got home and uncorked the cold chardonnay.

Later in the day one gleefully enlightened Arthur von Spittle II sat alone at a wobbly table beside a wobblier jukebox, playing one Grateful Dead song after another, giggling and talking to himself at Louie Louie's Lounge in Santa Maria, just 20 miles from the site of his Pacific Ocean satori.

"I will benevolently rule my kingdom of dopey wanderers." he said. "From now on you can call me Bud."

The bartender frowned.

"Tune it down, man," he said.

"Buy the house a drink," Bud said.

"You're the only customer here."

"Then I'll take a double."

The bartender poured four fingers of Old Snot, cheap artisanal bourbon distilled by smug bourgeois hipsters up the 101 freeway in Nipomo.

"I can see inside your head," said Bud after tossing down the shot.

"Out," said the bartender. "You're having flashbacks again. Get out."

"Your brain resembles Irish oatmeal."

"Out."

"Without clotted cream and brown sugar."

"Out."

"Mush."

The bartender jumped on the bar, menacingly waving his cocktail shaker like a ready-to-throw hand grenade.

"Like you and your deep-fried cerebellum have room to talk," he said, his skinny face flushing red as a Chile de árbol hot Mexican pepper.

Spinning on his stool, Bud pulled his multicolored beanie copter hat with the neon green plastic propeller low over the furrowed brow of his left eye and headed for the door wondering if the bartender was correct about his fricasseed brain matter.

Baked brain cells indeed appeared on Bud's daily menu for every meal no matter how meager. Burnt offerings included stir-fried brain cells for lunch and frizzled sizzled brain cells for dinner. Bud's daily brain cell buffet laid out an all-you-can-eat spread that each day laid out Bud. The man dug getting high. Check that. The man craved his highness the way a traditional prince needs an old-fashioned princess. Bud reigned as reefer royalty all rolled into one.

Vowing to resurrect peace, love, and vegetables the Woodstock Nation of burned-out hippies lost a long, long time ago Bud still stewed with zeal to save the world. One tough assignment for a high-tech nerd who gave back his full-ride scholarship in the Neuroscience PhD Program at California Polytechnic State University in San Luis Obispo, Bud had majored in artificial intelligence with a proposed thesis that could have and should have proven revolutionary.

When he quit college Bud had already created a brain in a casserole dish composed of thousands of living human brain cells. Once fully developed, he planned to teach the deep dish brain to write country music songs as well as perform them in Bay Area bars and maybe one day tour nationwide.

Gray matter matters, man.

Before dropping out of school Bud genetically engineered human brain cells from skin cells collected from sand grains he gathered on the beach in Pismo. Despite the project's Nobel Prize potential, growing a singing brain in a dish did not define his deepest passion.

"Bestie Bud Medicinal Balm" captured most of his short attention span focus. Of course Bud continued developing the pineal gland platter, treating the homemade organ as a dear friend he named Lee and nurtured into hyper-intellectual maturity. But the super cannabis-infused salve he invented soothed his savage head and prepared him for the future. Bud believed he owed himself and the world his newly patented pharmaceutical product to spread happiness by distributing the best homegrown potted product ever made. Blossoming cerebrums of young and searching Generations X, Y, Z and beyond would benefit from the sacred ointment.

On a high-flying Johnny Appleseed-type quest (in this case Johnny Reeferseed quest) to rouse long slumbering countercultural awareness, Bud dove deep inside his own brain, skipping through a mine field of plant-induced emotion. Bud gave full credit for the product's potency to the main ingredient of his powerful love drug balm, the essence centering on one-of-a-kind 100 percent pure Hoocha Weed.

Bud bought this freshly harvested elixir from a dune hermit named Mel Moyle, a gracefully aging freak who served as Bud's nirvana dealer and lived among the sand dunes near the little town of Oceano. Mel ate potent wild Hoocha Weed as salad, marinated the roots for his homegrown wine and ground the leaves into dope dust to use as natural seasoning in his homemade clam chowder.

Mel Moyle pretty much stayed to himself, although he politely dealt with others as he lived his days and nights among mellow sand shadows he considered his best friends. His relentless search for truth excluded other people because he no longer trusted other people the way he knew he should. One day that might change. One day others might join him in a more unsuspicious world.

More versatile than vintage Panama Red and Acapulco Gold put together, Bud only needed to dry Mel's fresh Hoocha Weed stems and pound them into a fine powder he mixed with beeswax and hand-squeezed avocado oil.

Voila!

"Bestie Bud Medicinal Balm!'

Rubbed into the human belly button as soft ointment ingested through the pores, its amoebic ingredients produced subtle bliss. If the paste had been available 2,500 or so years ago, Buddha would have rubbed balm on his belly and maybe even his butt, awakening years before he finally lost his mind in profound meditation.

"Bestie Bud Medicinal Balm," Bestie Bud for short, offered immediate peace of mind. Superior to even the powdered meal replacement products that gave time-constrained Silicon Valley techies more time to tech instead of eat, Bud knew Bestie Bud would one day exude enough good vibes to bring paradise down to Earth.

Nothing works better for terra firma heaven than a full blast zonkerbonker high. Reigning as a falling star in the Central Coastal California cosmos, Bud was king of the full blast zonkerbonkers. Cloud 10, one step above the accepted ninth pinnacle, provided extraterrestrial delight for Bud and his buddies.

Hoocha Weed forever!

LONG DOOBIEMOBILE RUNNING

HULKING and heavy, a bull-necked goon with a head crammed full of stolen prescription amphetamines waited politely outside Louie Louie's back barroom door. A faded pink carnation stuck in the lapel of his double-breasted black suit wilted in the heat. His breath smelled of burrito beans. He wore an uneven Fu-Manchu moustache.

Bud staggered from the bar, headed to the single room with a double hot plate he rented with the meager monthly allowance his father provided. Catching him by the neck of his torn T-shirt emblazoned with a smiley face on the front, the goon said, "You Albert von Spittle II?"

Paranoid yet fueled with a fresh hit of high-octane Bestie Bud balm he rubbed into his belly button five minutes earlier in Louie Louie's men's room, Bud said, "Yes, my pronouns are he, him, ham, and hum."

"Your father has a proposition for you," said the burly dark envoy.

"Ah, a proposition," Bud said. "Dear old dad is by all means a prostitute hooker crooker, a mean, deceitful tramp laying down and spreading his stock options for capitalism."

Built short and wide as a commercial fish cooler, the emissary held up his hands.

"Your father sent me with an offer," he said.

Bud rolled his eyes with the exuberance of a rookie head rolling his first jay. From the corner of his eye he spotted what at first glance looked like the Oscar Meyer Weinermobile parked in the lot beside the barroom garbage cans. Quickly realizing the long glistening white RV wasn't a windup hot dog after all, he scanned the tubular object.

Big as a mid-size Winnebago, the vehicle looked exactly like a big fat roach motel. The front end glowed red where automotive engineers had manufactured an unbreakable crimson plastic tip. The rear of the rolling joint resembled the curled, twisted end of a reefer. The biggest souped-up replica doobie in the world sat idling at the curb.

Stunned at the sight of this enormous head trip on wheels, Bud did a little buzzed dance the way he boogied at Louie Louie's disco night, shuffling left, shuffling right, pointing his index finger at the ceiling, tuning in, turning on, dropping out, digging excitable energy signals coming in loud and clear from scalp to groin.

The propeller of his beanie copter hat started spinning all by itself.

"Whoa," Bud said.

"Say hello to the Doobiemobile," said the go-between goon.

Sinking deeper into Cloud 10, Bud's cushy cumulus comfort almost smothered him as he cautiously approached the vehicle. Running his hand across the smooth vanilla finish, he listened to the sinister messenger explain his father's deal in slow sentences the way a mean zookeeper would try to persuade a chimpanzee to accept a lit match for a cigarette.

"Ever since California went ape shit over legalized recreational weed, your daddy's been calculating how to snare and monopolize the cannabis market and turn new consumer demand into unbridled profit," said the envoy. "Even with fast-sinking profits for tobacco products, your old man wants to hang on to what's left of his cigarette company."

"Greed is the most powerful drug," Bud said.

"So the boss is manufacturing instantly addictive nicotine tobacco leaf his mad scientists created in the lab and mixed with lousy pot too weak to sell," said the emissary. "He bought stale rotten weak weed at a dispensary chain going-out-of-business sale. Rolling the garbage weed with his instantaneously habit-forming tobacco leaf to make non-filter king-sized pre-rolled joints will provide a wired world with a brand new brand called Psyched."

Bud's eyes opened wide as the vegan pepperoni slices he devoured when he got the munchies.

"Take one pot puff and you're hooked on Daddy's primo pumped tobacco?"

"You'll smoke a whole pack by lunchtime," said the goon. "Mr. Spittle mixes pure mutated liquid nicotine with moldy tobacco leaves, squashed titan beetle juice from the Amazon rain forest and low levels of arsenic normally used as rat repellent plus a dash of baby powder. That shit grabs you soon as you step one toke over the line. The blitzed blend instantly hooks joker toker midnight smokers on tobacco while they think they're just inhaling pot."

The muscle head said, "Mr. Spittle is already planning to manufacture what he calls 'California Screaming' blunts wrapped in topnotch toxic tobacco leaf as big as whole ripe bananas."

Getting agitated, Bud sputtered.

"I kicked Spittle cigarettes years ago but still blow joints every hour on the hour," he said. "Bestie Bud primo weed belly button balm is where it's at. Safe. Kind. Nice. Bestie Bud won't give anybody lung cancer."

"Relax, mister," said the goon.

"I *am* already bigtime chill," Bud said. "Because I rub Bestie Bud round and round into my umbilicus and become one with the omphalos, the navel of the Earth. I'm opening the Nudie Navel Academy massage therapy school once we get famous. You should enroll."

Taking Bud by the shirt collar the goon pulled him close enough that Bud smelled sweet spicy nicotine on his breath.

"Look, nature boy, you can sell all the Bestie Bud love lotion you want on the side," the goon said. "But you and your pop are going into business together whether you like it or not."

Inside Bud's big bone head, miniature frizzles began short-circuiting brain waves like tiny frying pans sizzling eggs in a sputtering iron skillet.

"Your daddy wants to enslave masses of asses to devil nicotine with Psyched smokes," the goon said. "Why do you think they call it chain-smoking?"

Bud began nervously bouncing from one foot to the other like he had to pee which he did.

"And he wants me to drive the bus?"

"Prodigal son becomes power to the people pusher man," said the corporate bouncer.

The light finally lit in Bud's belly button.

"Sixties' holy man Ken Kesey said you're either on the bus or you're off the bus. Same goes for the canna-BUS, right?"

"Now you're cooking," said the goon.

Crossed wires in Bud's head burned with indecision. Fear and obedience fueled tense trauma from his childhood. Maybe Bud could find a way to beat gridlock in this deceitful trafficking jam with a one-way tunnel through the doors of perception and never look back. For the first time in his miserable life maybe he could pull one over on his old man.

Tossing the vehicle keys to Bud (who dropped them twice before picking up the ring) the company man of war walked away smirking.

"Daddy will be in touch with more detail," he said.

Sliding behind the wheel, Bud fired up the engine. Pulling up his shirt he rubbed a whole handful of Bestie Bud ointment into his belly button. No way in good conscience could or would he hand out the ton of pre-rolled shoddy pot and tainted tobacco leaf joints with which his father had packed the Doobiemobile. No way would Bud help hook comradely cannabusters and poor potheads around the world.

Driving the first eight miles in a daze, Bud pulled the Doobiemobile over to the side of Black Road between Santa Maria and Guadalupe. Spotting four farmworkers ending their shift, Bud bartered a 6-pack of Bestie Bud and four fresh Hoocha Weed joints in exchange for their unloading, dumping and covering his father's malicious mixture into a fallow field piled high with rotting broccoli.

"The stuff got poisoned at the factory," Bud said as the farmworkers blessed themselves like the obedient Catholics their mothers expected them to be.

Throwing the Doobiemobile into gear and pulling away he

watched in the rearview mirror as the farmworkers dug up what they had just buried and piled as many joints as they could fit into the beds of their dented, dusty and jury-rigged pickups and battered used sedans. Bud struggled to remember how to get to Mel Moyle's Oceano beach shack to pick up his latest load of pure Hoocha Weed to turn into herbal healing salve.

"Bestie Bud Medicinal Balm" would help save not sink the world. Thank the gods and goddesses for that grizzled hermit who tended the most potent cannabis plot in the universe.

"Viva Bestie Bud!" Bud yelled out the window of the Doobiemobile. In the distance the four hard-working vegetable laborers lit four joints, raising plastic throwaway lighters above their heads, flicking them on and off like seasoned stoners at a music festival. The broccoli cutters stared in Bud's direction, already a little stoned no matter how poor the pot.

"Viva Bud Light," one man yelled as the others bent over laughing.

Communing with his inner child, Bud steered the Doobiemobile down the road, happy to dispel all thought of his father's treachery like wisps of smoke disappearing into the breeze from a thin stick of Japanese sandalwood incense, or from a plump green Hoocha Weed joint so fresh it almost breathed by itself.

Like the man said, "Viva Hoocha Weed!"

EYE FOR AN EYE

TRIPPER and I park the truck we stole from the bandits in a shadowy space at the rear of a crumbling cinderblock motel with chipped sea-green pastel shutters and an empty swimming pool covered in algae scum. Strolling like happy honeymooners we take our time getting to the shadowy office to check in.

The clerk keeps his eyes on his gun magazine.

"Room 12," he says.

"I'd rather Room 13," I say.

Once we settle in I outline the plan.

"We'll dump the truck in the morning."

Tripper turns on the small TV tuned to a station that shows two senior citizen comedians playing with Mexican jumping beans for the first time, expressing astonishment at the hopping dancing frijoles which are actually caterpillar moth larvae trapped inside a shell beating their unborn heads against the walls going buggy trying to get out.

Tripper flips off the set.

"That's inhumane," she says. "Somebody should beat their heads against the wall."

"Focus," I say.

"OK," she says. "So how will we get to Sinaloa?"

"Take the bus," I say.

"Do we have to buy a ticket for Regalo?"

The scorpion rests on my shoulder like a pirate's parrot. After struggling to understand the Spanish 10 o'clock television news amid the din of the rattling air conditioner, Tripper falls asleep without removing her jeans and red plaid flannel shirt. I gently pull off her boots and tiptoe into the bathroom. Regalo curls up in a corner of the motel room, waiting for a rat or whatever else might cross his path as a midnight snack.

On the way south earlier that day we stopped only once for gas at an OXXO convenience store where we bought a large white Styrofoam cooler, bread, cheese, fruit, Pacifico beer, stick deodorant, toothpaste, toothbrushes, disposable razors and scissors. A continuing nod to growing up on the streets of East LA, I always keep emergency cash folded in my boot.

Removing a plastic razor and small scissors from the plastic grocery bag, I start cutting the long locks of black hair that hang to my shoulders and in my eyes. The four-inch goatee goes, too. The moustache remains thick and ominous as the midnight sky covering this tumbledown town.

Looking into the smudged, cracked mirror, I question who I see looking back. I'm a dead ringer for the ceramic or plastic face and head on countless Jesús Malverde busts disciples use as a centerpiece on personal home shrines throughout Mexico, the United States, and the world.

When I finish shaving, my cheeks soft from hot water and the excitement of a new authentic identity, I close my eyes and pat dry my cheeks with an itchy bath towel that smells vaguely of stale lemon disinfectant and body odor. Three seconds later, suddenly spinning I throw the towel in a straight-armed motion at slight movement I sense behind me. Tripper easily catches the towel in a fluid motion.

"Damn," she says. "I like you better as a long-haired hippie."

"People change," I say.

Tripper notices the dreamy look that fills my eyes as I gradually succumb to the trance that drops me like a malfunctioning elevator into another place and time. Knowing to leave me alone, Tripper fights the urge to reach out. Now she freezes.

Closing my eyes, I slip further and faster into the netherworld of my ancestral past. Whatever pulses in my subconscious spins vivid colors somersaulting in my mind, reminding me of the Zorro TV show reruns I watched on TV as a child in the comfort of the living room with my mother singing in the kitchen making hot chocolate and sweet honey buns while I wore a black mask I made from a cut-up T-shirt and waved a thin tree branch I found in the street as my sword.

My head pounds with the heavy gallop of horse hooves exploding in my ears. Sunshine blinds me as a red skull-shaped ball of fire rises fast from behind the mountains changing the landscape to a scalding madness I can taste. Salt from tears and sweat mingle in my mouth, drying quickly from fear and desperation.

Now I see them.

Men chasing me in the posse ride close on my tail. Closing fast, they surround me as I push my horse further and faster in a bid to escape. Dropping my head onto the black stallion's neck, I cling to the steed's thick mane, holding on until my grip slips and I drop to the ground, exhausted and fearing I broke my back. Dust rises in a cloud over my body as the bandits gather laughing so hard they choke on feverish emotion that makes them giddy from winning the chase. One man spits in my face as I lay in the dirt.

"Nowhere to run, Jesús Malverde," the man says. "The good news for us, bad news for you, is you have nowhere to go but up."

Dangling a thick tan sisal rope with a noose already tied at the end, the knot thick and brown with wispy hair that pricks like a needle to the touch, the man dismounts, showing me the end of the rope that signals the end of my life. With both wrists broken in the fall and my hands untied, I jerk like a marionette when the posse leader lowers the noose around my neck and tightens the knot.

Tossing the coil high with perfect aim over the lowest hanging branch of a torote tree, he pulls the rope tight enough around the elephant skin-thick bark to constrict human carotid arteries, break the neck and choke off the oxygen to the brain. Casually walking to his horse the hangman wraps the end of his lariat around the saddle horn and securely hitches the rope. The outlaw slowly walks his horse backwards. Tightening the rope around my neck, he drags me to my feet, then to the tiptoes of my boots, then off the ground.

Kicking to keep from choking and passing out, I hold on as long as I can, feeling rope burn into skin, watching purple, red and black flashes against the insides of my eyes as I rise. Higher and higher I ascend, kicking my legs and swallowing hard against the knot around my neck. The horse stops backing up. A man holds the rope, unties the knot from the saddle horn and knots it tight around the thick tree trunk. The men ride off without looking back at the jumpy man they left behind to die.

Afraid she lost me for good, not knowing what else to do to snap me from my stupor, Tripper slaps me hard across the cheek. Stooped and sagging, I remind her of the zombies at which we used to laugh together at the movies.

"Jesús," Tripper says. "Jesús, please."

Reality returns abruptly.

"I'm dead," I say. "I just don't know it."

"No," Tripper says. "Jesús Malverde lives."

After we shower and get dressed, we stand by the road outside the motel. She sees the bus before I do. Looking like a black prison neck tattoo, Regalo nestles above my shoulder before skittering inside my blue denim shirt to settle in the snug cloth beneath my armpit.

"Thirteen hours or so to Culiacàn," Tripper says. "That's a thousand mile pain-in-the-ass road trip."

"Better than fighting our way through bandit country in one of Uncle Arturo's trucks," I say.

"You think we'll make it?"

"My back and neck are killing me," I say. "You didn't bite me, did you, Regalo?"

FISH OUT OF WATER

BOLTING upright in bed Eeshell Martinez, 25, struggled to catch her breath. Fear gripped her mind. Uncertainty controlled her judgment. Pain flittered in her chest like a sick parakeet flying back and forth in a cage. Wide awake now, she listened to the Pismo Beach stillness through an open bedroom window.

A truck engine droned down the 101 freeway a few blocks away. The ocean slapped against jagged cliffs a few blocks beyond the tips of her unpainted toes.

Sliding easily from her bed, she dressed and walked carefully through darkness to the small living room. Eeshell (who sometimes politely reminded people Eee-shell rhymes with seashell) listened to the silver metal wind chimes singing outside her door. Stepping to the quiet narrow street she shuffled slowly to the edge of the salty sea. Sitting alone on this deserted western edge of America Eeshell thought about her nightmare and waited for sunrise.

An hour later with warm air refreshing her cheeks she walked to the water, kicked off pink beach flip flops and stepped out of cut-off white denim shorts. She removed her T-shirt imprinted with patterns of turquoise spiral nautilus shells. Awakening gulls greeted Eeshell with soft cries. Again she pondered the savage dream that attacked her restfulness as she walked slowly into deeper water torturing herself with questions about her unsettling vision.

Eeshell dreamed about coyotes, about wild animals killing and eating raw meat in their hunger for survival. Humans kill and eat meat, too, so what's the difference? Why did she face killer coyotes in her dream, beasts that let her live? Why do untamed creatures seek her out on land and at sea? Do birds of a feather really flock together? Why her?

Filling her lungs with fresh salt air, she dove, swimming underwater farther and deeper than ever. Rising, surfacing and gulping air after many long minutes, she wondered how she could swim so long and so far without taking a breath. Was she still dreaming? Did she fall into a meditative trance? Had she surfaced without remembering and then dove deeper?

Inhaling, she dove one more time, swimming with the smooth, strong, steady strokes of a mermaid. Of course, that cryptic thought crossed her mind as well. Wondering what superhuman force gripped her, propelled by a twisting, gliding natural movement, Eeshell became a pure force of nature loaded with animal energy. Surfacing again she checked her watch. Twenty minutes had passed on her plastic lime-colored watch that must have broken. No human can stay underwater that long.

Taking Eeshell by surprise, four dolphins blasted from the water like majestic natural torpedoes. Joining in the primitive fun of riding a gradually cresting wave, balancing lightly on the tip of the surge, all five mammals bobbed like sponges in a flash of silver momentum.

After joining together, five surfing females ruled the dawn, queens of the blue brine, playing majestically as they glided toward the shore of their ethereal water realm. Sharing abundant energy, these majestic sea goddesses then turned abruptly to swim back out in a swift underwater current. Squealing with excitement they made another turn for another run to ride the wild surf.

Exhausted as she stepped naked from the comfort of nature's sacred birthing pool, Eeshell put on her tie-dyed shirt, faded shorts and cheap rubber flip flops. Walking on tiptoes she bounced into a reawakening that felt like icy pin pricks all over her body. After a quick walk back to her tiny second-floor apartment, she headed to the Pismo Pier to sell her handmade Big Sur jade love beads that radiated peace of mind.

Eeshell's coyote spirit flourished.

Untamed.

Eeshell's dolphin spirit blossomed as well.

Sharing wild magnetic kinship with all creatures, animals together, living as one with nature, makes us part of a ticking planet - the way life's supposed to be.

 # DUNE WINE

TALKING to himself helped Mel Moyle better comprehend the chaos of the world.

"Don't get mad at the fish," he said out loud. "Don't blame the coyotes."

The Oceano hermit dragged his homemade seagull feather mattress to the top of the highest dune. Mel long ago calculated the 12-minute span for the climb by checking his breathing against his heartbeats and matching the numbers to the wristwatch he found on the beach and eventually threw into the ocean, letting go of his last man-made barometer of time.

"Free the fish," he said. "Free the coyotes."

People who don't know any better hate sharks when they attack humans. Of course they blamed the coyotes for the coyote dune attack. Adverse to interacting with strangers in most situations, Mel nonetheless steadfastly defended all non-human species.

As the last living Dunite, a direct descendant of bohemian people who lived full-time during the 1920s, '30s, '40s and '50s in these Central Coast dunes near the little town of Oceano, Mel understood how nature intersects in mysterious and often terrible ways. Individual existence is codependent. Humans dying in the water or on bloodstained sand simply illustrate another harsh fact of life in the food chain where people remain the weakest link.

Yet Mel sought peace for every sentient being, whatever sentient being meant. He once heard guru Allen Ginsberg recite that catchphrase 100 times at an unclothed body-painted poetry reading in Stinson Beach and tried to incorporate the phrase into his own lexicon. Calling himself "the ultimate truth seeker," Mel did his best to help whenever he could, which never seemed good enough for the mainstream world.

Self-professed as a low holy man, Mel Moyle christened himself the embodiment of those mystics, philosophers, artists, and outcasts who lived in shacks they built from driftwood in the dunes, setting the stage for San Francisco's countercultural beatnik and hippie explosions.

Despite the celebrity historical significance of President Chester Arthur's grandson, Gavin, writer John Steinbeck, photographer Ansel Adams and other world-class seekers who visited during the Dunite heyday, ignorance now ran amok. Society overlooked their power.

Not Mel Moyle.

Each day he gave thanks that 21st Century "civilization" had crowded and clouded his mind so much he had no choice but to flee the status quo to live in the purity of the Dunite moment, spending the rest of his life in the dunes seeking and finding blitzed bliss among dancing, talking flowers and waving sea grass.

Everybody needs a little buzz so Mel helped spread the news.

Spreading out his mattress, Mel stepped carefully to the middle of the soft bedding upon which he slept every night since he moved to the dunes to escape society's madness. Lowering himself onto his magic carpet, he crossed his legs into full lotus and settled into the downy cushion. Scooching forward, he felt sand shift beneath his butt as the mattress started to slide and his downhill run began.

"Yaaaahoooooo," Mel said, drawing out the notes the way he imagined Jimi Hendrix would sound singing the Star-Spangled Banner.

With brisk morning wind stirring strands of his uncontrolled white beard, Mel picked up speed as the futon flew down the sandy incline. Opening his mouth wide to gulp air and laugh, Mel raised his arms high above his head the way roller coaster riders do to get the best thrill. Within seconds a ferocious sense of freedom engulfed the nerve endings in the exposed bare skin on his arms, legs and chest. His face flushed with fun fever. His head pounded like a jackhammer of joy. Mel giggled all the way down the drift. No five-year-old with a silly streak had a better time at an old-fashioned amusement park. Mel fought to keep his eyes open as sand whipped in the wind and he took in the magnificent scene that passed in a blur.

The thought crossed Mel's mind that a grand finale trip down these dunes would be the best way to die. What a way to go. But Mel wasn't ready to die, not just yet, not as long as he could help even one guppy or gold fish that needed his help.

The stained seagull feather-stuffed mattress slid to a stop. Mel remained in full lotus, consciously breathing and meditating on what had happened at nearby Avila Beach shortly after he came to town. Word traveled fast about the great white shark attack that August day when the 50-year-old Santa Maria college professor went swimming near the pier and came out of the water dead.

Mel later read in a newspaper he found blowing in the wind how lifeguards training on the pier saw the attack and dove in to help. Shark teeth severed her femoral artery and vein. Other cuts and lacerations opened near the main bite on her left side near her hip and on the lower part of her right leg.

Based on the deep wounds, a California Department of Fish and Game marine biologist present at the autopsy estimated the shark length between 15-to-18-feet long, the news accounts said. Wearing a black wet suit and flippers, the woman might have resembled the silhouette of one of many seals eating small fish and swimming nearby.

Great whites eat seals but spit out humans. They're too fatty. Experts believe these sharks attack humans by mistake. Either way, the attacks are usually fatal. Experts believe this victim died in a minute or two. She loved to swim with the seals, friends later recalled to reporters.

By dusk the day of the attack talk circulated up and down Harford Pier about getting a shark posse together to hunt down the beast. Kill him, let God sort it out. Mel heard escalating rumors of vengeance as he scavenged discarded fish heads on the pier to make a base stock for his homemade clam chowder. The next morning Mel walked 10 miles back to the pier in his bare feet and made a sign from a piece of cardboard box he found in a garbage can outside the fresh seafood market.

"DON'T BLAME THE FISH! HELP THE COYOTES!" he wrote on the sign in a black marker he borrowed from Howie, a kindhearted veteran fisherman he knew from his years walking the beach near the pier. Then he walked up and down the pier until nightfall, fearlessly protesting with the nerve of a tough Teamster picketing against unfair working conditions.

When Mel finished playing in the dunes he headed home to his shack hidden deep in the sea grass. Screwing open a fresh jug of Hoocha Weed wine he made from his special pot plant leaves and grapes he raided from a nearby vineyard, Mel took three healthy slugs.

Noticing he was running low on what he lovingly called "beatific bong booze," Mel made a mental note to cook up a new batch in the morning. Cooking wine from Hoocha Weed offered one of the great luxuries of living alone in his wonderful wilderness. The world would be a better place if everybody guzzled Hoocha Weed wine, a truth Mel believed with all his being.

Thinking thoughtless thoughts brought him face-to-face with his face.

Looking back from deep inside the center of a sand mountain, undulating like a bearded wine jug with ears, the dune rippled like a mounting tidal wave. Unlike a normal sand dune, the center of this unique drift quivered with purple juice, flowing and brimming with vital life energy. A blue-green aura pulsed around the dune's eyes, nose and mouth, drawing Mel into the experience of witnessing a hallowed vision of himself that felt like finding a half-price version of a Shroud of Turin bath towel at a Pismo Beach outlet store.

Mel looked into what a Zen master would call his original face from the boundlessness that existed before he and any of his human ancestors slid from the womb. Like an ancient pagan deity experiencing a religious conversion, Mel moved toward the fantasy he called a yester-light-year. Mel yearned to eat the dune, drink the dune, breathe the dune.

"I am the face of the clam," he said, tapping into a glorious ancient secret kept quiet by Dunite teachers.

Dropping into his favorite seated yogic pretzel posture, he

rolled and lit a Hoocha Weed joint the size of a kazoo. Throwing back his head, he inhaled the sacramental smoke and warbled.

Gulls listened.

"Om," Mel Moyle chirped. "Om, om, on the range."

REEFER SADNESS

Up NORTH near Mendocino in the heart of the weirdest, weediest county in California, Reefer Johnson pined for the loss of his father.

Now just a flashback, Commander Fetus, head of the Weed Eaters White Man Christian Pot Militia, had been laid to rest with marijuana seeds dropped on the fresh earth of his grave so one day his genes might fertilize and sprout, bringing forth pounds of potent dope DNA in his powerful image. At least that's the spiritual tone to the eulogy his son Reefer provided when he spoke tearfully at the memorial service.

Built square and lean as a Texaco gas pump, Reefer Johnson stood solid as a freezer loaded with poached deer meat. Limber and strong, Reefer could do just about anything athletic including climbing redwoods in his bare feet like a lumberjack monkey if such a thing existed.

At 25 with a beard so thick a chain saw might get stuck cutting a hole through the brush to get to the leathery skin on his chiseled jaw, he was thinking about joining the Army, maybe becoming a diesel mechanic, a short-order cook or one of them Green Berets. Then his father got killed in a Northern California firefight with Mexican cartel banditos that changed life utterly for this lonesome young clodhopper.

At least that's what Reefer's Aunt Irma told Reefer about his daddy's passing, pounding the unproven killing narrative into his thick bonehead skull so hard and so often until he hated Mexicans so much he wouldn't eat a single Frito even if he were starving on a desert island. Yes, indeed, Aunt Irma said, he was killed in a Mexican cartel firefight with mustachioed Frito banditos firing automatic, semi-automatic and bolt-action rifles, screaming beneath Pancho Villa sombreros and bright wool serapes, cursing American greatness and Commander Fetus as commander of the Weed Eater paramilitary army.

In all honesty Irma had no idea what really happened to Commander Fetus and the Weed Eaters. Without witnesses whoever wiped out every member of the pot-growing hillbillies was anybody's guess. Those freaky old ladies who lived up the dirt lane from the firefight told police they didn't see or hear anything and were so scared they locked themselves in their sewing room and pulled their afghans over their heads. The shoot-out ended with one side dead and the other side gone. Irma told Reefer his daddy died a hero to the cause.

"Cause of what?" Reefer said.

"Cause I said so," Aunt Irma said.

As Reefer's long dead mother's sister, Aunt Irma went all gaga for Commander Fetus from the first time she met him, panting like a beagle hound on a dirt-encrusted sirloin bone, getting as close as he'd allow. That meant moving into his cabin shortly after her sister's funeral but not allowing herself to even think about common law marriage except for a couple of minutes every few months when the walls closed in, she felt depressed and took to swallowing amphetamine pills she traded at the bar for pot brownies she baked at home while watching love and marriage shows on the TV.

A damn dirty dog himself, Fetus loved Aunt Irma and all the ladies, as he liked to say, and they often loved him back usually after a night drinking and dancing at any number of hick roadhouse bars that lined the pot bush country back roads of Fetus' illegal dope domain. But Irma remained true to him even when a 19-year-old dreadlocked member of the militia propositioned her at the fishing derby and she slapped him across the face with a record-breaking grass carp.

That was rich because grass carp were the only fish the boys valued because of the marijuana connection to the word "grass." No black carp allowed, though, because they were white supremacists even though most of them couldn't spell "supremacist." So they just said "men" as in "white men" as in "white men militia" which they spelled "millisha" (which a loyal member actually named his newborn daughter: Millisha Benderhoff) on hand-drawn posters and leaflets they nailed to trees and handed out to potential supremacy sympathizers dumb enough to take them. The boys even had a secret handshake most of them could never remember.

"Your father was a louse, Reefer," Irma whispered at Fetus' funeral luncheon.

"Yes, ma'am," Reefer said.

"A stinking piece of skunk shit," she said.

"Yes, ma'am," Reefer said.

"I sure loved that man," she said.

Reefer obeyed Aunt Irma without question because the same blood that ran through her veins ran through his mother Zinnia's veins and all over the side of the road when she died bringing him home from the hospital. The door to the used bread truck in which she was riding flew open accidently after hitting a killer pothole (more than appropriate for weed country) and she tumbled head-first to the macadam still holding her new bundle of joy tightly.

New daddy Commander Fetus sure loved that bread truck saying it would make a good undercover assault vehicle when rapture came and the militia needed to pile men in the back for impromptu attacks on sinners before rising up to heaven. Looking down at his woman's broken neck and last breath, Fetus sighed in frustration.

"Guess I'll have to raise this little pecker head by myself," he said.

Doctors almost declared Reefer dead on arrival too, because no brain waves showed up on the EEG that records the electrical activity of the brain. The young man's brain wave status hadn't changed in 25 years. Even after Reefer's last all-terrain vehicle accident, few brain waves danced the pothead boogie on the electroencephalogram screen. Fact was Reefer was out jumping "cricks" in that very same ATV when the firefight that killed his daddy took place and didn't see or hear anything.

"My daddy was a great American," Reefer said during Fetus' eulogy, drawing hoots and oo-rahs from the assembled crowd of cannabis entrepreneurs and assorted bumpkin combat veterans left over from various wars who gathered in one particularly ragged backwoods and unchartered American Legion post, men and women who depended on under-the-radar THC for arthritis and alcohol for fortitude. Other mourners included ragtag flea-infested hippie stoners and acid burnouts drifting in from various parts of Washington, Oregon, California and across the nation to live as off-the-grid recluses in their timbered chunk of foggy, mossy coast.

Losing the entire local Weed Eater White Supremacist Christian Pot Militia all at once stunned these hearty souls. Nobody in that secretive mountain community ever imagined Commander Fetus going down in a fiery hail of bullets. Fate and simple bad luck took their hero leaving nothing behind but memories and a thirst for vengeance. Retribution bubbled hard in Reefer's head boiling over like turnip and squirrel innards soup overflowing the stove.

"That means we gotta set out for payback," Reefer told the crowd. "Find who killed my daddy."

Raucous applause greeted his vow as he bellowed his challenge. "Who's with me?"

The room got so quiet you could hear rat droppings hit the floor as they fell from the ceiling.

Reefer left Aunt Irma's house by himself that night, packing a German military rucksack with three flannel shirts all the same gray/black pattern of checks, two white long underwear shirts frayed around the wrists, a pair of black "dress up" jeans, a pair of baggy gray and white striped railroader bib overalls, two pair of white Fruit of the Loom briefs, six peanut butter and smoked frog leg sandwiches and 100 pre-rolled joints his daddy always kept on hand for company.

As you might expect, Reefer liked getting high, starting inhaling grass fumes about when he was old enough to walk. Commander Fetus' militia buddies thought it was funny blowing smoke into the toddler's little scrunched up face, watching him choke and cough and eventually space out to Allman Brothers' records blasting from the stereo.

Walking 12 miles to the road, Reefer stuck out his thumb and took the first ride that came along, a flatbed truck hauling logs to the sawmill 42 miles down the highway. When Reefer got out he gave the driver a joint the size of a sausage link.

"For your trouble, sir," he said.

"I hope you find what you're looking for, kid," the driver said.

"You mean who I'm looking for," Reefer said. "Who them Mexicans is who killed my daddy."

"Yeah, who," the trucker said.

"Who you calling a yahoo?"

"No offense, son."

"If the coonskin cap fits wear it," Reefer said. "I guess I am a yahoo. And proud of it."

Intellect and self-confidence not being his best qualities, Reefer pulled his homemade Davy Crockett cap with the almost bald raccoon tail low over his eyebrows and hiked off into the sunset, where a Day-Glo haze settled between the orange cloud cover and looked like the black light posters he saw hanging on the walls of his daddy's bedroom.

The next ride took Reefer all the way to Elk where he washed dinner dishes for his supper in a guest house on a cliff and grabbed a ride the next morning with Japanese tourists headed quite a distance to Central Coast wine country to taste the famous blood red syrah wine they heard so much about on the world cable TV news. When they bid Reefer goodbye at Exit 193 to Shell Beach Rd., so seriously stoned when they got out of the rental car they couldn't stop bowing at the waist along the 101, they watched him disappear in a blur into the abyss like a Japanese Yamabushi mountain monk in the land of the rising sun.

Standing alone by the highway, Reefer marveled at the green hills overlooking the Pacific Ocean and realized how much he hated rich people living above it all in mansions that sell for a million here and a million there while people like him search for a place to sleep under a bridge.

"Sumbitches killed my daddy. Now all that's left is me," he said.

No logical reason existed for Reefer to talk with hints of a Dixie accent. Maybe all those Southern rock lyrics went to his head and got stuck spinning around up there like loose grits before spitting out his mouth in later life. Either way he was on the hunt for truth and "them sumbitches" who killed his daddy. This mission might not bode well for anybody.

Reaching into his waistband, where most vigilantes would stuff a pistol, Reefer felt the sharp tip of the evidence he possessed that led him to the Central Coast: a gold-plated corkscrew one of his stoner fishing buddies found near the scene of the firefight that claimed his father and his marijuana militia men. When Reefer's fingers wrapped around the thick redwood handle, the corkscrew seemed to pulse, alive with energy powerful enough to pull the tightest cork from a wine bottle. Carved into the wood, the words "AVILA BEACH" seemed elegant, signaling a serene destination vacation.

Reefer's next ride suddenly appeared at the top of the hill cresting the horizon with the ease of an orange, black and white speckled monarch butterfly gliding from its grove at the top of a fragrant eucalyptus tree. Rubbing his eyes to make sure he was really seeing what he thought he was seeing, Reefer started to laugh a big belly laugh that started in his lower intestine and worked its way up to shake the rippled muscles in his 12-pack abs, his double-wide shoulders and down the vast expanse of his mighty back. The oncoming driver seemed to hear him because he laughed too, a maniacal fit of cackling chuckles that rose and fell in pitch like a bagpipe band on drugs.

Pulling the Doobiemobile to the side of the road, Bud leaned across the seat, threw open the passenger side door and asked, "Where you headed, partner?"

"Don't ask me why but I'm hungry for clam chowder," Reefer said.

"I know just the place," Bud said.

Down the road awaited the face of the clam.

You can call him Mel.

MOON WOMAN

IN REMISSION from her sickness for years, Zita felt ready for action. Her son, Jesús, told her she couldn't possibly be a witch. Witches don't get lung cancer, he said.

Zita laughed.

Tell it to La Santa Muerte, she said, lighting a purple candle to recognize the spiritual presence of the revered death saint who always walked by Zita's side. Like the living spirit of Jesús Malverde, La Santa Muerte offered hope to countless needy Mexicans, often needy people who never gave up, never gave in, and rarely got the simple life pleasures they deserved.

Wearing a purple hooded gown over her body and bony skull, La Santa Muerte protected both the hopeless and the strong, including Zita whom La Santa Muerte baptized as one of her rare mystical daughters.

La Santa Muerte wore various color robes for different reasons. The purple La Santa Muerte stood with Zita as goddess of magic, assisting with shamanic spells. A gatekeeper between different realms, La Morada, the purple La Santa Muerte, helped with Zita's health including her psychic abilities. Holding a globe, scythe and sometimes both, La Santa Muerte exercised dominion over the world. In return Zita burned sage to comfort her guardian and offered water to quench her thirst for death and ancient Mayan chants to soothe La Santa Muerte's mind that churned and burned endlessly.

Graciously accepting the threat of death always lurking in the back of her mind, years after mostly quitting two daily packs of Spittle King Non-Filter cigarettes, Zita breathed consciously and deeply during morning and evening trances that carried her far into her powerful psyche. Still, Zita wondered if somebody other than the tobacco company had personally cursed her, an unknown enemy who monitored her progress or despair. No one had, but always alert, she wondered anyway.

Arthur von Spittle came to mind, the man she read about in the newspaper and saw interviewed on television speaking as the head of the cigarette company who condemned her and countless others, sentencing them to death and misery for profit. Spittle ruled as society's special kind of demon, a walking, talking, American-made executioner who needed to feel the curse of retribution. For good measure Zita should declare war on all cigarette company executives, CEOs, who deserved to suffer and die all at the same time. But she could not erase them all.

One would suffice.

Mr. Spittle had to go.

Yet every time she planned a fatal attack against the smoking cartel chieftain, she asked herself what baby Eeshell would think, this beautiful child she loved more than the sun and the moon who opposed conflict and violence of any kind, a young wonder woman who proffered purity and innocence to fight wanton mayhem that gripped the world.

Back in 1999 while living in East Los Angeles, Zita heard from witch friends on the streets how a young mother blamed her son Jesús for her pregnancy. These allies from the barrio advised Zita to take action, to keep an upper hand on the situation. Within days Zita spoke to the parents of the skittish pregnant teenager, compensating the 19-year-old with what little money Zita had saved. With soft hypnotic suggestion, Zita persuaded the young woman and her parents to turn over the child, sternly telling the teen gangbanger to go on with her life. With the meager cash windfall came a red leather jacket and expensive sneakers, luxuries that helped her easily forget the child she never named as just another bad trip. One year later the reckless young woman died in a crossfire between warring gangs.

Bullets killed her, not Zita's magic.

After arranging a new home for the new baby with Mr. and Mrs. Martinez, middle-aged friends Zita knew from Culiacán who had moved to Santa Maria, the couple embraced the child and continued working hard, she in the agriculture coolers, he chopping broccoli dug from the black dirt of many fertile fields. Their new daughter never lacked for babysitters. Neighborhood women argued over sharing in the infant's joyous company. No one questioned the new addition to the Martinez family.

At a private baptism a Catholic priest and undercover warlock from Cancún, who respected the Maya ways, poured water over the child's head. Mrs. Martinez held the baby tightly with new "godmother" and undisclosed grandmother Zita standing nearby watching over the little one with the same adoring intensity La Santa Muerte exhibited watching over her.

With rich Maya ancestry on Zita's mother's side, they named the baby in honor of Ixchel, the Maya goddess of the moon, fertility, medicine and happiness, who Zita believed instills the core of radical feminism in all female beings. Zita spelled the name "Eeshell" so the essence of the sacred title would be heard whenever properly pronounced. Of course Ixchel and La Santa Muerte attended the secret christening, offering bittersweet gifts of wisdom and retribution, a double-edged sword capable of manifesting swift justice.

As Eeshell grew up, she wanted and asked for nothing, exhibiting smooth dignity from the time she could walk. Zita doted on her with weekly telephone calls and regular visits from LA.

Jesús never knew the edgy teenager wearing an embroidered peasant blouse, tight white jeans and green snakeskin boots he met when he was 20 and working security at a Voodoo Glow Skulls concert took seed with their child after the show.

Eshell never knew either.

The same night Jesús went to prison for beating a man to death in a Santa Maria bar parking lot, Eeshell's 15th birthday, Zita went home to Culiacán to hone her witchcraft skills to an edge as sharp as a new machete. Jesús never knew his daughter lived in Santa Maria near Preisker Park in the very town where he would eventually work as a newspaper columnist after his release from prison.

"I must go," Zita told Eeshell, the loving teenager whose deep green eyes glistened with tears. "One day you'll understand."

Zita never told Jesús she was leaving Los Angeles. She just

disappeared. As much as temporarily deserting her son hurt, Zita headed back to her roots where she would remain until her wayward boy discovered the mighty resolve and courage of the original Jesús Malverde and promised to follow in his footsteps. Honor must guide her boy for the rest of his life, the sole requirement his holy ancestor needed to one day anoint him as a vessel of goodness necessary to right wrongs.

Fighting to save the world mattered even when you failed.

The battle itself mattered most.

Of course Zita suffered in the absence of her son and granddaughter. In her heart she knew Eeshell would blossom into the fine young woman who now lived in a small second-floor Pismo Beach apartment as a disciplined artist who crafted necklaces from nephrite jade she gathered at Jade Cove near Big Sur and sold to beach tourists.

Out of respect for her madrina, Eeshell lit candles she lined up on the La Santa Muerte shrine she constructed in the living room of her apartment after talking to Zita on the phone about her power and reading online about the death saint. The shrine grew larger and more intense over the years, what some might call dangerous, teeming with dried fish skeletons, small animal skulls Eeshell found on hikes in the surrounding hills or bought at flea markets and polished as well as a dozen unidentified jaw bones and teeth bleached from the sun.

A second altar in Eeshell's little apartment honored Maya moon goddess Ixchel, upon whom Eeshell depended more than anyone knew. Her namesake offered a psychic connection that rippled in her innermost self whenever Eeshell thought about the ancient Maya civilization that worshipped the powerful deity.

Like Ixchel, Eeshell could and would give life. Eeshell could and would punish when the need arose. As much as Eeshell loved peace she understood violence, natural selection, survival of the fittest. Still, Eeshell craved peace more than anything.

Ultimately we all do.

Small rainbows Eeshell crafted from jade hung from the ceiling in her apartment. A bare-chested statue of the moon goddess took up a corner of Eeshell's bedroom. Stuffed animal sea turtles and other soft creatures lent testament to Ixchel's life-giving and death-dealing power.

Zita counseled Eeshell to learn patience, to only ask questions that do not disrespect privacy. Eeshell respectfully agreed. Whenever they talked on the phone Eeshell always winced at hearing the first deep inhale Zita took, the long, first drag she drew from her Spittle non-filter cigarette, a sound deeply rooted into Eeshell's mind. Somebody should pay for dispensing such evil, Eeshell thought, as if she had read her godmother's mind. Tobacco is as bad as heroin or fentanyl, maybe worse.

Somebody should pay.

DANCING HOOCHA WEEDS

"OK, SISTERS, time to make the weed wine," Mel said.

At the sound of his voice about two dozen young female Hoocha Weed plants, growing in a damp spot near a small hidden lake carved out behind a small dune, began to undulate to the left and undulate to the right, twerking their little stems back and forth in time to the music of the universe.

Mel spoke in his melodious singsong voice.

"You dig helping me make Hoocha Weed wine, don't you?"

Not embarrassed by the attention, one Hoocha Weed spoke up.

"You want to dance, Mr. Toker?"

Mel's nerve endings tingled as he began to boogie from the center of his soul man core. With the stern but soft guidance of a seasoned Zumba instructor, the chief Hoocha Weed danced along, explaining the benefits of doing just a little dance in the morning as she watched Mel's moves.

"Shake-shake-shake my leaves," she said. "Dig deeper into moist loamy sand with my roots to get to the water here by our little hidden lake. Hot in the morning but I bathe in sunshine's early luster. Energy builds in my roots and the roots of my roots."

On a whim Mel somersaulted, rolled and stood on his head for morning yoga as the Hoocha Weed continued to preach.

"I started stretching way back in my beginning, even before I cracked the seed and burst from the shell to push my way into the light," she said. "That rising flash from the sun helps me grow and gets me high."

Upside down Mel listened, focusing on the merit of her message.

"We're a lot more than pot plants," she said. "We're pioneers born here in the dunes. You're the only one who knows we live here."

"Shhhhhh," said Mel. "Don't tell anybody."

Casting off his homemade loincloth, Mel now moved into a naked warrior pose. In the summer he communed as a Buddhist, in the winter a nudist. Or was it vice versa? The plants didn't mind. They too lacked inhibition. Minus the brainwashed installation of prudish self-consciousness, they all grooved together in sunshine and health. Now Mel kicked into the Twist. The Hoocha Weed dancers joined him in exercising exuberant beach blanket gyrations.

"Maybe it's the blend of soil, sand and water, night cool air blowing in from the ocean," said the Hoocha Weed leader. "Maybe it's the mountains behind us and the fog that rolls in from the sea. Maybe it's the blend of elements that come together and produce the right recipe for Hoocha Weed wonder. Whatever factors make us potent."

"Power to the pistils," Mel said.

"We need to touch more people," said the lead Hoocha Weed. "We need to pollinate the people."

"Pollination to the people," Mel said.

Gathering up his winemaking ingredients, Mel inventoried his stock, everything he needed for a fresh batch of Hoocha Weed wine displayed in front of him on the sand: One pound of stems, one pound of leaves. No seeds ever because they make the wine taste lousy and don't have any THC in them anyway. Four cloves, two oranges, three limes, ¼ tsp cardamom, ¼ tsp nutmeg, ½ tsp ground cinnamon and 3 large clam shells that act like soup bones in a ham and bean soup. And grapes. A multitude of grapes. Plus what Mel called "Hoocha Weed squeezins," secret ingredients he kept in a pillowcase buried in a hole he dug under his shack.

Wherever he could confiscate grapes Mel stockpiled the luscious, sugary ripe orbs until he was ready to crush and use the fruit alongside the rusting metal sieve he used for draining spaghetti and sat waiting to be filled. Pinot noir grapes, chardonnay grapes, syrah grapes, cabernet grapes, any kind of grape worked to produce yet another masterpiece batch of the Hoocha Weed wine.

Dumping all the fixings into the pot he placed on the fire he built from driftwood, he added extra orange peel for appeal. Vitamin C empowered the citrus fruit, slamming more bang into what weed gods call the dope Entourage Effect that kicks in when the sum total is greater than the power of each individual part.

Next Mel boiled the mixture at a slow gentle roll for two hours, scratching around in the brew with a stick whenever the urge itched to make sure the magic potion didn't evaporate too much, then adding brown sugar and a couple dozen raisin bread crusts he saved up over the past few weeks. Sometimes he used prunes to keep the brew regular. Leftover hard Christmas candy worked wonders. Grabbing the colander, he strained which wasn't a strain at all. Pouring the mix into bottles, jars and jugs, he capped them, wrapped the bottles in swaddling clothes and buried the containers in the sand.

Weeks later Mel would dig up his stash and drink until his brain followed El Sol and dropped below the horizon, keeping his product to himself although he did recently share the nectar with Bud whom he met one day when Bud got lost on the beach walking in circles looking for his mind. Mel liked Bud because Bud often didn't know where he was. Mel always knew where he was so they made a good pair. Bud was hooked on his weird belly button salve but was fast becoming attached to Hoocha Weed wine.

Loud exhaust backfires sounded in the distance, moving closer and closer until Mel spotted the 24-foot-long, 14-foot-high identified rolling object (IRO) Doobiemobile cresting one of the shifting dunes that led to his hut. Rubbing his eyes, Mel wondered if he finally lost what was left of his mind. The closer the vehicle got the more the motor on the cruising groove tube purred like a Cheshire cat wearing a top hat in a made-for-LSD cartoon. Bud rolled into the enchanted land and came to a stop. Stepping unsteadily from the bubble-nosed cockpit, he and his hitchhiker shook seriously stoned stupor from their heads.

"From one deep fried doobie to another," Bud said. "Mr. Moyle, I'd like you to meet Reefer Johnson."

"You boys are just in time for Happy Hour," Mel said.

Startled, Reefer looked to the dune and took Bud by the arm.

"What was that moving over there?"

"Dancing Hoocha Weeds," Mel said.

"Weeds can't dance," Reefer said.

"Tell that to the dancing Hoocha Weeds," Mel said.

READ ALL ABOUT IT

IN MUSTARD morning sun Culiacàn smells of crisp corn tortillas and peppered eggs fried with shrimp, onions and jicama. The street teems with aromas tangy as a Persian lime grove after a steady spring shower.

"You ready for this?" Tripper asks.

"After our showdown at the border, what could go wrong?" I say.

"Your favorite uncle learned more about the birds and the bees than any of his twisted sexcapades ever taught him," Tripper says.

"A little overkill if you ask me," I say. "But I have a feeling word's out in Culiacàn about my late Uncle Arturo and company."

"I'm still super freaked out by honey bees that gave your uncle the biggest buzz he ever ran into in his miserable life," Tripper says.

Pointing to *The Culiacàn City News* daily color tabloid head-quarters across the street from where we stand, Tripper says, "You, my hero, are on your way to orientation at your new job. Think you can handle living the quiet life of a crusading crime columnist lined up against the evil banditos?"

"I can handle anything," I say. "Even you."

Tripper glides in to playfully jab me on the upper arm. I easily slip the punch. The orange front doors to the newspaper building shimmer in the blistering midday heat. A green neon business sign the size of a food truck shows bullet holes. Breaking news is always just a trigger pull away.

Sitting on his haunches beside the entrance, a stooped man wearing white whisker stubble watches me with runny eyes as piercing as hot needles. Asking if I'd like a shoeshine, he seems harmless and looks hungry. Appearing more gringo than homegrown in my blue hand-tooled boots, I know my roots burrow deep into ceme-tery soil that holds the remains of my ancestors. The old man senses purpose. One look at my freshly cut coal black hair and trimmed moustache gives me away.

I am Jesús Malverde, the Mexican angel of the poor. The devil goatee that once made me look sinister is gone. My unruly long hair has disappeared. A sculpted and dignified persona is on display for all Mexico to see.

"A shine for free," the old man says in English. "To polish the past."

Reaching into my jeans pulling out a small peso bill, I slip the money into the front pocket of the old man's faded pink cowboy shirt.

"To the future," he says.

Tripper pops two pieces of Bubbaloo plátano chewing gum into her mouth and puts the small yellow pack back in her purse.

"I'll meet you here in two hours," she says.

As soon as her teeth bite into the liquid center banana-flavored gum, the building across the street explodes sending bricks, splintered wood, sharp metal and torn chunks of burned flesh into a bright fiendish flash of terror. The blast originates in the newspaper lobby where a few customers gather to pay bills and order back copies of the gruesome chronicle that concentrates on cartel violence ranging from murder, torture and other drug-related events, including lavish weddings. Unscathed by flame or debris, Tripper spins and dives beneath a churro truck parked beside the paint-chipped curb.

I leap with outstretched arms over the hood of a taxi, touching the ground with the fingertips of my right hand, rolling up my outstretched right arm and shoulder and land on my back in a classic jiujutsu break fall. Standing in one smooth motion, I run to Tripper and kneel beside the truck's back right brake light.

The smell of grilled meat fills the air.

"The shoeshine man is dead," I say.

"So is he," she says, pointing to the gutter.

The blast blew the well-meaning yet still timid editor/publisher from his swivel chair in a second-floor office where he was going through the motions of announcing to the staff news that he had hired a two-fisted news columnist to provide spark to the paper. The blast propelled him through the window and into the street, his body and head crushed and oozing on the sidewalk. Tiny flames lick the pinstripes of his dark blue suit. Smoke curls from his still buttoned pinstriped vest.

Splattered gray brain matter looks like steaming hot cereal spilled from an earthen breakfast bowl. As sirens begin to wail, a stray mongrel dog runs to the medium rare corpse, sniffing with his tail between his legs, fearfully approaching the mystery entrée as an unexpected gift.

Disheveled and sloppy in an olive drab police uniform, a traffic patrolman thin as one-ply toilet paper appears and points a pistol at my forehead. Hissing his words, he says, "Freeze."

Regalo skitters toward the policeman's ankle.

"I'm a journalist," I say.

Pressing the barrel tight against my head, the cop shows a dirty grin exposing a green speck of jalapeño pepper stuck to his gold front tooth.

"Journalism is a crime," he says.

I slowly point to the newspaper offices consumed by fire and smoke.

"I work there," I say.

Walking to the smoldering corpses, the unshaven lawman moves the pepper stuck to his tooth with his tongue, spitting on my murdered editor's charred ear that lies on the road a foot away from the rest of his head. Sneering, the cop nudges the editor's body with his bloody black boot.

Looking up he says, "Looks like you'll miss your deadline."

VIVA LA SANTA MUERTE

GUNFIRE slays all hope for tranquility.

In a makeshift camp 100 yards from Arturo's picked over remains, not knowing how else to behave, the few ragged survivors of the late renegade drug boss's cartel fired guns into the night sky, trying to shoot down constellations and blow holes in the moon.

Bad move.

Real bad move.

Drinking tequila and shooting since noon, what remained of what Arturo called his "empire" called his name, fought with knives, argued, cried, and mourned, screaming drunken oaths of vengeance for hours after their leader's demise.

"Arturo!"

Bang!

"Arturo!"

Boom!

"Arturo."

Bang, boom!

For all his ugly faults, Arturo commanded this inner circle of low functioning underlings for years with direct orders, fear and above average intelligence that worked well in the local yokel drug trade. Once considered a potential captain among established Sinaloa cartel chiefs, Arturo eventually betrayed his compatriots and struck out on his own.

With pistols, rifles and a new bazooka discharging into the mountainside, Arturo's men wallowed in mayhem. Free but fearful, they knew Arturo would never have accepted such reckless displays of weak emotion or the careless waste of ammunition.

A terrified rabbit family huddled at the edge of the river. Three desert cottontails, a mommy, daddy and baby hare, stared from a clump of brush. Standing above the bunnies, a hazy figure reached with a skeletal hand into a black satin bag and produced a handful of fresh wild green chard. Stooping and extending her gift, the bony woman wearing a purple shawl over her head called to the rabbits in a soft voice that comforted the animals.

Sniffing, wriggling his nose, daddy rabbit stretched a furry neck to the chard and nibbled, burying his face in the cushion of vegetable bounty. Mommy rabbit moved cautiously to the offering, gently biting into a corner piece of leaf. Just as baby bunny mustered the courage to lean forward for a taste, a nearby shotgun blast erupted. Panicked and skittering back against the warm folds of his mother's belly, the tiniest bunny closed his eyes and shivered.

Kneeling on dusty earth, the woman lightly placed the handful of chard on the ground. Standing to full height, she turned to the sound of explosions and started to walk toward the gunfire. Wearing a bleached bat skull necklace around her throat she seemed to be floating. Gunfire stopped when she came into sight and continued gliding toward the pack of unruly men. Another shot rang out, kicking up dirt close to her bloodless, ashen feet. The cadaverous shape kept coming. Another shot and now the crack of a bullwhip snapped close to her left ear. The woman stopped.

"One more step I snap off your ear," said a bandit wearing a $300 black Cuernos Chuecos cowboy hat with a satin crown lining.

"Look into the bat's eyes and threaten me again," the woman said.

The man saw tiny red sparks flash from the empty bat skull sockets.

"What man among you will look into the devil's eyes? Who will risk losing his sight as his pupils shrink like plump grapes turned to dead shriveled raisins?"

"We are sorry, La Santa Muerte," said another bandit. "We didn't know it was you."

"You are all cowards," said the Mexican death saint who makes even the hardest men tremble. "Weaklings scare bunnies. Your scalps will look lovely as part of my new winter shawl."

"We beg your forgiveness," said yet another bandit. "Please, La Santa Muerte, we will not sin again."

If these losers feared her as the ultimate demon magician, believed she carried the perfumed scent of a corpse and spoke directly to their ancestors, especially to their grandmothers and mothers, why did the gangsters live lives of rotten debauchery and immoral degradation? Why did these skittish scarecrow souls keep hurting people?

Suspicion ruled as the man holding the whip snorted and turned away so quickly that the shining crystal-studded black embroidery on the back of his jacket flashed like lightning. A man chewing a piece of straw and holding a pump action shotgun snickered and walked to a new black pickup and opened the door. Throwing the heavy weapon against the passenger side door, he slid behind the wheel, slammed the door, turned over the engine and pulled away in a cloud of dust. Another bandit scratched his blue embroidered cowboy shirt encased beer belly that poured over a polished silver belt buckle adorned with a carved stallion rising on two legs. Looking at the ground, he alone deferred to the goddess of death.

"Please forgive us," he said.

Spitting into the dust, La Santa Muerte bared teeth in a twisted sneer that shined like green jewels from Hell.

That solitary man would later swear under torture from rival cartel members that he saw the devil's sharpened fangs glisten with blood. Her eyes flashed crimson. Screaming until he passed out as his torturers peeled his skin from his body to make new flesh-tanned boots, he denied betraying the Sinaloa cartel.

About two miles away the buzzing began again, this time from angry killer bee stragglers who missed the first attack on Arturo. Now they initiated their own assault streaming through the pickup truck's open window to cover the driver's face. Newly blinded, the bandit drove the black pickup off the road where the truck overturned and burst into flames. The cruel cowboy with the whip lost his sight as fire bees roared into his eyes. The last of Arturo's once macho desperadoes dug fingernails into their faces for relief as bees swarmed and burned life from the living who believed like fools they would live forever.

Driven to frenzy by nature's increasing imbalance, climate

change and global dysfunction, the bees would dominate more and more of the land, adapting to breeding conditions and clime where they had never before prevailed.

Ossified and looking fried from scalding sunshine, the satisfied skeletal woman still had the touch. Would her power wane in the 21st Century turning her into just another folky memory whose fury disappeared like ice cubes in a margarita glass left on the bar until morning?

Unlike the bandits she would see.

 **GOT POT?**

BEFORE his daddy died, Reefer's only two big item possessions included a used backhoe and a used girlfriend. A well-oiled machine and somebody to love made his rustic world fire on all cylinders no matter how cold winter got on the mountain.

Branch loved him back too, or so she said.

Reefer once told Aunt Irma how he felt about the ex-waitress at the winery where he dug the sewer line for free.

"Branch is hotter than homemade possum pie right out of the oven," he said.

Aunt Irma slapped him in the back of the head with the telephone book she was about to use to balance the kitchen table that leaned right after the leg broke and Reefer tried unsuccessfully to fix it with black electrician's tape.

"You can't fix nothing," she said. "Now you're walking around with that hussy's boobies bouncing around like swollen water balloons in your head. Not to mention she got a baby swastika tattooed on her forehead. A real woman woulda got a big one on her chest."

Humiliated, Reefer retreated to the garage where he changed the oil in the back hoe and slapped another new bumper sticker on the side door. Daddy opposed public announcements of any kind that might alert the feds, but since nobody saw the bulky piece of equipment except like-minded neighbors in the know, Reefer's relatively dull political expressions by West Coast standards didn't really matter.

"Got Pot?"

"God Made Weed. In God We Trust."

Reefer rebelled in his own mellow way. Daddy flipped when he found out Reefer used the hoe to dig the sewer line for that skanky nutcase of a terrorist his men claimed was related to Charlie Manson. The hometown militia was supposed to keep a low profile. A blood relative Manson groupie was just too much to take.

"I only did a favor for the girl I'm gonna marry," Reefer said.

"You'll get us all locked up."

"Sorry, Pa."

"When's the wedding?"

"November 10."

Commander Fetus, pro-life champion of unborn prisoners of war wallowing in wombs and esteemed exalted leader of the Weed Eaters white man's militia, chewed his lip and thought a bit.

"The wedding's off," he said.

"Why?"

"That's the same day as the Marine Corps' birthday," Commander Fetus said.

"You wasn't no Marine, Daddy."

"I coulda been."

"Thank you for your service," Reefer said.

All those baffling family memories now just pushed up severe mental illness images like wild flowers on the settling graves of every Weed Eaters' member killed in the Mexican butchery. Reefer had no idea it wasn't Mexican at all, an historic event on the pot frontier that rivaled the Gold Rush for personal significance as far as Reefer was concerned.

A whole white man militia headed up by his own flesh and blood was gutted by Mexican bandits who got away scot free after setting fire to his girlfriend, Branch. How his poor old lady got in the middle of that blazing shoot-out and burned to a crispy critter was beyond him. With everybody dead, though, Reefer knew he had to get even.

Getting even was as American as a man could get.

Truth be told, he was relieved the bad citizen soldiers were all dead. Finally free to live life the way he wanted, Reefer decided against his initial impulse to seek revenge. Now, since meeting his new best friend Bud, he would hold off for a while longer.

Freedom is just another word for nothing left to bruise. Maybe Reefer'd be lucky enough to find himself another girlfriend, maybe a dental hygienist in faded green medical scrubs who could fix his teeth and get him high on laughing gas nitrous oxide. Tired of taking hits, not bong hits but blows to the heart, depression ruled his life since he was ten.

Chill, be cool, he told himself.

Stay stoned.

Lighting up a joint on the Oceano sand as Mel and Bud slept by their bonfire beneath more falling stars than Reefer had ever seen, he felt the smoke clear his lungs and work its way into his bloodstream. Tiny specks of blue glitter flashed in his eyes, looking like confetti dropping from inside his skull. Life looked good. Reefer flushed with independence. But what about them south-of-the-border desperadoes who killed his Pa? A new one-man Mexican-American War would have to wait.

At least now he had a pal.

Settle down.

Enjoy the ride.

Later the next day, he and Bud slid into picnic table seats for lunch at a roadside food truck and scanned the menu. Reefer focused on the entrées.

"What's a camarón?"

"Shrimps," said Bud.

"I'll have a couple of them camarón shrimps," Reefer told the cook.

"Make mine two," said Bud.

Again Reefer seemed dismayed.

"Is a camarón shrimp one shrimp or two shrimp?"

Now Bud froze with paranoia as he asked the cook a question about the menu.

"Is camaróns one shrimp or two shrimps? Or is it two shrimp?"

The cook's smile started draining from his face. More than a little wrecked himself on the pure sativa flower he smoked before work in his favorite swan-shaped water pipe, the cook got anxious. So unsure was he of the answer he had to call his wife to check.

Bud wiped sweat from his brow.

Reefer nodded.

A woman in a loose purple and green tie-dyed dress that ended at her ankles appeared out of nowhere. Smelling of apricots and See Canyon apple slices, her words sounded soft as lamb's wool feels at the Avila Barn petting zoo.

"Would you two handsome boys like to buy some of my love beads?"

Both men later agreed Eeshell reminded them of a mermaid, although Bud said she also looked like she could fly. Both men fell deeply in love at the very same time.

After Eeshell got home that night and ate a 100 mg vegan edible THC purple gummy bear made with plant-based pectin, she reflected on the best day she ever had in the love bead business. Two guys high as an asteroidal midair collision bought three dozen jade necklaces she carried in her hippie bag.

The next morning Eeshell walked to the beach and went for a long swim. When she emerged from the water she sat alone on a cliff combing thick black hair that hung to her waist. Watching a sailboat in the distance she imagined pirates headed to shore only to crash among the slimy green moss-covered rocks at her feet.

Why did she feel so mystified, like somebody knew something about her she didn't, data she needed to know? Why did she feel alone? Empty. Almost desperate.

What would Ixchel do?

PEACE OF MIND

STIRRING fresh ripples with a lime green straw stuck in a double margarita, Tripper raises her head and locks eyes with me. Only a few customers sit scattered outside in the shade of the small bar near the Malverde Capilla (Capilla de Jesús Malverde), the chapel dedicated to the man, the myth, the legend. I can tell by her eyes she's got a big question.

"Did you see the falcon in the sky after Arturo and his men attacked?"

"I did."

"You see the glimmer when the same bird swooped over the flames of the newspaper building?"

"I did."

"What else did you see?"

"C'mon, Tripper, I saw it and don't know what to think."

"What'd you see?"

"A silver peace sign medallion."

"I knew it," Tripper says.

Pulling the straw from her glass, sucking on the end and slapping it on the table, she raises her almost full glass and drains her drink. An observant server races to her side, presenting even teeth as he wipes smooth hands on a clean white apron.

"Would the lady like another?"

I cover my face with both hands and slowly shake my head. Sensing the tension, Regalo looks up from enjoying a margarita droplet on the floor. Tripper places her chin in her palm.

"What did you call me?"

Ill at ease the server steps back.

"Please, madam. What did I do?"

Offering a weak smile, I intervene.

"Get us another drink before this radical feminist cuts off

those poor sexist balls of yours and racks them up on the pool table. I won't tell you what she'll use as a pool cue."

Again Tripper sees the falcon, the glimmer, the peace sign.

"Please forgive me, friend," Tripper says. "I am sorry. And, yes, I'll have another double margarita, please, when you have time, mi amigo."

Looking skyward, I follow the bird as it flies through deep blue sky that offsets the bird's sandy brown plumage and distinctive "moustache" stripe pattern from wing to wing. Climbing with a full wingspan, the bird tips its wings like a fighter pilot as if to salute us, rising to continue its path over the city. Tripper gives me the gentle eyes of a first-grade teacher addressing a new class of children.

"Wally Wilson was our friend," she says. "Wally died for us when he lit himself on fire to help protect the world from his madness, OK? His sickness. His violent insanity. Wally gave his life so we might live free from responsibility for our sins."

I nod in agreement as she continues, her voice rising like an escaped parrot on the run.

"And he took Syrah, that nut voice inside his head with him," she says. "Wally didn't know how else to get better."

"Like a Buddhist monk protesting the Vietnam War and Jesus Christ put together," I say.

"Wally did away with his part in evil that never dies," says Tripper. "Our conscience helps us decide what we see and what we hear. We make decisions every day. We fight temptation. Remember the Garden of Eden?"

"Syrah meant well," I say.

"Until she rented a room in your head and trashed it," Tripper says.

Stroking my new moustache, I say, "OK, good riddance, Syrah. So how do we get better, heal, do good things?"

"We learn from Wally's kind legacy whether he's guiding us from another life in the sky or whether he's just plain dead and his grisly imperfect example is all we have to remember. Wally was a world-class serial killer, but the most lovable serial killer anybody could ask for."

Leaning across the table close to Tripper's face, I say, "So how do you explain the peace sign necklace Wally's mother gave him to wear that he wore until the day he lit himself up like a Roman candle? How'd the talisman get on the bird?"

"The falcon could have picked it up by accident," Tripper says. "You ever watch a sea turtle struggle to remove a plastic 6-pack ring after getting entangled? Or, if you believe in witchcraft or reincarnation, the bird could really be Wally reborn. What do you believe, Jesús?"

"I believe in uncertainty," I say without thinking too deeply.

"Either way Wally's on our side," Tripper says. "Wally's always been on our side, on the side of good. His sainted hippie mother Mary Jane would be so proud of her baby."

"I hope she doesn't show up," I say.

"You never know, man. What I do know is Wally's guiding us, watching over us, helping protect us," she says.

"People see what they want to see. I don't buy into all that supernatural mystical bullshit on either side of the border," I say.

"Tell it to Zita," Tripper says. "Your mother's the witch."

"My mother's a believer."

"I'm serious," Tripper says. "Like evil, like Syrah, witchcraft lies in the eye of the beholder. Ask your favorite lynched ancestor about rising from the dead or walking on water. Ask the Pope about his miracles. The only Miracles I'm sure of are those who sang backup for Smoky Robinson. But that doesn't make people's experiences bullshit, just unexplained stranger-than-science symbolic lessons of life."

"I see," I say.

"Yes, you do. People see what they want to see."

"What do you see, Tripper?"

Reaching to take a full margarita from the server's shaking hand, Tripper sits silently sipping from a fresh straw stuck into a fresh glass packed with sparkling cracked ice.

"Trouble," she says. "I see nothing but trouble."

"No peace?"

Tripper looks at me like I'm not even here.

SMOKING ALLOWED

ASSEMBLY line workers smoked like fiends at the Spittle Cigarettes sweatshop factory outside the Santa Maria city limits whether they wanted to smoke or not.

Employees and others smoked everywhere in work spaces, toilets, conference rooms, the employee cafeteria, and the fitness center—mandatory and illegal, of course, since management can't force workers to smoke cigarettes in a warehouse where smoking is against state and federal law anyway.

But Arthur von Spittle controlled all the action with bribes to government officials, intimidation, violence and fine grain tobacco leaf shipped by air express daily from North Carolina to Spittle's illegal manufacturing plant to be turned into cigarettes sold mostly to undocumented Mexicans on the Central Coast, all fresh, cheap, and dangerous to your health.

In the same plant Spittle also manufactured his new cannabis hybrid, a product that blended high-intensity toxic nicotine infusion and a minor THC buzz created in the building's basement where special secret workers paid a dollar more an hour added supercharged lab-produced nicotine to the tobacco smokes.

Spittle butts and ash littered floors, desks, hallways and staircases in the three-story brick building. The place stank of stale smoke. Nicotine stained workers' fingers and lips a deep brownish yellow as they toiled in a toxic environment. You want to work you have to smoke. Even sales people lit up as soon as they entered the lobby. You want to do business with Spittle, you smoked Spittle cigarettes.

Nobody complained or filed formal complaints. Most workers smoked anyway and needed the work however demeaning their shift schedules, treatment, or conditions. Besides, they got all the free cigarettes they wanted for the first year of their employment.

One health condition they knew nothing about, though, took place in the boss's body. Each day for the past month small parasitic worms crawled through CEO boss Spittle's intestines, inching their way to his heart, meandering slowly as fat heartworms do, finding their way across his duodenum where they mixed with bile from the gallbladder and digestive juices from the pancreas. Laying eggs as they slithered the little worms grew into big worms, some a foot long that found their place snuggled against the body walls where they created and reproduced more maggots, grub and larva.

Arthur von Spittle asked for the truth.

The physician stared at his shoes.

"You got worms," he said.

Arthur von Spittle sensed movement in his rectum.

"Worms like I've never seen, like these nasty wrigglers. Most the size of one of your cigarettes, about 2 and ¾ inches long," the doctor said. "That's what the worms in your heart look like."

Arthur von Spittle tried to sit stoically on the thin white paper that crinkled beneath his expanding behind. Trying his best to exert some type of executive privilege, he poked a forefinger in the doctor's face and asked a big question.

"What can we do about it?"

"I'm worried if we open you up the worms will move so fast trying to escape they'll clog the chambers and shut down operation of the heart muscle."

"Plan B?"

"We let you go living as long as you can with the worm farm."

"How long do I have?"

"Based on what we know from dog research, I'd say six months."

"Guess I'll have to get cracking then."

"Meaning?"

"Meaning I have to ramp up the sales plan for my new and improved discount weed before I check out."

"Why not just relax, enjoy the time you have left? Why spend your last months hustling to make money, desperate for cash you won't live to spend?"

Arthur von Spittle checked his Rolex with a blue face and a

Jubilee band.

"It's not the money. It's the power to do as I please."

Smiling as he stepped into the hallway, Arthur von Spittle punched in a West Coast number on his high-end cell phone, waiting for fifteen rings with no voicemail before his long-lost wastrel son picked up.

"Mellowyellowhellow," Bud said.

"You never change," his father said.

"My underwear occasionally," Bud said.

"We need to sit down and shape a plan to take over the cigarette slash pot slash vaping trade on the Central Coast," Arthur von Spittle said. "Billions of dollars in profits await in Santa Barbara County alone. I'll give you fifteen hundred a week to manage the business."

"A grand or nothing," Bud said.

"Deal."

At that very moment they fused a slick transaction, a final father/son family business destined to overshadow the plump vineyards and skunk stinky pot grows popping up all over this aristocratic picturesque county loaded with bloated plutocrats and overfed wine merchants.

"Can I keep the Doobiemobile?"

"It's yours."

"Can I toke and drive?"

"Anything to make my boy happy."

"Aw, dad."

When he hung up Arthur von Spittle felt nauseous. The kid was a lost cause but had the kind of overcharged super brain required to cut through the red tape in an already out-of-control pot industry and see light at the end of the spliff. Once the business got underway, though, Arthur von Spittle would punch a one-way ticket for his offspring to spend the rest of his life in an asylum for the terminally damaged stoner, out of the way and legally committed against his will into a nice designer strait jacket so dear old dad could relax and enjoy his final days.

All Arthur von Spittle needed before he died was one big

personal score to fuel his ego to show he was better than all those smart-ass Cali aristocrats drinking chardonnay and now sucking down designer Frankenjoints. Before you know it, they'd be loading up commercially available caviar balls with THC. They'd make rolling papers from gold leaf. These pompous bastards always thought they were better than anybody with a tobacco background, including a vicious cheap tobacco cigarette manufacturer who would soon show them who was boss.

Arthur von Spittle would hook the moneyed beautiful people's pampered pompous kids on high-powered deadly nicotine, ingested through hipster-sucking vaping and oversized joints of bad weed. Arthur von Spittle's legacy would continue as do-gooders tried to crush cigarette companies out of business.

Even dead Arthur von Spittle would survive.

Of course, nobody was better equipped than Bud to drive the Doobiemobile through the doors of perception and eventually off a cliff into the ozone.

What neither Arthur von Spittle nor Bud knew was that Zita, a chain-smoking, cancer stricken witch in Culiacán, Mexico, had cursed the nicotine tycoon with an agonizing death spell—the only way she could stop smoking her favorite Spittle brand and show La Santa Muerte she was worthy of respect.

"Time to butt out," Zita said as she prepared to work her magic.

DUNE DEVILS

BLAZING bonfires fueled with driftwood, charcoal lighter fluid and fractured frames of used furniture ripped from abandoned and rusted recreational vehicles illuminated the foggy dune buggy encampment where Adam convened a motorized posse of men and women who shared common bloodlust under a black and white skull and crossbones flag.

Calling themselves Dune Devils this ragtag gang of buggy mutants ruled with an iron transmission. Revenge bubbled in their veins even though they weren't quite sure what Adam expected them to do about the fatal coyote attack. Abbie died and he needed vengeance on the animals that gutted his wife. Wild coyotes wouldn't stand a chance against unstable duners chasing them down at full throttle until the beasts' bones crunched beneath their buggy wheels.

Oceano Dunes State Vehicular Recreation Area is heaven and hell, the only California state park where you can drive on the beach, a vast 1,500-acre natural wasteland beset by a subculture of primitives who have the collective brain power of jellyfish that lack a thinking organ yet feel pain.

As much a testosterone proving ground as the Bonneville Salt Flats in Utah for jet engine land speed records, the dunes exist for raw men, women and their already brainwashed children willing to take risks and buck the odds of living. Death in the dunes happens frequently. More than 50 have died since 1992. Duneheads long ago got used to loss of life and wore the prospect of grave passage like a badge of honor.

Adam sometimes snickered after hearing of a fatality, often somebody he knew.

"More beer for me," he'd say.

With Abbie's hearty party days over, her prime mate now

sought the sense of justice that usually went missing in his world. To accomplish that elusive goal, he decided to live more like an animal than he already did. In his prime Adam stood tall among misfits. Even before he hit the dunes to claim chiefdom amid the sand mountains, he proclaimed himself king of Bakersfield, a lanky ruggedly handsome numbskull who had enough of what it takes in a crusty hard town to win a used muck queen amid leftover debris. Once, high on Everclear high-proof grain alcohol, he pulled his own eye tooth with a pair of needle nose plyers to win two tickets to the Bakersfield Monster Truck Pit Party.

Abigale also had what it takes with pot breath and beer stains on her Sunday dress she hemmed up thigh-high and wore to Bible school for the 13-to-17 class. Nineteen-year-old Adam needed a younger woman and Abbie's sweet 16 sure enough did the trick.

You could say the two teenagers loved each other, showing deep affection in fundamental ways like the first toot off fresh made meth for him or a gift of cold crab cakes and limp fries displayed on a greasy wax paper wrapper from the Portuguese food truck for her. Love comes wrapped in different packages. Tattoos do, too—a mouse with crossed eyes for her, a grinning sewer rat with a penis for him. They named their rodents Adam and Abbie. Now she was gone, chewed apart, eaten to the bone, slaughtered by a pack of ferocious predators in a supposedly safe place where she adored her role riding the dunes beside him.

The dune devils waited for their instructions.

"Kill," Adam said.

About 50 faithful outliers who considered themselves the baddest bad-asses among a normally badass subculture went silent. They represented the worst of the worst, thick untamed primates who roamed the dunes like zombie demolition derby survivors intent on staying drunk and disorderly no matter what the intoxicant. Getting even was a Bakersfield trademark for hundreds of years that only added to the thrill of the pursuit.

On the other side of these dunes, wildlife unfolded more gently. Watching three furry coyote pups rolling and tumbling over the dunes coming his way, Dunite hermit Mel Moyle clapped and started to whistle, kneeling as he egged on the pups.

"Here boy," he said. "Here girls. Good doggies. Good doggies."

One male and one female, two lively, lovely critters eager for attention from this hairy creature so willing to welcome them, bounded into Mel's arms, knocking him backwards as they licked his face and whimpered with excitement and joy. You couldn't call them fluff balls with prickly strands of wiry hair exploding on end from their heads and pointy ears looking like punk rock band members bowing after a ragged show, but feral affection permeated every staccato breath, slobber and cumbersome step they took romping through sand country.

Mel had found them earlier huddled in a sand hole while their parents roamed dune peaks looking for food, so disoriented after the unexpected storm the parents briefly left the pups alone. Naming the children (yes, he called them children) posed a minor problem. The names had to fit their character and motivate Mel to laugh and feel joy whenever he observed them. Cute as they were, they didn't really need names to instill great wonder and love in his heart. But, out of his love and respect for a simpler past, the names Hugo, Ella, and Elwood, three legendary Dunites, made the final cut.

From the bluff Theo and Sophia (the names with which Mel christened Alpha Mom and Alpha Dad) watched in rapt silence, not sure what to make of Mel's motives with their offspring. Reaching deep into the canvas newspaper bag slung over his shoulder, the kind of gray coarse cloth bag armies of kids once depended on to deliver newspapers across the country, Mel pulled out chunks of dried fish he personally caught and smoked over an open fire. The three pups ran in circles, wetting themselves with glee as they vied for Mel's affection.

Looking on from the sand ridge Theo and Sophia fought the urge to charge down the hill for their own treats, leery of their new natural surroundings since they now walked with fresh blood on their breath, human blood they knew would soon draw a crowd of hunters who would do their best to kill them and their babies. Amid excited animal whimpers and eager fish flesh nips, the pups got lost in primitive reverie. They, too, lived as hunters, taking life and death as it came, surviving with instincts and wiles intact but always on high alert.

When the three pups heard Adam's bugle blast they froze in mid-chew, ears up, ready to escape. Ready to fight Theo and Sophia tensed. Mel stood to full height, looking into the distance as dune buggies roared closer. Off and running, the cubs raced to their parents, who ran wide patterns around their offspring so they might herd them to a safe place in the vast expanse of sand.

Leading a dozen or so mad dune riders, Adam's thick helmeted head with green eagle's wings painted on the sides appeared over the horizon. Holding and blowing a copper bugle with one hand and the steering wheel in the shape of a skull with green glass glaring eyes with the other, Adam led the mad platoon behind the swerving tail of his blownout, heavily modified sand machine.

Bellowing, drunk and drooling once they saw the cubs, the hunters throttled up, increasing speed as they tried to encircle and snare the animals with reckless dune runners, ATVs, tricked-out dump trucks with oversized tires, customized used Jeeps and hand-painted pickups when the first shot rang out. The bullet missed its mark. So did the oncoming lead fusillade, allowing the swift cubs time to scatter and disappear into the dunes.

Theo ran straight, fast and hard, leaping high as the buggy adjacent to Adam made the crest of a hill at about 45 miles-per-hour, using all the strength and spring in his legs to catch driver Petey Borda at the bottom line of his square sculpted jaw, sinking his teeth into his unshaven chin. The coyote's weight sent the driver into the air then sprawled hard on the sand. Never one to wear a safety harness, Petey had ejected from his seat. Screaming until his voice box broke, Petey wrapped his hands around the furry head and neck that reeked of foul breath stinking of rotten meat as he lost consciousness, his throat torn out by the wet fangs of a berserk coyote dad whose children almost perished as he stood by helplessly and watched.

A shot louder than the rest now erupted, echoing in the vast expanse of sandy wilderness. Wounded, Sophia went down, grazed but dazed nonetheless.

Spinning into a frenzied leap, Theo hit Cynthia Varner in mid victory yell, taking her down in a heap of black combat fatigues the woman had chosen as her look-at-me uniform among the pack that drove all the way from Fresno to camp in their own adrenaline-packed, gasoline-charged, alcohol-driven world. Reacting to the power of the tackle, Cynthia crashed into the ground head first, breaking her neck immediately on impact, landing so hard she heard the distinct crack of bone before losing consciousness and succumbing to her injury after a series of involuntary muscle spasms and herky-jerky movements of her limbs.

Sophia continued crawling for shelter, watching as the woman expired.

Now springing at Randall Breckenridge, half holding a child on his lap, the baby braced against the handlebars, Theo snarled and bit through the muscles in Randall's face. Resilient after being thrown and landing, Randall Jr. bounced in the sand and rolled down a dune like a cantaloupe, not knowing what jarred him from his dead Dunehead daddy's arms.

Another shot from another dune raider rang out, just missing Theo's snout and right eye. Sensing terror, the scrambling baby started to cry as Theo tore off Randall Breckenridge's left eyelid and cheek before vanishing behind another sand mountain where Sophia left a bloody trail after crawling to safety to protect her pups.

Sand shifted.

Dunes glistened.

The heavens listened.

Existence highlighted ugly cycles of sacred mystery and beautiful despair.

Mel Moyle appeared at the top of a swirling sand peak. Preening like Moses in "The Ten Commandments" movie (Cecil B. DeMille filmed the 1923 movie in the nearby Guadalupe dunes), alone and unafraid, he raised both hands into the air in a "don't shoot" pantomime. Glaring, he exuded white-hot defiance.

Throwing into low gear the monster yellow and black dune buggy flying a flag emblazoned with a picture of a hornet, Adam accelerated, picking up speed as he crested the top of the tan mountain, sliding to a stop in a spray of sand beside Mel's frail weathered body. Neither man moved as Hugo, Ella and Ellwood serenaded them with baby coyote howls in the distance, brave notes that carried in the chilly air.

Giving Adam Hazzard what Mel Moyle called his "moonpie" smile that turned his face into one sweet oval, Mel pointed to the sky where a prairie falcon circled lower and lower before climbing higher and higher.

"That bird is wearing a peace sign," Mel Moyle said. "That bird knows war is not the answer."

# WATCH OUT FOR SHARKS

IN A cold metallic voice the woman whispered, "Wake up."

Opening her eyes Eeshell looked left and right, spotting a sliver of moonlight flickering on the far blue wall of the tiny bedroom in her tidy Pismo Beach apartment, a perfect place for her to live above the America the Beautiful Restaurant where delicious smells of onions, peppers, home fries and eggs greeted her every morning. Goose bumps rose on Eeshell's arms. A chill snaked up her back. A cramp bit into her right ankle. Fighting the urge to throw up, she tried to lie still. Afraid and alone, she shivered.

"Who are you?"

Silence met her fear of the unknown until again Eeshell heard the woman's squeaky voice.

"I am Syrah Wilson."

Eeshell's vision spun as she took slow, conscious deep breaths to keep from fainting. Again the voice spoke, whiny now, seeking support, maybe pity, even comfort.

"I'm a widow. I heard you need a roommate," said Syrah.

Swinging long legs over the edge of the bed, Eeshell stood in a smooth move that balanced her weight on the balls of her bare feet. Acting relaxed as she could, she tried to ignore the voice and justify the interruption as remnants of a dream. Moving with the ease of a practiced country line dancer doing a two-step on hard wood, making her way past creaking floor boards and heading outside, Eeshell walked to the cliffs and made her way down a well-worn path to the ocean's edge.

Stepping into cool water without removing her cutoff gray sweat pants and black T-shirt, she walked slowly until she pushed off from her toes and fell face forward, keeping her chin tucked and arms outstretched, pressing fingers tightly together as she took her first stroke into the water world from which life on planet Earth long ago emerged.

Eeshell felt Syrah's presence all the way into deep water, the scary spirit mirroring Eeshell's motion like a twin shadow whose swift steady strokes took her a hundred yards into rough churning swells and into the open sea. Eeshell tried to clear her thoughts as Syrah did her best to torment and disturb even the thought of peace of mind.

"You could drown," Syrah said. "You're lucky I'm here."

Eeshell ignored the sense of dread gurgling in her gut. Turning her cheek to the right and away from the water, Eeshell twisted her body and inhaled through her open mouth. Turning back to the sea, she buried her head and face. Exhaling through her nose she heard bubbles. Eeshell kept swimming.

Syrah persisted.

"You afraid of sharks?"

Determined to ignore the voice in her head, Eeshell stroked harder, losing herself and Syrah in the buoyant cushion of wet reality. Now Eeshell turned onto her back, floating, wondering if she could sleep in the water. Pedaling, she slowly moved both hands along her sides, staying afloat and alert as she breathed in and out in a determined bid to maintain self-control.

"I think I see a great white," Syrah said in a language drawn from an ancient indigenous Mayan language of Yucatán, Mexico, Eeshell suddenly understood but didn't know how.

Eeshell wondered if she might just sink, go underwater forever. Is Syrah real? Does she exist only in Eeshell's mind? Does she pose a danger? Where did she come from? Flipping over again, Eeshell headed back to shore.

"I'm just kidding,' Syrah said. "I'll protect you."

Back on shore Eeshell climbed the cliff and walked home to the apartment above the morning breakfast smells of vacationing tourists and locals who know a good deal when they see one. Sunshine warmed her shoulders. The fresh air made her feel good. Without changing clothes she walked three blocks to the Pismo Beach Drug Store.

The grandfatherly white-coated pharmacist behind the counter looked up from filling a prescription for Valium. Scratching her arm, Eeshell studied the reddish irritation more enflamed now than it was when she first noticed the discoloration on the walk back to her downtown neighborhood.

Extending her right arm, Eeshell said, "I have a rash."

"That's odd," said the pharmacist. "Looks like fish scales."

"My little mermaid," said Syrah, her voice pounding in Eeshell's head.

ADIÓS MY SON

NOT FAR from where I stand a 20-something widow collapses on freshly hosed sidewalk outside the Jesús Malverde chapel entrance in Culiacán. An hour earlier, her cherubic husband doubled up on the same concrete, dropped by a single bullet fired by a local drug enforcer who didn't like his angelic looks.

Before pulling the trigger the drunken young outlaw said, "I don't like your soft face."

"Tell Rosa I love her," the young victim whispered to his killer standing over him in triumph.

"No, I won't," said the murderer, unwrapping a candy bar, taking a bite and holding the creamy dark chocolate out to his human sacrifice just in case he wanted a bite of a last meal.

Now Rosa wants to die, to join her handsome groom in heaven.

My mother Zita walks to her side, passing an open palm over the young woman's head, blessing her, relieving the crushing grief and fear the new widow feels in her loss. Slowly getting to her knees, rising slowly, the young woman kisses Zita's hand, sniffling as tears drip on bloodstains that discolor zigzagging cracks in the broken cement.

Zita says, "Jesús Malverde helps the living avenge the dead."

However the young woman understands, she understands. Zita's power passes from eye to eye, invisible but compelling. A powerful witch offers blessing or curse so her target quickly feels pain or pleasure.

Turning to me, Zita says, "You, too, must seek his help to live free of fear and recklessness. Jesús Malverde died for you."

Removing my new stiff white straw cowboy hat, I step slowly into the small prayer room packed tightly with flickering votive candles, expensive bottles of unopened tequila, Cuban cigars, brown caramel candy, photographs on walls and the ceiling, statues of saints and a large ceramic bust of my great-grandfather positioned on an offering altar arranged at the center of the room.

As a Jesús Malverde doppelgänger, a dead-on look-alike so explicit people start pointing at me and blessing themselves, the spitting image resemblance between me and my outlaw saint blood relative is startling. A man with a pearl-handled pistol visible in the waistband of his pants sees me, drops to his knees, takes my hand and kisses the knuckles.

I whisper to the main statue at the center of the room.

"I ask only for guidance," I say. "I'll take care of the rest."

A woman faints.

Turning to leave, I raise my hand. The crowd that now packs the shrine with sweating, weeping men, women and children parts. People reach to touch me. Their touches feel like marshmallow kisses. A woman holds out an infant whom I cradle, hand back and keep walking.

"You can't save Culiacàn," Zita calls out. "Culiacàn must save itself."

I try not to cry and face my mother.

"I'm only going back to the Central Coast because you promised to stop smoking if I do," I say. "I want you to live. I want you to come back to Santa Maria with me."

Zita laughs.

"Quitting the coffin nails is easier said than done," she says. "I will stop smoking cigarettes when Spittle stops making them. I'll return to the Central Coast shortly. In my own time."

I give Mamá a look that makes her eyes fill with tears.

"You always act in your own time," I say.

"Never forget you are the pure materialization of Jesús Malverde," Zita says. "You embody his legacy, his everlasting life, his mission for goodness. But you are needed elsewhere, where you will be safe."

"Unlike Rosa's husband," I say.

"Pistoleros share blood with the devil," Zita says. "They have explanations but no excuses for them trying to steal the heart of your ancestors."

"Will they ever put down their guns?"

"One day," she says. "One way or the other."

Together we stare into the abyss.

All I can do is try.

Taking my mother's hand, I ask, "When will you join us?"

"Soon," Zita says. "So we can hide together in plain sight like tens of thousands of Mexicans who do the hard work in Santa Maria gabacho white people resist."

A tear rolls down my cheek.

"Your flight leaves early in the morning," Zita says, kissing Tripper on the cheek before wrapping her arms gently around me, her baby.

By early evening the next day Tripper and I are checked into rooms my old homie El Maloso booked as a belated wedding gift for us at the Santa Maria Inn. We head out for a walk, exploring already familiar streets.

"All I want is a couple of fish tacos loaded with avocado and Valentina hot sauce," Tripper says.

"And a bottle of pinot noir," I say.

"My, my, haven't we become the Chicano snob," she says. "No bottle of rotgut tequila, a 6-pack of Tecate and a fat spliff?"

"Those days are gone," I say.

COCK-A-DOODLE-DO

OUT OF sight around the corner from the Santa Maria Inn two brilliantly colored fighting cocks circle each other in a ring of men gathered in the alley behind Mucho Loco Cantina. Roosters at their most ferocious, the birds feint and bob like professional bantamweight fighters, ready to strike when an opening appears.

A red and green bird darts rapidly toward the exposed neck of his opponent. Slipping the attack, the puffed up blue and yellow bird heads off the strike, sinking its beak into his attacker's eye.

Nearing the ring, Tripper and I stop talking when we hear a rooster crow, a skittish clamor that blares again and again.

Now I crave tequila.

Lots of it.

Instinctively sensing confrontation I flash on that long ago night pretty much across the street from the hotel where we now rent a room when I took the life that sent me to prison for eight years. Except for the occasional fire-breathing shot of tequila on very special occasions (like right now when I crave a bottle), I fight to limit my alcohol intake. Since the fatal fight in the bar parking lot I also swore off the late nightcap toke, blow of coke or any other illegal substance that could get me locked up and tied up in emotional knots.

An outlaw sometimes wants to go straight.

Staying clean and ramping up my aikido martial arts practice as the way to peace and harmony help keep me strong. Adding aiki-jujutsu, aikido's root combat application and a fast way to break opponents' bones, keeps me balanced, stable, sane, and calm. Maybe one day I'll even stop drinking, eat loads of yogurt and tofu instead of dreaming of cow tongue and bull's eye tacos washed down with a bottle of Patrón Silver.

Like my old pal and meditation martyr Wally Wilson used to say, more meditation, less medication. Nowadays, though, since full-scale legalization slammed California like a runaway tractor-trailer loaded with hay bales, all anybody wanted to talk about was weed. Weed this, weed that, weed makes the world go 'round. But I held back, hesitating to respond to the lure of getting lit. I admit I like weed. I like getting high.

Grabbing a leather drawstring pouch from her hippie shoulder bag, Tripper finds a thin pre-rolled rocket she hid in an empty lipstick tube. Pulling the stick in and out of her mouth to "baptize" the joint so it burns slowly, she lights the tip, inhales deeply and exhales.

"Want some of this?"

I narrow my eyes.

"You bring that with you on the plane?"

"I forgot I had it until now," she says.

"Like your mind?"

"Smoking gives me a clear head," Tripper says. "I can see through your skin all the way to your bones."

"Aren't you worried one day you'll bend over and brain cells will fall out of your ear like Cheerios?"

"Speaking of ears, are yours hearing that cry?"

With the urgency of a three-alarm animal rights inferno, increasingly loud rooster screams interrupt our teasing the way we do when we're a little on edge.

"I can't let this go," Tripper says. "Let's go see."

A small group of men press tightly in a circle behind Mucho Loco, leaning into the action that sends feathers skyward and dark droplets of rooster blood flying several feet into the air. Without a word, Tripper pushes her way into the circle, elbowing her way past a plump man wearing a black denim jacket with red embroidered horses stitched across the back.

Without speaking Tripper stoops and scoops up a fighting bird with her right hand. Spinning, she bends to scoop up the other bird with her left. Like they know her, the birds relax as if the life and death fight has left them and they know they are saved.

Gliding easily into the ring of cursing men and taking a cue from Tripper, I keep my mouth shut. For now my surprise presence keeps the strangers at bay. With my shoulders squared against the cloth of a tight white T-shirt that fits like extra skin across my chest, I move to Tripper's side and grab one of the roosters.

A middle-aged cockfighter with a bean pot belly bites down on a wet cigar stump as he reaches for my throat. Before he knows what hit him, his front tooth and cigarillo hit the dust. The event enforcer spits blood into a small pile of loose blue and yellow feathers.

I know how to punch. Spinning and moving fast, I snag Tripper by the arm, rush down the alley and around the corner. Still holding a bird she turns and grins.

"No harm, no foul," she says. "Or should I say 'fowl.' "

LUCHA LIBRE LOSER

BELOVED Mexican wrestlers regularly become national heroes.

Wannabe gangster and heavyweight Santa Maria wrestler "El Chapstick" lived life not as a role model for youth but as a laughing stock for young and old alike. Successful local gangsters nicknamed him after a commercial lip balm because of his pathetic obsession with legendary Joaquin "El Chapo" Guzman, the Sinaloa drug cartel chief doing life plus 30 years in a Colorado federal Supermax prison.

Practicing his "High-Flying Crack" trademark aerial grappling technique by bouncing as high as he could and leaping spreadeagled off the edge of the bed in his rented room, the local professional "lucha libre" loser and aspiring cartel hitman landed in a thick pile of blankets and bubble wrap he had folded and piled on the floor to break his fall.

Meant to crack and splinter bones in his opponent's neck, in real life matches the "Crack" never worked. So ineffective was the move El Chapstick's acrobatic assault once resulted in a tear along the inside seam of his bright yellow wrestling togs that opened to expose the crack in his hairy behind, resulting in hysterical roars of laughter from the crowd. Of course, El Chapstick mistook the howls for support. Bowing deeply at the waist in a gesture of gracious appreciation caused the seam to completely come apart and send his shorts dropping to his ankles which caused him to trip when he took a step and fall to the canvas mat with dangling private parts exposed like a plate of chorizo sausage and fried eggs in a glossy restaurant menu photograph.

An outraged deputy sheriff hired as security threatened to arrest El Chapstick for child pornography because the local public access television station broadcast the match live and innocent little ones might be exposed to the obscene display of sausage. Kicking off the shorts bunched around his ankles, El Chapstick ran from the high school gym with both hands covering genitalia shriveled like a plantain left to wither in the sun.

Although his wrestling career failed to bear fruit, stubborn persistence drove him to set one other unachievable goal. Killing Jesús Zarate, now wanted by several cartels in Mexico, would make El Chapstick famous. After recognizing Zarate from when he wrote local newspaper columns in Santa Maria, all El Chapstick had to do was snuff the man already rumored among local teenage gang-bangers to be the manifestation of Jesús Malverde.

Assassination would ingratiate El Chapstick to cartel bosses throughout Mexico who hated Malverde. Not everybody wanted Sinaloa to win. Sometimes Sinaloa didn't even want Sinaloa to win. Any number of competing bosses hated Malverde for one reason or another. If nothing else, El Chapstick would garner enough clout to at least claim a new nickname. El Exterminador sounded good even if most Mexicans in Santa Maria would mistake him for termite control.

Mostly, El Chapstick just wanted his chickens back. Like a mother hen he missed the dependable creatures he raised from chicks and managed as fighting cocks all over town like desperate bantamweight boxers ready, willing and able to die in the ring. But the birds seemed terribly willing to fly the coop, refusing to resist when that white woman birdnapped them. She sure was white— blond, blue-eyed, white on white as a Michoacan coconut paleta ice cream bar. As much as his chickens seemed to love him they also seemed to want out, to retire, to chill. Who wouldn't appreciate being snatched by the nice woman who smelled of overripe bananas and mezcal?

Convinced these birds would become champions, El Chapstick would profit from the hens' prowess unlike the defeated cock-fighting arena roosters that would find themselves simmering in a thin soup with corn dumplings instead of receiving tender loving care from some female warrior animal lover.

Nobody but El Chapstick knew the birds weren't roosters. Until now nobody knew he glued big red fake combs on their heads and wattles. Nobody knew their vibrant tail feathers originated from his sister's feather duster she used at her job with housekeeping at a beachside motel. Still, so far the hens won every bout. As you might expect, living with El Chapstick provided them with attitude.

Now that untamed gringa hanging with Jesús Zarate ruined everything. For that she would pay. But he couldn't kill the new generation Jesús Malvede all by himself. El Chapstick needed help.

Pacing sticky yellow kitchen linoleum in his furnished studio apartment at the Falafel Villas on North Broadway where dozens of hard-working farmworker families stayed, El Chapstick dropped his head into his hands and realized the depth of his predicament. Other Mexican grapplers who wrestled professionally enjoyed better lives, not much better but better. For El Chapstick, saddled with a nickname that mocked his very existence, the future looked worse than the bean-encrusted burner on his hot plate.

El Chapstick's so-called amigos from the local wrestling world wouldn't help and couldn't be trusted. Most drank too much beer, tequila and aftershave lotion when the money ran out. Others used Loco Toro pills made up of amphetamines and bull tranquilizers that together combined into an explosive mixture of testosterone and errant brain waves that sent countless imbibers into rages that after an hour's burst of energy quickly dropped now comatose dope fiends to sleep, sometimes forever.

Unless he found his birdnapped chickens, all he could hope for was that Arturo's renegade cartel would expand to Santa Maria where he could work for the gang as an enforcer. They were losers like him. That's why El Chapstick decided to relinquish whatever self-respect he once possessed. That's why El Chapstick decided to rat out the new narco-saint and his old lady. After finding Arturo's cell phone number boldly listed online (as a true man of the people Arturo often boasted he would talk with anybody anytime of the day or night), El Chapstick dialed the number.

Counting the number of rings that echoed in his head, he popped five pieces of cinnamon-flavored cannabis-infused chewing gum into his mouth, each piece containing 10 milligrams of THC and just five calories. El Chapstick let his mind wander while he waited.

Maybe he should lose some weight. Get a girlfriend. Get married. Belly fat bounced in at 356 pounds when he last stepped on the digital scale. Waiting for Arturo to answer his cellphone and anxious for the high to hit, El Chapstick chewed and imagined himself as a made man, a cartel captain and feared executioner.

"Arturo's not here," said the voice that answered Arturo's cell phone in Sinaola.

"Who's this?"

"Me, Juan Gomez."

"My older brother, Juan Gomez?"

"Who else, you tub of shit. Arturo's permanently down with a terminal case of hives," said Juan Gomez. "I'm the new boss. He left me his phone in his will."

Just what El Chapstick didn't need. Big brother Juan Gomez lived his life obsessed with crossing the border and snagging gigs as the best Bruce Springsteen impersonator in Santa Maria, singing "Born in the USA" in Mexican and maybe even playing an Elks Club wedding for Republican farmers and ranchers. Truth be told, Juan's act stank and he almost got shot several times in Culiacàn when he stepped on a rickety stage to perform New Jersey hits in Spanish.

"Jesús Zarate stole my chickens," said El Chapstick. "My only friends."

"Jesús Zarate is in Santa Maria? We've been looking all over for him."

"The man trimmed up and is the spitting image of the Jesús Malverde pictures and statues," said El Chapstick. "People say he is 'The One.' "

"Which one?"

"The chosen one, the rightful heir to Malverde's legacy."

"Zarate is also who we were supposed to kill before the bees jumped us and killed Arturo."

"What if I capture your target for you?"

"I'll be impressed," said Juan Gomez. "If you get him, hold on until we get there."

"You're undocumented. How are you going to cross the border and get here?"

"We bought fake American passports," said Juan Gomez. "I even got a Bruce Springsteen tattoo."

"Born in the USA?"

"Sí," said Juan Gomez.

DANCING WITH THE SEA

PLANNING her journey north and thinking back to when she introduced Eeshell to the sea, Zita cherished her memory of taking the 4-year-old by the hand and walking the child into soft foamy waves that lapped at their ankles.

Sticky humidity brought out the bugs that day at Imperial Beach south of San Diego as Zita stared at the high orange rusted metal wall that separates Mexico from the United States. Looking toward calm water she tried to imagine the official governmental maritime boundary line that distinguishes national property rights, a mishmash of bureaucratic regulations that mean nothing to her.

No border exists in the sea as far as Zita is concerned.

Borders exist only in our minds.

The two had driven first from Santa Maria to LA, then the next day from LA to San Diego, a great adventure for the child and her guardian that took them though a Southern California Eeshell had never seen.

"I want you to see the border," Zita told Eeshell. "I want to teach you to swim."

Standing in tepid water, Eeshell pointed. Four dolphins surfaced 50 yards offshore, diving, frolicking and rolling over each other like leaping acrobats in a tent circus.

"Our friends are waiting for us," Zita said.

"Hi, fishies," said Eeshell.

Tender awe turned frightful as they walked into knee-high water.

"The water is biting me," the child said.

"No," Zita said. "Mother Ocean is telling you she wants to dance."

"I like to dance," said Eeshell.

"Then we will dance with the sea," said Zita.

Human life began in the sea. Few see ocean rhythm as choreographed. Those who do learn to appreciate natural patterns that provide movement and balance to our bodies. Water stays with us from the womb until our last breath, gently washing our organs to lubricate and quench our thirst for existence. Swimming shapes the core of the human dance that connects us to the cosmos.

"Bend your knees and bounce on your toes," Zita said.

Eeshell giggled, moving on little springy legs to the music of the waves.

"Mother Ocean likes you, Eeshell," Zita said.

Deep in the child's psyche, atomic energy expanded, lightly pulsing to make constantly changing shapes Eeshell felt in her thin body, radiating electric comfort that made her feel safe and light as a gull feather. Falling face forward into the water, stretching her legs behind her, Eeshell began to glide. Beneath her belly two dolphins acted as cushions, lifting and moving her into deeper water.

Zita swam beside them, taking long, smooth strokes as an expert swimmer at ease in the deep, keeping up with the pace of the other mammals. Eeshell imitated Zita, paddling seriously with both arms, cupping her hands as if she truly were swimming.

An adult life of chain-smoking Spittle non-filter cigarettes began to steal strength from Zita's breath. She felt a tiresome weight in her lungs, pulling on her the way gravity pulls stones dropped into a turquoise lagoon. When the two unoccupied dolphins sensed her discomfort they dove, tenderly surfacing beneath Zita's body to spirit her to shore.

Back on the beach Eeshell looked for attention and approval.

"Did you see me?"

Once again in control of her breath, Zita sat on the sand with her knees pulled to her chest.

"You are a creature of the sea," she said. "Water is life."

"Fishies are people, too," Eeshell said, laughing.

Years later Zita stood in that same spot, watching rippling whitecaps beneath a jumbo rainbow that arched over the western horizon from Mexico to California. One day soon Zita would again dive deep into that holy water, this time alone. She would make a final trip north, this time to unify her past, present and future as one in the same.

One time.

One world.

One way.

Unity defined Zita's purpose and the purpose of her teachers—Jesús Malverde, La Santa Muerte and Ixchel. Zita would soon join them as another powerful guide to goodness, an experienced sorcerer who would call on her spiritual team to help people in need the way she once needed her guides' help.

Nature defied and defined humanity.

Yes, Zita thought, fishes are people, too.

ANIMALS IN THE ZOO

"THREE Die In Second Killer Coyote Attack" declared the bold print, top-of-the-fold headline in the Santa Maria Mirror, a dull daily broadsheet in a tight-ass cow-town steeped in heart attack-inducing tri-tip barbecue, oversized rodeo belt buckles and white Republican farmers who controlled the newspaper content, the status quo, and countless strawberry and vegetable fields.

Punching a hole in the front page with a fist still clutching a Pabst beer can, Adam Haggard threw the newspaper across the 1991 Ford 30-foot camper he called a motor home and "bought" in exchange for a new washer and dryer he stole off a delivery truck and three pit bulls in need of distemper shots. He and Abigale called the Dumpster-on-wheels home until she died in the first coyote attack.

By sunset the cops had removed the yellow crime scene tape. After the massacre Adam buried his riot shotgun in a wooden compartment he built beneath the camper where he kept a few pistols, a live hand grenade and an M2 Vietnam-era flame thrower with a backpack he stole in a recent VFW social hall burglary.

Adam gave his witness statement to police, helped the coroner identify bodies, rustled up as many TV interviews as he could and prepared to settle in to the sandy campsite to plan Abbie's funeral service. He'd hold a bring-your-own-bottle (BYOB) memorial event in the dunes where she died because he didn't have enough gas money to make it back to Bakersfield and bury her there. With enough publicity he might make a profit out of this mess, maybe even cut a deal for a screaming streaming Netflix movie.

Dune devils needed to stick together. Woke hippie left-winger libs still congregated everywhere and were taking over the country. Dune devils would fight them to the death, taking back America one way or the other even if every American died in the process. If Adam could get his hands on a nuclear bomb he'd nuke Washington, the state or the nation's capital didn't matter.

Adam and his ilk would gather in Abbie's memory to flaunt their superiority over the hominid species, partying like heartless heathens despite proclaiming deep belief in Jesus Christ, one righteous holy man the Bakersfield hicks considered Caucasian, heterosexual, and on par with Waylon, Willie, and Buck Owens.

Do-gooders wanted to ban dune buggies, mocking working-class people like Adam who worked straight manual labor jobs when absolutely necessary and whose primal instincts manifested in gratuitous violence and daily boorish behavior. So what if their maniacal mechanized conduct damaged the land, sending sand specks blowing like poison dust clouds into disadvantaged communities.

Who cared if they disturbed snowy plover nesting sites or encroached on Native American burial grounds? Screw them indigenous Chumash Indians and their clam shell mounds. Cry me a whiskey river over noise and erosion and air pollution and fossil fuel. If Adam died from a fractured neck after drunkenly flying through the air over a dune cliff in his off-roader, that was fate and his own goddamn business.

Come to think of it, maybe Adam could hijack a jet taking off from San Luis Obispo Airport and kamikaze nosedive into the Pismo Pier. Go out like a berserk Roman candle when he leaves God's green Earth to become the top story at 11 on the Bakersfield TV news.

USA, USA, USA!!!

Adam especially hated that old man Mel Moyle who wanted to save the world. In Mel Adam saw the end of human nature, not the continuation or the beginning of a new and better America where jug bands with a washtub bass, spoons and a comb and tissue paper played the National Anthem. No Jew's harp allowed in the jug band, though. Adam hated Jews. Jews killed Jesus and ruined Christmas. Easter too. Smug bastard Jews didn't get drunk on St. Patrick's Day.

Mel loved everybody.

The dune monsters overrunning the sand would only get worse. Sincere litigious attempts to ban off-road driving and camping in the Oceano dunes failed dismally. Judges simply overruled common sense. And in 2019 alone the local economy sucked up about $500 million from the gloom-and-dune set.

When Adam's breed won Mel initiated what he deemed a "PEEceful" protest, a one-man environmental outreach campaign, not hurting anyone, of course, just urinating each night into the gas tank of a single camper or RV parked on the beach, hoping his salty act of defiance might at least dissuade a buggy brain here or there from returning to ever again foul sacred land.

Two mornings after the mauling, the coyote family crept from their hideout Mel dug for them beneath the steps of the hidden driftwood shack he built in the non-vehicle area a few miles away in the natural preserve. Theo and Sophia came first, the three pups following, already back to normal nipping at each other's hind legs, tripping and rolling in the sand.

The smell of Mel frying surf perch, potatoes, onions and eggs caught their noses. After Mel and the pack ate breakfast, the animals went their separate ways. Unlike people, coyotes take care of themselves and each other. Mel headed back to the beach campsite to see what Adam and his lynch mob had to say for themselves.

Noticing a small crowd standing at the water's edge, Mel heard Adam's high-pitched squeaky voice. Adam had called an impromptu press conference. Falsely claiming he could still see Abbie's blood in the sand, he felt empowered by how several lapdog reporters looked down and seemed to scribble his quote as if they, too, could see Abbie's DNA shining in the wet grains.

Mel couldn't help himself.

"Don't blame the coyotes," he said, loud enough for Adam to hear. Refusing to defer to this trashy Bakersfield gladiator with early morning bourbon on his breath, Mel gathered all the courage he could muster to face this beached bully.

Adam went off like a lit M-80 dropped into an empty quart beer bottle.

"I blame you, you, you, lunatic," Adam said in a voice wailing like a flat line alarm in a hospital room.

"We're all animals in the zoo," Mel said. "I broke out. You and your herd are still caged. I run free."

"Nobody runs free," Adam said. "In my world we all burn in Hell together."

SKULL RACKS

LIVING as a spiritual daughter of La Santa Muerte created tests Zita never underestimated. Matters of life and death required solutions. Nobody took care of business better than La Santa Muerte. She expected the same results from her disciples.

As a purveyor of dark prophecy, Zita emulated her Maya ancestors who stacked men's, women's and children's skulls on racks cemented side-by-side like bricks in a California ranch house patio wall. The skulls hung as mute testament to human sacrifice and idolatry.

Warriors sometimes killed their victims to serve as honorable gifts to Maya gods which entitled the dead special privileges in the afterlife. The living heaped praise on their spirits as well. By making these human sacrifices the Maya kept their gods alive and preserved the health of the universe.

Stacking skulls made sense to Zita so she stacked her own trophies beside the spices on a wall rack in her kitchen - small sugar skulls, of course. Candied craniums provided far more joy than bittersweet human bone, carrying no spiritual flotsam from enemy ghosts who might cry out in the middle of the night. Sugar skulls tasted better, too.

Zita gave up stacking real bleached human skulls years ago when she kept only a half dozen or so on display, all awfully bad men, of course, who insulted life itself and paid dearly for their misdeeds.

Compromise meant everything to an evolving civilization. Like the fraud of believing the Virgin Mary gave birth to the Son of God and the Dali Lama can accurately choose reincarnated holy men from the bodies of children, a time must arise when reasonable people realize religious hustles are deceptive and rational thought must prevail. True faith required reason.

While gods constitute fantasy, a deity's power in the mind of a person often determines life or death. La Santa Muerte's power is no different than Allah or Yahweh, living and dying in our minds, taking root as fact or fiction, inspiring a human to kill, offer mercy or never even give homicide a passing thought.

To Zita La Santa Muerte appeared as a comely ageless woman who agreed Zita could age gracefully as an elder priestess, allowing Zita to dabble in the occasional minor spell and incantation. Before mellowing, however, Zita had to carry out one last grand finale. Zita must once and for all kick the vile cigarette habit that racked her chest pain, ate away at her diseased lungs and sapped her willpower.

Zita gave her word to Jesús she would stop smoking. In order to keep her word and again relocate to Santa Maria, she had to dig deep into the core of her addiction. When Arthur von Spittle stopped producing cigarettes, Zita would finally free the nicotine demon from her body. All attempts to quit in the past had failed to rid her of the loathsome habit that owned her as much, if not more, than La Santa Muerte.

When Arthur von Spittle died Zita would regain strength she needed to make the swim to freedom from Mexico to that same special border spot where she taught Eeshell how to swim so many years before. Instead of paddling out a few hundred yards from the American beach, this time she would start on the Mexican side. After swimming about a mile into the Pacific she would turn right and head toward the United States. Maybe she would swim all the way to Santa Maria. No woman could swim that far, could she?

But first Arthur von Spittle must suffer for the evil he has caused.

Lighting one smoke off another, Zita exhaled into a small glass fishbowl. Two blue cat's eye marbles rolled around on the bottom of the bowl as smoke clouded the sides. At work in his plush warehouse suite at the Santa Maria cigarette factory, Arthur von Spittle sensed irritation first in his left eyeball then in the right. A burning sensation made him rub both blue eyes with the knuckles of his hands.

"I got something in my eye," he said to an assembly line worker who ignored him for fear of missing one of the 100,000 cigarettes her job required her to inspect each day.

Both eyes began to cloud before his vision went from gray to black. Not only did Arthur von Spittle breed hungry worms inside his body and suffer continuing fresh cigarette burns on his skin, he now went blind. Three weeks later stumped doctors shook their heads in awe when their patient's sight mysteriously returned.

To hear Zita later tell the story to the other witches, the man long ago lost sight of morality and ethics. When his time to die finally arrived, Zita would make sure to exhibit his skull as a special trophy. For now she'd just place another small sugar skull on the shelf and chalk it up as a sweet reminder of a small man who would soon no longer exist to cause pain.

Zita finished smoking her cigarette, lit another off the butt and got down to business.

RINGWORMS OF FIRE

PINKY-FINGER-SIZED worms squeezed through Arthur von Spittle's ears.

Under the warm embrace of local anesthetic, he lay still as doctors removed one slimy invertebrate after another from the waxy canals and dropped them into a chemical solution that preserved the helminths for study. Stopping in mid-pull the doctor examined a second severe condition.

"You've got fresh burns on your arms," said the doctor.

Arthur von Spittle shuddered with fear.

"Cigarette burns," the doctor said. "They look like new cigarette burns."

A world away in Culiacàn Zita took a deep drag of a Spittle non-filter. Removing the lit cigarette from her mouth, she touched the tip to the center of the raggedy effigy's forehead, pushing the red-hot butt deep into the handcrafted doll's pale flesh-colored face.

Smoke rose.

Straw sizzled.

Shocked, the doctor noticed a brand-new burn appearing on Arthur von Spittle's forehead. Second-guessing himself, the doctor thought maybe he had missed that raw mark. Maybe his patient had earlier harmed himself on purpose, feeling guilty about addicting and killing countless cigarette smoking customers. No, thought the doctor, probably not.

Despite having no conscience, Arthur von Spittle sensed the end would come to him with poisonous worms slithering from several sweaty orifices and seeping, festering open wounds appearing all over his body, a condition modern science could not explain.

After surgery more worms appeared.

More burns, too.

Awake all night in the recuperating room, an exhausted and

terrorized Arthur von Spittle wondered if he might be cursed. At 6 a.m., at the very moment he asked God for help for the first time in his life, Arthur von Spittle felt his left eye begin to sizzle. In another world so very far away, Zita pushed the glowing tip of a Spittle cigarette deep into the center of the limp rag doll's left eye.

When the coroner examined Spittle's fresh corpse he demanded to know who tortured the patient before the man's heart gave out and he died, incinerating his left eye to a crisp so badly the pupil, iris and sclera looked like an egg charred in a scalding hot pan on the stove.

A long skinny worm struck dead crawling from the deceased's eye socket resembled a strip of bacon burned beyond recognition.

The worm had turned.

WHY IS THE SUN BLUE?

SHAKING the plastic aftershave bottle until the last blue drops plopped into his palm, Reefer slapped icy cool Aqua Velva on his cheeks.

"You smell like a gumdrop farm," Bud said.

Reefer Johnson blushed through raw hamburger-red cheeks.

"I ain't never had a real date with a girl before," he said.

"This ain't no date," Bud said. "I mean this isn't a date. We're driving Eeshell in the Doobiemobile up to Jade Cove to replenish her supply of stones."

"Stoned?" Reefer asked. "Did you say stoned?"

Bud pulled a joint from behind his left ear where he usually stashed an emergency joint that made him look like a retail clerk with a #2 yellow pencil tucked behind his auricle.

"Jim Doobie to the rescue," he said.

Reefer blinked and blanked.

"Who's Jim Doobie?"

"Never mind," a perpetually ripped Bud said, not sure who Jim Doobie was himself.

"I'm in love, buddy," Reefer said.

Lifting four thin strands of Big Sur green nephrite jade love beads he bought from Eeshell and refused to remove from around his neck since they first met, Reefer said, "I'm gonna ask her to marry me."

"Keep talking like that and Eeshell won't need to go to Jade Cove," Bud said.

Again Reefer blanked, his mind exhibiting all the depth of a greasy empty pizza box.

"You got all the rocks in your head she needs to make a year's worth of necklaces," Bud said.

Reefer still didn't get it.

"I told you, man," said Bud. "Eeshell digs me."

"How bout we have a smoke-off to see who gets her," Reefer said.

"Who gets her, as you so crudely put it, is not up to us," Bud said. "Eeshell decides."

"So let's make her the contest judge," said Reefer.

"We can't *make* her do anything," Bud said. "California is a free country where women make their own decisions about their own lives. Eeshell's not a prize like a bowling trophy or a deer head you mount on the wall of the hunting cabin."

"We ate the deer heads in soup," Reefer said.

"And people ask why I'm a vegetarian," Bud said.

A scowl crossed Reefer's brow.

"What if Eeshell doesn't want either one of us?"

Bud reached up and gave the plastic propeller on his multicolored beanie a spin.

"How can she resist, man?"

Standing beside the Doobiemobile like dutiful valets opening the door for a princess, Bud and Reefer believed Eeshell would fall for one or the other. Driving her to Jade Cove to replenish the supply of raw green stones upon which she depended to make her jewelry helped the boys feel like they mattered, that they served a power greater than themselves.

As soon as they picked her up Eeshell laid down the law.

"No, thank you," she said nicely but sternly, baffling them immediately with her hesitancy to take a hit off the joint they just lit.

"You'll have to put out those joints you're smoking if you want me to accompany you," she said.

Flummoxed, Bud whimpered.

"But, like, smoking a joint in the Doobiemobile is like wearing your seatbelt," he said.

"I don't smoke," Eeshell said. "Secondhand smoke kills. I try my best to inhale into my lungs only clean fresh air. With increasing pollution that's hard enough as it is."

Reefer got lost in the translation. Eeshell's words banged around his head. Bud quickly snatched Reefer's reefer from his fingers, snubbing out his own joint and Reefer's on the sleeve of his tan fringe rawhide jacket.

"Here's the good news, boys," Eeshell said. "I'm loaded with super-duper infused dancing gummy bears."

"You had me worried there for a nanosecond," Bud said.

"Never ever used nothing *but* joints," Reefer said. "God made joints same as he made man."

Eeshell smiled that smile that launched a thousand potheads and handed out a smattering of multicolored gummies.

"None for me," she said. "I'm driving."

Reluctantly handing over the keys, Bud watched Eeshell slide behind the wheel of the Doobiemobile.

"I hate to say it," she said. "But this mode of transportation has got to go, too."

Reefer and Bud looked like they had arrived a minute after closing time at their favorite cannabis dispensary. Wearing a stungunned look, Bud said, "I live in this mode of transportation."

"Me, too," said Reefer. "At least I think I do."

Kind but firm, Eeshell said, "A rolling joint is no way for future non-smokers to behave, now is it, kids?"

Trying to outdo his pal in vying for Eeshell's attention, Bud got the jump on Reefer's response to Eeshell's power of suggestion.

"No way, man," he said. "I hate smoking."

Reefer jumped in.

"That's right, Ma'am," he said. "I quit."

Ten minutes up the freeway the gummies kicked in.

"Why is the sun blue?" Reefer asked.

"To match the trees," Bud said. "Why else?"

Hearing a telephone ring in his head Bud turned to Reefer and said, "Would you please answer that?"

"Um, hello," Reefer said, listening and nodding for a whole long minute as if somebody was talking to him on the other end of the long distance line. Finally getting his head sufficiently together to reply, he said, "Sorry, man, wrong number."

Eeshell drove north doing the speed limit thinking sweet thoughts of black cherry blossom incense and red-striped peppermint candy.

The phone rang again.

"Bud's not here, man," Reefer said.

 HE PUT THE ASS IN ASSASSIN

"NICE tattoo," said the border guard.

Five Mexican hit men lined up at the crowded U.S. entry point froze. Stepping forward, lead assassin Juan Gomez touched the outside of his upper arm with the tip of his thick forefinger.

"You mean this work of art?"

In faded ink the tattooed blue depiction of legendary rock star Bruce Springsteen looked more like a skeletal stick figure a troubled child drew in art therapy class. Still, you could make out the outline of a guitar and a raised arm pose that resembled the photo of the Boss portrayed on one of the bootleg records marked "Borned in the USA" album covers Juan bought at the market in Mazatlàn when he was 12.

"Born to run, amigo," said the American border patrol agent.

"Tramps like us," Juan said, quoting his hero and raising a fist in a symbol of national solidarity. The cop winked, handed back Juan's forged American passport and motioned the other four undocumented band members though the gate. The other four bogus American citizens raised scrawny fists, waving forged American passports with more exuberance than the Marines raising Old Glory on Mount Suribachi after the Battle of Iwo Jima during World War II.

With Arturo dead Juan and his men had a shot at making a name for themselves on both sides of the border, maybe even jumpstart the renegade cartel Arturo started before he got forever buzzed. That's the way they referred to his death by bees—buzzed, like he was on an eternal drunk in the afterlife when he really was just another grub at the bottom of a mezcal bottle.

With their combined low-level criminal experience in Culiacàn, stealing a car was as easy as shoplifting bags of spicy tortilla chips for the drunken drive up the coast to Santa Maria. Juan's little brother El Chapstick was already there getting details for the hit, if in fact the suspect he eyeballed in town really was Jesús Zarate.

All this Malverde business was probably just the result of all the weed El Chapstick smoked, pot paranoia finally going to his head and staying there like a marine layer of sea fog that never lifted. Malverde's legend haunted only those fools Juan viewed as weak, those who took to heart Malverde's presence as if he truly lived and wasn't merely a symbolic saga who appealed to the poor. But what the peasants lacked in money, they more than made up in the priceless gift of faith.

Juan only believed in himself, trust that one day soon would make or break him.

REEFER COME HOME

AUNT IRMA missed her little Reefer something awful.

Time to go look for the little critter.

Survivor's guilt as the last of the Weed Eaters white supremacist Christian pot warlords' elders (the only woman to boot) made her yearn for her moody nephew even though she usually couldn't stand sitting in the same room with him burping, scratching, and eating chocolate THC rice pudding with his fingers. All she and Reefer had in common was smoking dope for hours every day. Through deteriorated and shared sisterly DNA, Reefer remained Aunt Irma's only blood relative. Among her tribe blood is thicker than cannabis-infused rice pudding.

Reefer's daddy, Commander Fetus, remained forever in Aunt Irma's heart but now enjoyed Valhalla where she knew he felt right at home among other barbarians who broke all the rules. As much as Reefer would like Valhalla, the man-child was a loner, a troglodyte who would never make the grade.

State cops had impounded and kept all the compound's vehicles during the investigation of the Weed Eaters' massacre that killed the dozen or so neo-nutcase paramilitary members. Of course, K-9 dogs found drugs stashed in every nook and cranny of the motor pool.

So Aunt Irma packed an overnight bag and a big Colt Model 1873 pistol Commander Fetus stole from a local collector. Standing in the middle of the mud road that led to the compound she pointed the old-fashioned six-gun at the windshield of the first car that rattled her way and crouched in a combat stance, promising herself to track down Reefer and the Pancho Villa-inspired Mexicans who killed her man.

About eight hours later she pulled into a Shell Beach motel with no assigned stars in the AAA travel guide. After checking into her cramped room she looked out the window and noticed five Mexicans skinny-dipping in the leaking moss-encrusted swimming pool.

One of them reminded her of Bruce Springsteen. Aunt Irma hated Bruce Springsteen worse than lima beans baked with sugar and tomato sauce. And Aunt Irma really hated lima beans baked with sugar and tomato sauce.

Maybe these Mexicans knew where Reefer might be hiding out.

But when she asked, all the leader of the pack said was, "Sorry, lady no speekee dee English."

DANCING WITH BEARS

WITH ONE EYE peeled on Adam's crusty camper and the other watching the road into the Oceano Dunes State Vehicular Recreation Area, known by tight-ass capitol bureaucrats in Sacramento as Oceano Dunes SVRA, Mel Moyle remained alert despite massive amounts of THC that pulsed through his system steady as the mechanical throb of a healthy human heart.

Venturing deeper each day into himself, Mel's mental health kept him active. His physical activity kept him healthy. A cannabis conundrum of intoxication and esoteric exercise helped him thrive on crane-like Qi Gong movements and mindful breathing, living the Dunite lifestyle of careful creature comfort based on basic existential need. Not luxury. Need. When Mel cut out unnecessities it didn't take long to realize need is luxury.

"Things are out of whack," Mel said out loud to himself. "I'm bringing back the whack."

The thought hit Mel as particularly profound.

"Bring back the whack!!!" he yelled, his words catching on the wind and disappearing into the ozone. "Bring back the whack!!!'

The whack meant everything to Mel who was as whacked as a Dunite could get.

And that was a good thing.

About 90 miles up the coast Bud, Reefer and Eeshell spotted a '66 VW camper painted bright blue, green, yellow and purple with psychedelic amoeba swirls parked near the small side road entrance to Jade Cove.

"Dude," Eeshell said to the driver when she slid from the traveling joint.

Gumball blue eyes floated in a face full of caramel-colored suntan as the van owner pushed back a lock of hair blond as fresh straw sticking from a hay bale. Wide-eyed, he stared at the Doobiemobile.

"Dude," he said.

Eeshell cockishly tilted her head.

"Wanna trade?"

Pointing to Bud and Reefer the dude said, "Those two don't come with the transaction, do they?"

Eeshell whispered, "Wish they did."

"Deal, dude," he said.

Eeshell tilted her head so a foot of black hair slid over her shoulder like a lava wave in a crash pad lamp. Reminding the dude of pictures he saw of Grace Slick at Woodstock, she offered him a citrus gummy and popped an orange cannabis candy into her mouth.

"You don't mind if I paint dancing bears on the sides, do you?"

"I was just getting ready to ask you the same thing," the dude said.

An hour later after exchanging owners' names, addresses, insurance paperwork and more gummy bears, two dudes happier than nudes on ludes drove off into the setting sun—the VW loaded with a new stash of raw jade, the Doobiemobile loaded with one seriously loaded dude.

Back down the coast, Mel suddenly felt alone. Time had diminished the weatherworn recluse's sense of self-reliance, creating a need for companionship he had rarely before sensed.

Mel wanted friends.

Mel needed people.

Love is like that, you know.

MEETING OF THE MINDS

SEVENTEEN miles south of Oceano, Jesús Zarate pulled into the Santa Maria Inn parking lot driving a metallic purple custom-built 1949 Mercury Eight.

"Tell me you didn't steal it," Tripper said.

"My man El Maloso's people told me he wants me to have it as a gift," he said.

"Gangbanger El Maloso?"

"I beg your pardon," Jesús said. "El Maloso heads a fraternal organization more prestigious than the Elks Club."

"Members in both clubs carry guns," Tripper said. "What's wrong with driving a Mustang? We're in rodeo country, right? These cowboys dig horses, right?"

"My new hot rod matches the color of the grapes in the vineyards," Jesús said.

"As long as nobody picks us off with a bazooka while we're cruising," Tripper said.

"That's what I like about you, Tripper. Forever the optimist. Let's go for a ride."

From where Mel Moyle stood at the entrance to the Oceano beach, he spotted the violet lowrider followed by a VW bus he momentarily hallucinated as a giant plum. Both vehicles converged near the guard shack by the dunes. Not all was well at the beach.

Stumbling drunk down the steps of the camper, Adam geared up for another off-the-cuff press conference. Mel shuffled in duct tape repaired flip flops to where members of the national and local press had set up. Eeshell parked the van and stepped onto the hard sand. Bud and Reefer followed. Jesús and Tripper pulled in and got out of the vintage cruiser.

"Nice car," Eeshell said to Tripper.

"Nice bus," Tripper said.

Bud and Reefer gawked at Jesús.

"You look like a Mexican movie star, man," Bud said.

"Don't screw with Zorro," Reefer said. "I'm picking up a weird vibe like he could eat us for lunch."

Jesús gestured at the small media gaggle.

"What's the attraction?"

Noticing the spontaneous get-together, Adam ridiculed the lively group to the press in a booming voice.

"Just what we don't need," he said. "Tree-hugger environmental kooks here to protest our human right to self-defense over the coyote invasion."

Turning to Tripper, Jesús said, "Coyote invasion?"

"Pretty boy over there looks like the leader of the pack," Adam said pointing to Jesús.

An electric shiver ran up Jesús' spine, not fear, not even close. Adrenaline rippled cold throughout his body. Hair on the back of his neck bristled slightly. His pulse slowed. A turned-down smile made his face look like a cornered varmint baring his teeth in the face of danger.

Breathing heavily, slobbering down the front of his chest, Adam balled his fists and railed at the lanky middle-aged man who stood quietly in faded blue jeans, a fake snap pearl button matching shirt and polished black cowboy boots.

"You want a piece of me, faggot! Do you? Come get it then!"

A falcon circled high above Adam's head, gliding in a graceful arc. Catching himself before emotion transformed into violence, Jesús turned away from Adam's fury.

"You look like you could use a drink," Mel Moyle said to Jesús.

Almost on instinct Jesús accepted the green glass gallon jug Mel held out. Assuming the contents to be homemade red wine, Jesús twisted off the cap, raised the bottle to his lips and swigged, swallowing two healthy gulps of Hoocha Weed wine that warmed his throat and pooled in his stomach like a swirling hot tub on a seaside cliff.

Jesús would later swear he heard his taste buds giggle.

"Go ahead, son," Mel said. "One more time."

After another guzzle, Jesús handed back the jug. Not one to be easily surprised, Jesús sensed immediate revelation in the wine that tasted sweetly dry with hints of chocolate, salted caramel, honey and red pepper flakes, all of which Mel had dumped into this most recent batch of Hoocha Weed wine.

Draping his arm around Mel's shoulder, Jesús said, "What *is* this, brother?"

"Weed wine magic," Mel said. "Good for what ails you."

Bud sidled up to the old-time beach prophet he had met a while back, literally bumping into him while walking the beach during a storm. After discovering they were both Geminis, Mel agreed to supply Bud with discounted Hoocha Weed for his ointment in exchange for bags of pistachios and black licorice Bud bought at Trader Joe's.

"I sure could use a hit off that flask," Bud said.

Mel passed the magic jug.

Reefer stood nearby, dazed as usual and outfitted in a white man's militia uniform of black jeans and scuffed work boots unlaced without socks. Frayed crimson strings hung from his shoulders where he earlier cut off the sleeves of his black and red checked flannel shirt, his daddy's lumberjack shirt he stole from Commander Fetus' closet a few weeks before the white supremacist militia leader passed, as they say in the mountains, passed like a methamphetamine-fueled trucker hauling loose logs roaring past a lost Silicon Valley tourist looking for a road sign and exit ramp to point the way to the sequoias.

Eeshell glided up to Mel and kissed him on the cheek.

He blushed.

"I heard what you did and want to thank you for standing up for the animals," she said. "Nowadays, everybody hates coyotes."

"Not this guy," said Tripper, jerking her thumb at Jesús. "He thinks he is a coyote."

When Eeshell and Jesús momentarily locked eyes, she noticed he looked away first. Then he looked back. Something clicked between the two. Mel motioned for everybody to take a hit off the bottle. As he wiped his lips from a fast swig, another vehicle pulled into the parking area.

"Uh-oh, we're in trouble now," Reefer said, wiping his mouth with the tail of his lumberjack shirt.

Moving with a speed spry for a supposedly dour and depressed lonely heart, Aunt Irma stepped from the vehicle she had commandeered to demand answers from her spaced and wayward nephew.

"Glory be, boy," Aunt Irma said pointing a forefinger upward toward the heavens. "I prayed to Commander Fetus for guidance and he steered me here."

As coincidence and divine intervention would have it, Reefer looked relieved, super-duper wrecked but relaxed. But as soon as he tried to babble out a response Mel cut him off.

"I just got a brainstorm," he said. "Why not get ourselves a big old house and move in together like a reborn Dunite commune against the world? Get along and get away from maniacs like that."

Mel pointed at Adam who stood glaring and slobbering on the sand as reporters lost interest in his tirade and drifted away.

Everybody else looked at each other, wondering if such a move could actually take place. Each person had ample reason to want a family and live as brothers and sisters in a nonviolent world. Bud perked right up. The proposition sounded good.

"Let me think about this," he said.

Everybody else looked at each other again. Who was this old beach bum anyway, suggesting a commune 60 years past California's commune heyday?

Breaking the silence a familiar hit rock tune from the '80s blasted from the open windows of an approaching black SUV. When the stolen Tahoe slid to a stop, five skinny Mexicans jumped out. Pointing to his Bruce Springsteen tattoo, the leader said to Jesús, "You can call me Brice."

"You mean Bruce?"

"No, Brice. As in Brice Springsteam. I front a Springsteen cover band. Brice Springsteam and the C Street Band. C is for Culiacàn. I altered my name to keep from getting sued."

Jesús recognized the accent as pure inner city Culiacàn. Brice recognized Jesús as the marked man he and his clown cartel had been looking for. Reefer recognized the smell of strong cheap weed clinging to the men's bodies.

Eeshell kept looking at Jesús who could hardly hear her voice when she finally asked, "Don't I know you?"

Confused, Jesús looked away.

DRIFTING WITH DOLPHINS

"I CAN'T wait to see you," Eeshell said.

"We have a lot of catching up to do," Zita said.

After firming up details on the phone of where and when Eeshell would pick her up, Zita walked upstairs and gave her apartment key to the landlady who was sincerely sorry to see her go.

"When will you return, señora?"

Zita leaned in and gently kissed the woman on the cheek.

"No matter where we live," Zita said. "La Santa Muerte will continue to watch over us both."

Walking to the bus station she thought about how surprised Eeshell would be to find out Zita had a son living in Santa Maria. And how shocked she would be when she learned the whole truth of their existence.

Relieved Jesús didn't ask how or when she planned to make her way back across the border without a legal way to enter the United States, Zita took the stuffy bus all the way to the beach. During her 20-hour ride from Culiacán to Tijuana, she finished two thick avocado and cheese sandwiches with hot sauce, sharing her third with a mother and her five-year-old daughter from Guatemala she met on the trip.

"Hot sauce makes my tongue laugh," the child said.

"We're going to America to work," the woman said.

"And meet Mickey Mouse," said the child.

Shaping a tender blessing in her mind, Zita cast a soft spell to erase the capitalist rat from the girl's dreams, replacing America's corporate rodent fantasy with happy thoughts of singing and dancing avocados. America needed more singing and dancing avocados, she thought.

So did hungry masses huddled on the Mexican side of menacing border walls. Imagining the dreams of countless migrants who risked and often lost their lives in their trek to freedom, Zita tried to conjure the sense of desperation men, women and children felt fighting their way through jungles teeming with snakes, bandits, and other unknown dangers.

During the long bus ride Zita watched through the window as countless peasants from throughout South and Latin America as well as other nations as far away as China marched along the roadside, packed into fields and parking lots, even riding atop speeding trains that raced through the countryside on their way to the border. Of those migrants who made it to the border, most would be turned away by armed guards, many of whom claimed Mexican descent. Mexican Light, Zita called them, watered down company men and women who turned their backs on their real heartland. Zita sent a pointed blessing their way, too.

"Dream of the rat," she invoked, summoning a nightmarish rodent to disrupt their sleep.

Nobody knew how many border patrol agents would awaken screaming that night, paralyzed, sweating and crying for mercy as diseased rats crawled beneath the covers and chewed off their toes. Even a dream can traumatize, especially a dream that reoccurred night after night.

Zita understood revenge could backfire, that retribution signaled ignorance, that getting even sinks civilization deeper into a moribund mental morass of mindless mire. But now she had aged into another body, an old shell, a dried human fava bean covered in auburn chili powder the kids called "old school." Relinquish cultural evolution to the new generation, to Eeshell's peers who might save what was left of the world if anything worth saving remained.

Still, for her grand finale as a witch Zita got even. La Santa Muerte would be proud. Arthur von Spittle was dead and gone. Perhaps Zita would visit his grave. Dig him up. Bring him back to life. Kill him again.

Beautiful as ever, the beach at Tijuana stunned Zita with its vibrant color and flowing energy. Thinking of all the unseen and unknown living species beneath the water cover, Zita felt as powerful as ever. *We come from the sea*, she taught Eeshell. *We are the ocean*, she said. Eeshell understood immediately that day they swam together as one with dolphins that now came again to meet Zita. Clapping her hands together Zita greeted the mammals who, like her, understood the secrets of the sea.

Kicking off well-worn brown leather huaraches and stepping out of faded blue jeans and underwear she bought four-for-five-dollars at the market, she pulled over her head the Berkeley sweatshirt she bought at a yard sale in LA, a lucky find because she once read of the revolutionary zeal for free speech that took root there. Free expression meant everything, even to a witch.

Looking down at the cracked skin and nails on her feet she thought about getting her toenails painted when she finished her trip. No, that's too American, too gabacho, one of Zita's favorite words. Spoken as an insult against white people, gabacho also could be used in an endearing manner. Not often, though. In her mind Mexicans could be gabacho, as well. Chicanos and chicanas, too, a Mexican-American breed too often comprised of coconuts, brown on the outside, white on the inside.

No, no toenail polish. Fingernails were different. Zita promised herself once she got settled in Santa Maria she'd make an appointment with Sinaloa Lucy who produced not only the best designed fingernails in Santa Maria but in all of California. Women in Sinaloa had already heard and talked about Sinaloa Lucy and how she planned to open a franchised shop near the Jesús Malverde shrine. Zita planned to get the face of the greatest saint emblazoned on her fingers. Her wayward son would shake his head at the familiar bright image.

"Looks just like you," Zita would joke.

A lone fisherman caught up in his own thoughts failed to notice as Zita stepped into the water, walking slowly until only her head appeared and she pushed off the calloused balls of her feet, disappearing beneath a gentle wave that splashed her face as she submerged into a world below the surface of natural human experience.

Within seconds the first dolphin nudged her left side, bumping playfully against Zita's bare skin. The second nudged from the right, bouncing off and coming back so softly she felt like a loose feather from Zita's down pillow tickling her in bed. The dolphins accompanied her about two miles into the ocean.

Even for an excellent open water swimmer, two miles in the ocean can be exhausting. Yet Zita gained strength in her stroke. Turning her head right and then left and then right again she found a delicate, balanced cadence in her breath. Sensing she would soon arrive at the zone where she belonged, she pushed to its center. One hour later she turned north. Home in the zone she closed her eyes.

The long journey passed like a sound sleep with vivid dreams of fish and other brilliant creatures Zita didn't even try to identify as she marveled at their shapes, vivid colors, patterns and easy navigational skills.

Once a whale surfaced nearby and her four guides expertly maneuvered her from harm's way, zigging and zagging on another route that suddenly immersed Zita in a school of flying fish. Hurling their bodies from the water, this majestic ancient species soared through the air, speeding faster than her dolphin guides. Zita could have joined their spectacular aerial flight, she imagined, if she truly had bewitched the environment and wasn't hallucinating from sacred mushrooms she nibbled during the bus trip.

Maybe she was dreaming, traveling in a deep trance through unseen vibrations and frequencies from one plane of consciousness to another. Maybe a fishing boat crew picked her up delirious in the water and delivered her safely to Eeshell's open arms. Maybe La Santa Muerte took care of travel arrangements, conspiring with Ixchel and even alerting Eeshell who waited patiently on the Central Coast expecting the arrival of the woman she believed to be her godmother.

Numerous ways exist for a witchy woman intent on reaching the U.S. to achieve her goal, especially a seasoned wizard and favored daughter of the one and only death saint. Nowadays, Zita was never sure what was real or imagined. Imagination is part of the fun of living as a sorceress, not knowing the difference between fantasy and reality but knowing how to use supernatural talent when the right time arose.

The time had come.

As four sweet dolphins safely bumped Zita toward shore at Guadalupe Beach, Eeshell spotted the sparkle in the water erupt bright as a comet in the midnight sky, recognized the friendly creatures from so long ago and rushed into the water from the desolate sand that retained creation's primitive imprint. Dynamic freestyle strokes thrust Eeshell about 50 yards offshore where Zita treaded water without the aid of animal guides that chattered excitedly in high-pitched whistles, chirps and squeaks while circling their old friend. Eeshell nuzzled each of the four dolphins before turning to Zita.

"Follow me, child," Zita said.

Diving, she disappeared underwater. Eeshell did as she was told. Together they plunged deeper until leveling off and heading for shore. Brightly lit beneath the surface of the sea, a world unfolded Eeshell had never seen. Startled by shocking blues, greens and an ominous purple seascape, her eyes opened wide to specific detail among the living movements of plant and fish life that surrounded her and made her feel secure.

Sensing Zita had gifted her with a secret panorama, not knowing the full extent of Zita's power, Eeshell felt the subconscious bond that drew her even closer to her godmother's presence amid splendor in the depth that gave birth to their species. Surfacing together they swam to shore and stepped on land they would share as long as they could.

At times both women wondered if they had dreamed the same dream that night, if what they remembered of their time together in the water had actually happened or if they just lost their minds together while experiencing the same beautiful vison of love.

Both women answered their own questions by simply going with the flow.

The day after the reunion, Zita called Jesús.

"Guess where I am?"

"I'm afraid to ask," said Jesús.

 **HOMECOMING**

"I CAN'T believe you two know each other," Jesús said.

Pushing two overcooked fried eggs around on his plate with a fork, he shook his head and stared at the yolks that seemed to stare right back. Eeshell stared even harder at Jesús than she had that day at the beach.

"From almost as soon as she smiled her way into my world," Zita said.

"I like freaked out a little when she told me she was meeting her son," Eeshell said. "I'm freaking out even more now that I know it's you."

"We met the other day," Jesús told his mother.

Turning to Eeshell he said, "You from Pismo?"

"Grew up in Santa Maria," Eeshell said, spreading orange marmalade on her toast.

"You ever read me in the newspaper?"

"My favorite columnist," Eeshell said. "I wrote a letter to the editor they didn't publish when those new owners from Iowa fired you."

"I wrote one, too," Jesús said. "Got the same response from the children of the corn."

Eeshell laughed.

Jesús didn't ask why Zita kept her relationship with this young woman a secret, why she hadn't mentioned to him the lifelong responsibility of serving as her godmother. Eeshell respected them both not to question either one. Some things are supposedly better left unsaid.

For now.

 # SWEET MYSTERIES OF LIFE

A FEW DAYS later, comfortably adjusting long legs that embarrassed her as the teenager whom mean girls called "Spider," wrapping one inside the other in a pretzel-like lotus position Eeshell sat straight and sober on the sand outside the VW bus double doors.

Feeling balanced and healthy, having harmless fun hanging out with Bud and Reefer, she gripped a tie-dyed T-shirt shred to polish a chunk of black-green jade and contemplate her kaleidoscopic world.

What makes a witch, anyway? Magic or morals? Mythical moments define existence from beginning to end—better yet, from no beginning to no end. We start from nothing. We're a magic bean breakfast that develops from a microscopic sperm and an over-easy egg that grows out of nowhere, connects and morphs into what the greatest minds of our species believe is the most complex, intricate actuality to exist. To the best of our most advanced mathematically precise knowledge, we're the only living matter in a cosmos with no start or finish, a celestial bandwidth that expands infinitesimally, growing bigger throughout time and space.

Extraterrestrial atoms come together to make life. Without alien atoms we're nothing. Most atoms originated billions of years ago. Helium and hydrogen (almost 10 percent of each person) joined itty-bitty lithium atoms left over from the Big Bang when everything in the Big Nothing exploded. Bigger, heavier atoms formed to create plant, animal and human life on Earth. Oxygen atoms in our lungs, carbon atoms in our muscles, calcium atoms in our bones, iron atoms in our blood all started inside a bubbling star before our planet began spinning around the sun.

All those interstellar outer space atoms come into play at that all-you-can-eat predator breakfast buffet on Earth that perpetuates human life. Yet nobody has come close to deciphering how our quivering body organs originate from nowhere, how they develop, grow and gain pulsing vital energy to live until they die.

The brain?

Don't even try to figure out brain waves while using your brain to analyze the human consciousness computer. Your brain will block your thoughts from entering because your brain grew in your head all by itself without your help. The brain functions without your assistance when you're awake, sleeping or unconscious. Your brain works by itself. Your brain doesn't need you. You need your brain.

As for God, humans thought him up. Humans developed countless gods, some female, because they needed to explain, simplify and trivialize everything in the midst of their own stupidity. Christians who killed and continue to kill for their three-in-one God (Father, Son and Holy Ghost) are the worst. Casper the Friendly Ghost makes more sense. Above all, please remember the mind. Dementia will strike sooner or later. As we age, the mind forgets itself. Call the process the ultimate mind blower? Then we just disappear.

Eeshell meditated on the glow of a glorious rainbow that suddenly appeared. Rainbows carried unique significance. When she was little Zita told her how Ixchel, the Maya moon goddess after whom Eeshell was named, creates rainbows whenever and wherever women need them. Because men dislike bending, adapting and adjusting to changing circumstances, men resist the color and glory of the great arcs across nature's spacious sky. Male resistance always fails to stop the feminist potential of a rainbow, Zita said. Eeshell bore the symbolism of life-giving rainbows the way wayward men carried death-giving swords. Eeshell battled the evil so many men carry out.

Ixchel gave Eeshell strength.

"Morning, dudette," Bud said stepping from the bus wearing a red and green plaid kilt and his beanie copter hat.

"I see you dressed for lunch," Eeshell said.

Eeshell held up the jade chunk that caught a glimmer of sunlight that flashed a mini-rainbow in Bud's eye.

"Whoa," he said. "Far-out."

"That might be a sign," Eeshell said.

"Of what?"

"Equality," she said.

"Whoa, dudette," Bud said. "That is deep."

The jade piece Eeshell slowly turned in her hand resembled a heart. Spotting the shape, Bud put on a conspiratorial look, cupped his hand beside his mouth and said, "That heart reminds me of anatomy. Did I ever tell you about my deep dish brain?"

Eeshell stopped polishing.

"Continue, please," she said.

"Creation is like making Chicago pizza," Bud said. "I create a real brain in layers like a four cheese pie stacked with mozzarella and sauce and Swiss and sauce and cheddar and sauce and Muenster and sauce only I stack cerebrum and cerebellum cells from brains no longer staying alive like John Travolta dancing in that disco movie. I collect cells. Some I buy from the Chinese internet although they aren't all Chinese. Some I scrape off the beach."

Intrigued with Bud's freaky impromptu metaphysical rundown, Eeshell cocked her head and listened.

"I make my brain in a casserole dish with extra amygdalas," Bud said. "I have one finished and another one in the oven. The finished one, the smart one, her name is Lee."

"Lee's living in a dish?"

"I'm using a Crockpot for her," Bud said. "The brain forms from nothing in the head that forms from nothing in outer space, then slow cooks into wisdom. Life is nothing but something that returns to nothing."

Just kidding but half-serious, Eeshell teased her friend.

"Are you slow cooked, too, Bud?"

"I'm stir-fried," he said, "and best served high."

 **PRIMO NOIR**

"I'm creating a pop-up Hoocha Weed wine startup," Mel Moyle said to Jesús and Tripper when they visited him one afternoon. "I'd like you and Tripper to work with me as partners. Bud says a little birdie told him to bankroll the whole operation with the windfall his father left him when he died."

"You don't even know us," Tripper said.

"Good vibrations," Mel said.

Without a job and no way to support himself at the moment, Jesús paid close attention.

"Hoocha Weed Primo Noir," Mel said. "Like pinot noir but primo noir, like primo bud."

"I'm surprised you want to go into business," Tripper said. "I would assume you hate capitalism and the whole establishment grind."

"I do," Mel said. "We'll give the shit away."

"How do we make a living?" Tripper asked.

"Bud envisions an anti-corporate commune," Mel said. "He offered to pick up the tab for everybody for everything. His now deceased billionaire father already bought that big house on the Oceano hill. Bud says everybody can live there."

"It sounds too good to be true," Tripper said. "All of us living in that big old twenty-room Victorian house overlooking the ocean."

"Your two chickens, too," Jesús said.

"And Regalo," said Tripper.

"I'll keep my place in the dunes as a summer cottage," Mel said. "Eeshell says she'll miss her little second-floor Pismo Beach apartment. But she's excited to live in a commune and make jewelry in a corner of her room."

"She's great," Tripper said. "A radical feminist, I might add."

"Bud's father bought the house and lived here on weekends

when he opened the manufacturing plant and warehouse in Santa Maria," Mel said. "The old man left the house and money to Bud in his will."

"My mother is staying with Eeshell," Jesús said. "Can she live here, too?"

"Reefer and Aunt Irma, too," said Mel.

"We can all look after each other," Tripper said.

"By the way," Mel said. "One more thing everybody should know about our new home."

Jesús and Tripper held their breath.

"No smoking allowed," Mel said.

 # HOUSE OF THE RISING HOOCHA WEED

THE OCEANO mansion came complete with an oval driveway, extensive grounds with avocado trees, a sculpted Roman sundial, a pillared entrance way, and a number of additional buildings on the property.

The estate also held a supernatural history.

One wife of a previous owner disappeared. The original owner went mad. He and his wife had a baby who grew up to be a California executioner in the state prison system. The dog went crazy, too. As for their rabid tabby cat with crossed eyes, the poor thing got locked in the cellar and ate itself.

Empty when Arthur von Spittle bought the house, he pumped loads of money into remodeling. Within a month of buying and moving into the long-abandoned manor, he gave the place a do-over makeover that sparkled and provided modern luxury to the run-down features that had once shined. Except for a few large, dark and crusty stains made by an unknown substance on the foyer hardwood floor, everything returned to its original spotless sheen.

The timeworn structure had once served as the Radiance Sanitarium for Tuberculosis patients who improved from the salt air and care provided by people from a local utopian society who staffed the facility. Countless terminal sufferers benefited from their hands-on philosophy that stressed no treatment worked better than truth.

One sufferer received a standing ovation in 1947 from other patients and staff (the echo of clapping could even be heard from a patient inside an iron lung) when she announced "TB or not TB, that is the question."

"TB," said the doctor who within weeks pronounced the woman dead. Pointing to the smile on the corpse's face, the physician proclaimed in a metaphysical magazine the utopian community published that his patient died happy because she prepared for her deadly diagnosis by receiving ample support to send her on her way. Following her death the woman often visited the home in the form of a reincarnated monarch butterfly everyone sitting on the sun porch recognized by the little smile on its face and called by name.

Even when Arthur von Spittle spent time elsewhere in one of his other homes in New York and London (where he planned to market cigarettes to chain-smokers from Beijing to Moscow), he made sure groundskeepers and servants kept the Oceano home in tiptop shape. Lucky for Bud, who had no domestic skills and would have been happy living out of the VW bus for the rest of his life as long as he could get high.

Life had changed utterly.

With the old man's estate planning acumen (because he knew Bud lacked any financial or common sense) and a high-tech security system that kicked in with the push of a button, the communal compound was ready to rock.

Reefer's sound system provoked neighbors to call police and complain the very first night everybody spent together on the property, the Cove as Aunt Irma called her new home whenever Reefer called the place a bunker. Instead of turning hipster, Reefer reverted back to a modern mountain man look more suitable to his frothing at the mouth temperament.

One night while braiding his beard with tiny red, white and blue beads he stole from Eeshell's workshop he asked Aunt Irma, "You think them Mexicans who showed up here had something to do with killing Pa?"

"Mebbe," she said.

Reefer took that as a "yes."

"Is that skinny man with the American flag handkerchief sticking out the back pocket of his jeans really Bruce Springsteen?"

"And I'm Aunt Jemima," Aunt Irma said.

Reefer also took that as a "yes."

No hierarchical leader existed at the Cove as each housemate followed an independent muse, particularly Bud who regularly got paranoid, prone to anxiety attacks and downright cranky.

So did Aunt Irma.

As expected, Mel Moyle periodically turned grumpy.

Still, for the most part they got along, chilled and gelled like a non-animal product lime gelatin dessert complete with grapes and pineapple chunks. Common purpose remained elusive as weed wine served at room temperature was as close as everyone came to sharing a community common denominator.

The strongest bond existed between Zita and Eeshell.

By now everybody had stopped smoking joints and anything else that took a flame to light. With Eeshell's anti-smoking campaign underway, Zita's persistent coughing hung on with increasingly bad bouts, alarming everyone in the house, particularly Eeshell, who lectured regularly how smoking doomed existence.

Nobody wanted to talk about Bud's dad's death, but everybody wondered about the cause of death since word filtered back about his father's demise attributed to creepy crawlies and dime-sized third-degree burns that emanated from inside his body, a spontaneous internal combustion, according to one renowned pathologist who refused to go on the record for fear he'd be labeled a quack and driven from his very profitable profession.

Weed wine fueled the group, personally and professionally, which they considered one and the same, an under-the-table enterprise like a starship equipped with a metaphysical profit margin designed to improve vibes on the planet and cool the land with mellow, laid-back contentment good for all living creatures.

People in the house particularly respected Mel Moyle each time he recounted daily conversations with Hoocha Weeds which spoke back, treating them as living, breathing little pot people who saw life from the ground up and were more than happy to share their wisdom. After all, enlightenment was the whole point.

The words "Hoocha Weed Wisdom" appeared on each handmade back bottle label the commune produced and Eeshell wrote in longhand. Like mini-prayers from a Bible for a smarter generation, Eeshell said the wine labels would serve as propaganda for the commune's outlook of life, pamphlets for a new and better world even braver than the last.

Each back label said, "Hoocha Weed Wine soothes the soul

however you choose to define the core of your spiritual substance. To commune with nature and the universe, just sip from this bottle, jelly jar or glass and look into the sky. When you see your original face or the face of the clam—and you will—you're enlightened."

The front label on the wine bottles also served as an eye-catcher with a portrait of La Santa Muerte, no longer just a skull but a mystical woman in the flesh, a real woman wearing a purple cowl, holding marijuana in one hand and half a glass of Hoocha Weed wine in the other.

Eeshell sometimes asked a question that never received a suitable answer from the rest of the family.

"Is La Santa Muerte's glass half empty, half full or both?"

FROM ME TO ME

"DEAR DIARY" is no way for a man like me to begin my secret journal. The homeboys would laugh me off the cell block. Still, I'm just an out-of-work killer ex-con newspaper columnist who almost can't believe I did eight years for a fatal fair fight I fought in self-defense. A jury NOT of my peers decided I did the crime, so I did the time.

When I first moved to Santa Maria my main man from prison, boss of the Los Matadores west side gang here in town, El Maloso, helped me out. He's still helping me out even though I'm not sure if he's dead or alive. I can't say too much more about El Maloso. Let's just say I'll always owe the man. Now I don't know who, if anybody, to trust on the street. So when it comes to the shit storm that's headed my way I'm on my own. I don't want to pull Tripper back into this chaos any more than she's already neck deep in the swamp. I trust and love her.

I hate to bring it up, but I got a call on my cell this morning from a guy who calls himself El Chapstick. Said he got my number from his cousin and wants a meeting he says could save my life. Not sure what I'll do. Most likely take the meeting.

This is all on me, I know. Me and you, Jesús Malverde. My all-seeing mother tells me I'm channeling my main male genes, my most influential genetic traits, manifesting you, my grandfather and father into my life, epitomizing you mostly, dear great-grandfather, as my personal savior.

You. The original "sinner" of the Malverde family. You. The man who started the legend. You. Who now shapes me until La Santa Muerte takes me and anoints another to carry the torch of personal liberation.

Definitely some weird shit, but my mother sees things nobody else sees. I've seen her in action. Ask my late Uncle Arturo. Dude never knew what bit him. That's a joke, by the way. I know, not funny. I miss writing newspaper columns. That's why I was headed to Culiacán to spread truth and light on the frontier when my mother's brother, my own flesh and blood, jumped us. He knew I was coming and why—to right wrongs and stop him from establishing his splinter cartel.

To stand against oppression the way you, the first and most powerful Jesús Malverde faced down the enemy. Now our own kind hijacks your name. From now on we decide who uses our name. My mother says I face the same enemy you did. You and I are one. I am your living legacy.

I didn't want to believe any of this occult bullshit, but also never believed I could become a giant coyote, one predator taking on another animal. Until I did. Winning with blood on my teeth surprised me. I hate to admit it, but victory tasted good. You understand.

You are Jesús Malverde.

So am I.

TOMATO SAUCE

UNDULATING red waves of clots and gore flowed up and down the outside surface of the Oceano mansion's front door. Screaming without words, Reefer's mouth opened and closed like a lingcod gasping for air on a seagull shit-specked dock.

"Ahhhh, ahhhh!"

Pointing to the flashing crimson arched entryway with both forefingers like a heavy metal head banger minus his pinkies, one extremely stoned Reefer looked like a mad symphony conductor taking a fit in a burning orchestra pit.

Bud opened the door and stared at his commune-mate standing on the front porch.

"What, man, what?"

Reefer babbled.

"I'm drowning in tomato sauce," he said.

"Oh, that," Bud said looking at the red waves. "Light show, man, like those amoeba lights at the Fillmore back in the day. Humans got our start as amoebas. Bending bright beams is my tribute to mankind. A hippening, hoppening happening, dude."

Unable to accept reality Reefer continued to wail.

"Ahhhh, Ahhhh."

Bud shook a crooked finger in Reefer's face, a visual reprimand that left enough bright trails hanging before Reefer's eyes to start a hiking club. Chastising his new friend, Bud at least tried to be truthful.

"And if you ate my whole bag of missing supercharged "THCee The Light" gummy bears, you'll be tripping so bad you might not land for a week. You might want to fasten your seatbelt."

Reefer fumbled with the black leather belt he wore around his waist.

Until now, THCee The Light gummy bears took center stage

amid Bud's cannabis consumption—until he drank Mel's Hoocha Weed wine down in the dunes, that is.

"That vino is primo," Bud told Mel about a dozen times after his first few swigs at the wine and Cheez Whiz bash Mel threw Friday afternoons for anybody who happened to be around. Mel loved Cheez Whiz even though the processed cheese sauce spread contained chemicals bad for humanity. Recognizing weakness, Mel convinced himself a true societal renegade has to slouch a bit every now and then.

"You need to come down a little or the crash will be like a rough landing on the moon," Bud said to Reefer.

With the simple mention of the word "moon," Reefer watched Bud's face contort, resembling the man in the moon wearing his pouty, puckered mouth amid a yellow cheesy oval portrait. Blubbering more nonsense, Reefer increased the volume of his mantra.

"Ahhhh, Ahhhh!"

This time, though, he had reason to fear. Standing behind Bud, holding a chicken by the neck in each hand, Aunt Irma, wearing a bandana decorated with skulls wrapped around her head, smiled for the first time since the Weed Eater Massacre that ended the white supremacist Christian militia that once meant so much to her and Reefer.

"Lookie what I found, boy," she said. "Chicken soup's gonna taste real good for supper."

Bud went ballistic.

"Those chickens are Tripper's pets," he said, the octaves in his voice shooting high into soprano range and beyond what alert dogs can hear. "You better get them birds back where you got them."

Grudgingly, yet without malice, Aunt Irma asked herself what life must be like to be cooped up all day. She felt much better after dropping the chickens off in nearby Arroyo Grande Village where untold numbers of feral rosters and hens lived free in trees, on fences and sidewalks and have the run of the town.

Tripper would understand because Tripper understands freedom.

 # WEIRDO WINERY

MORNINGS in the windswept dunes Mel played with the coyote pups that grew bigger and stronger each day. With fangs sharp as buzzsaw teeth, the animals developed individual personalities each as unique as the other and as similar as their parents.

Watching Adam through rusty binoculars he found near 75-acre freshwater Oso Flaco Lake that provides an oasis in the dunes, Mel observed the moody dune slug devolve even further than the primitive larva that first rode into sacred land pulling a jerry-rigged buggy behind his corroded camper.

Pity drove park rangers to agree to ignore Adam's presence and let him park for a week or so along the ocean in violation of the rules. In his gut Mel wanted to turn the coyotes loose on this marauder. But his evolving sensibility toward peace and love overwhelmed the primitive urge for blood, a predilection coyotes couldn't change but Mel could.

In the meantime Hoocha Weed wine helped sooth Mel Moyle's nerves.

Mel hauled two canvas sacks loaded with dried herb to the shed at the rear of the Oceano mansion where Tripper and Jesús had stockpiled other necessary ingredients on Mel's shopping list. Bud had taken a lengthy piece of driftwood he planned to turn into a surfing safari longboard, but donated for the new outlaw winery's sign, into which he carved a question mark he painted purple.

"Our logo," he proudly announced.

"I don't get it," Tripper said.

Bud mulled over the matter, allowing the words to linger in his head like a beat poet dawdling over an eviction notice and a mug of hot wine and woe. Bud put on the gleeful look of a vintage freak stepping into a new pair of recycled bib overalls.

"Please allow me to explain," he said. "Ingest Hoocha Weed

wine and all you can do is question whatever goes on around you. Like, whaaaaaaaaattt? I mean, how many times have stoners responded to whatever anybody asked with that long drawn out question 'Whaaaaattt?'"

On a roll Bud continued: "So if you drink Hoocha Weed wine and sense the dune magic, you might see through the abyss into the next circle of the realm where something is nothing and nothing is everything and all is well until the clock strikes 13."

"Evolution is like my brain-in-a-dish friend Lee," Bud said, referencing the deep dish being who didn't speak but communicated with mental telepathy, which Bud called telempathy because Lee felt his pain as much as he felt hers.

"I mean, she doesn't have a mouth, man, so how else would she talk?"

Unanswered questions become answers themselves, Bud told Tripper.

"Get it now, Trip?"

"No," she said.

"Exactly," Bud said.

That's why Bud easily understood how the question mark logo meant a world loaded with Hoocha Weed wine and magic. Even Jesús Zarate got psyched when he heard Bud's trippy explanation.

"When do we bottle and give away the first batch?" he asked.

"Tomorrow we're ready to fly," Mel said.

In her normally nice way Tripper politely asked another question.

"Why is it still illegal for vintners to mix pot and alcohol for sale, Mel?"

"Big brother wants to keep separate both profit margins so one doesn't interfere with the other," Mel said. "Keep the peasants paying pumped prices while cannabis corrupters lobby, bribe, cajole and coddle the government booze and weed brutes spinning the hamster wheel."

"Turning with no power to the people," Tripper said.

"Not us," Mel said. "As long as Bud finances our communal winery we'll market our bandit brand free, outlaw Hoocha Weed the way it's supposed to be - given away. Which is legal, believe it or not, my dear brother and sister."

Robbing from the rich to give to the poor appealed to Jesús, sending him into soft reverie and contemplation of a less explosive future until a Harley-Davidson Fat Boy broke through the closed oak living room pocket doors. Reefer Johnson appeared shaking off wood splinters and plaster that dropped from the top of the doorway.

"Look what I found," he said, sliding to a sideways stop on the hardwood floor.

Jesús and Tripper quickly noticed the sleeveless leather vest he wore.

Jesús snapped at him.

"Where'd you get that motorcycle?"

"Nice, huh?" Reefer said, smoothing out creases in the black leather vest with "CRUSHERS" stenciled across the back. "One of the goons took it off at the tattoo parlor and I grabbed it on my way out. Didn't even have to hot-wire the bike like when I stole scooters in the mountains. Dumbass left the key in the ignition."

Jesús stepped close to Reefer.

"How many Crushers were at the tattoo parlor?"

"Fourteen," said Reefer.

Jesús stepped even closer.

"Did anybody follow you?"

Puffing out his chest like one proud peacock, Reefer said, "No way, man."

Jesús breathed a sigh of relief.

"They'll stop by later, though," Reefer said. "I yelled out my address twice real loud just to make sure them punk-asses knew I wasn't ascared of no Crushers."

 # NO BOMBER JET PLANES

WAITING for the monarch butterflies overwintering migration arrival, Bud sat nude, cross-legged and alone with his thoughts beneath a eucalyptus tree, meditating on the disruptive state of the world.

"Not good," he said over and over, reciting his mantra 100 times a day as a vow of peace.

World War III loomed large on the cusp of Bud's brain, expected at any time in the form of a nuclear missile from Russia, China, North Korea or the Midwestern part of the United States itself. Underground silos buried beneath barns across the Great Plains from northern Colorado into western Nebraska and throughout Wyoming, North Dakota, and Montana bothered Bud more than any potential overseas projectile headed his way. A couple of hungover Air Force duds could launch a full-loaded nuke by mistake, sending a LGM-30G Minuteman III intercontinental ballistic missile or ICBM into Pismo Beach instead of into a penthouse Kremlin suite in Moscow.

"Woe is us," thought Bud before a mood change hit causing an abrupt change of attitude.

"Whoa," he said. "Just whoa."

Adding to Bud's dilemma the monarch numbers were diminishing. Almost 90 percent fewer monarchs showed up in the Pismo Beach grove than 25 years earlier. The destruction of milkweed the creatures need to shelter, flourish and survive added to their demise.

Flittering above the tree the first butterfly Bud saw landed in the branches. Then came two and another and another and by the time Bud left the small grove thousands of Monarch butterflies had landed in the treetops of the tall eucalyptus and Monterey cypress trees, coming to the beachside haven each year for warmth and nourishment to hold them over until they headed to Mexico.

"Just like me," thought Bud who wanted one day to migrate south to surf, eat shrimp tacos, drink cold beer and find love nestled in south of the border sand. Hoocha Weed, too, of course. Bud would infuse everything he could find with as much Hoocha Weed as his slim body and mind could hold. Maybe grow Hoocha Weed in Mexico.

Mel, Eeshell, Jesús and Tripper would do well with the weed wine. Reefer and Aunt Irma could go either way. All Bud knew about their past was they had come from the weed hills of Northern California and were looking for revenge for some unknown slight they called a Fetus. Bud promised himself to help make the weed wine until he decided to split south of the border.

Looking skyward toward the west, Bud spotted a UFO circling high above the butterfly grove, rising and falling at a pace that seemed to signify peace from a pilot in no rush to land. When the UFO climbed and suddenly turned to dive, Bud ducked. A glint of light temporarily blinded him as the sun caught the edge of a small disc attached to the UFO before the object climbed again and disappeared from sight. Looked like a silver peace sign.

Taking the UFO as a good omen, Bud flapped his arms like a bird. For a second he thought he'd take off. Of course he didn't. You can't have everything.

 **LIZ**

Bᴜᴅ ᴡᴀsɴ'ᴛ the only one looking for love.

Regalo searched everywhere he crawled, checking out corners and crevices hoping to find a kindred spirit on the ground where he skittered and scattered tiny prey he attacked and ate, including other scorpions and lizards.

If only he could find something that crawled his way with a smile. Nothing slithered better than a lizard, especially the one he saw giving him the eye one day as he ran from bush to bush hungry for a meal. Backing her into a corner, he reared up ready to strike.

"You don't look so tough," the lizard said.

Defiance always boiled Regalo's adrenaline.

The Great Basin Fence Lizard was commonplace in these parts, but since Regalo stayed to himself he wasn't at all sure what to make of her. He didn't know, for example, she could consume him as easily as he could consume her. Instead of a killing instinct, though, Regalo felt his little arachnid heart beat all the way to his growling belly.

"I'm Liz," she said.

Although scorpions rarely blush, red hues tinted both sides of Regalo's body behind his tympanal organs that function like CIA listening devices, incredibly sensitive organs that allow scorpions to hear the faintest sounds. Scorpions have great eyesight, too, but Regalo balked at checking Liz out up and down and all around. Sexism is a given in the scorpion world, but Regalo wanted to be respectful. Smitten, not bitten, but suddenly shy, Regalo didn't know how to react. No female scorpion had ever expressed interest in his wiles and charms.

Now a fearless lizard named Liz was coming on to him. At least that's the way it looked to Bud who sat in the backyard watching the lizard approach Regalo who didn't seem to know what to do.

Rare for a predator, his sudden timidity seemed to disorient him.

"Go on, man," Bud said. "Tell her your name."

Looking up at Bud, the scorpion took off through the grass and headed for the house.

"I'll talk to him," Bud said to the lizard, taking a prolonged hit off his Hoocha Weed Wine as he watched her sashay to a small hill where she stretched out to sun herself on a rock.

Regalo sat on the porch.

He looked stoned.

I AM YOUR SOUL

As SOON as Jesús spotted the nametag on the black biker vest Reefer stole, the unmistakable identity jarred him with the raw power of a baseball bat crack to the back.

"Animal Jr." read the red outlined stitching. "Prezdent."

Of all the ferocious bikers in California, Reefer had to steal the vest and scooter of the son of the man Jesús killed months ago, if, in fact, he did black out and slaughter the late Crushers Motorcycle Club enforcer "Animal Sr." while in the transformed embodiment of a massive animal spirit coyote.

Rarely nervous, Jesús felt anxiety for the first time in years. The Mexican rocket attack and assassination attempt freaked him out, but this encounter put him on a cutting edge so sharp he could feel doubt slice through his black and red cowboy shirt, up his spinal column and into his subconscious.

The Crushers obviously elevated Animal's son to a position of power in the club, only giving him the nod because longtime Crushers' president Wallace abandoned the outlaw life and made friends with Jesús, Tripper, and Wally. When Wally killed himself, Wallace and his partner Rose disappeared into a mountain Zen retreat never to be heard from again. Jr. had no doubt returned to the Central Coast with a hunting party to look for his feral father's killer.

Pacing the house to get his thoughts together, Jesús unconsciously lifted the lid of one of the cut glass candy dishes Bud placed all over the house. Popping two juicy lemon gumdrops into his mouth Jesús chewed and swallowed before realization struck. Too late to spit out the gummies, Jesús realized he would soon be flying on Bud's always potent Hoocha Weed-infused candy he made in the kitchen as often as Aunt Irma made fudge.

Crawling up his spine into the deep crevices of his medulla oblongata, the dynamic cannabis strain struck before Jesús could count to ten. When he hit eleven the flashback whacked him swirling bright and colorful, carrying the physical and mental impact of the duel that left Animal's blood running in the gutter and glistening on Jesús' hands.

Jesús could see Animal's death like the scene was happening all over again. Just minutes before Animal died in Jesús's grip beneath the lit red neon Shell Beach liquor store sign, Jesús felt serene, better than ever, maturing and happy, on the road to a new peaceful adventure. The mark of the beast changed his identity as an unfamiliar and primitive presence tore through Animal's throat and snuffed out his life. Survival of the fittest lent evolutionary zeal to an otherwise starry night.

All Jesús Zarate saw that night was a dangerous "Animal" about to attack two friends when he stepped in. But what about that giant coyote Tripper and the others saw, that six-foot beast rising and standing on hind legs before springing into action like one of those teenage werewolves in the '50s movies he still loved to watch on TV?

Was Jesús that beast? Was he the great coyote that interceded in a human confrontation as a wild protector across species? Could Jesús continue to think like a man but kill like a beast? If so, did the creature remain inside his otherwise strong shelter of human body and mind? Could and would the coyote emerge again? If so, who would Jesús kill again?

Man is a beast, an animal, Jesús thought, always and forever a more dangerous beast than any coyote or great white shark. Jesús had sensed his coyote's guardian presence for many years before, knowing men who shared his prison cell block who swore they looked into the coyote's eyes at night and feared his power.

Would the coyote kill again?

A STATE OF MIND

MEL STOPPED talking.

From now on he would communicate only through messages comprised of single letters of the alphabet on his Ouija board. Bud would accept the responsibility of putting letters together into words and sentences and translating Mel's message for anyone interested in what he had to say. Mel called his communiques "Dune Vibes" and considered them part of his directives from the cosmos to be published in a collection of poems and essays in his prospective monthly magazine.

Back at the mansion Bud busied himself painting all the rooms in the house including the floors and ceilings, alternating bright colors because he always wanted to live inside a rainbow. Eeshell told him rainbows held the secrets of the macrocosm. Recognizing that living life from a metaphysical perspective by turning into a human rainbow would be a commendable goal, Bud also declared himself to be a Dunite.

Mel preached you don't have to live in the dunes to be a Dunite. Dunite is a state of mind.

When Bud carelessly painted himself into a corner of the common downstairs living room, he just stood there waiting for the paint to dry. To pass the time he listened to Lee lecture. The imaginative brain-in-a-dish friend he created in the science lab sat across the room in her casserole dish expounding out loud about how the human mind is an even itty-bittier bit than the most itty-bitty miniscule material at the core of the cosmos.

"Cosmic consciousness thinks for itself," said Lee. "Not like humans think, mind you, but on an infinite level that incorporates all elements from the periodic chart that combine to create human life. The cosmic brain decides which way to move infinity and how to live as the atoms of the past, present and future."

Bud nodded in agreement.

"I can dig it," he said.

"The cosmos reasons reasonably," said Lee. "Infinity lives. Human intellect, if you want to call our species' devolving brainpower intelligence, matters not at all in the mind of the cosmos that expands, gets bigger and decides for itself which way to go."

"Like an over-the-road trucker deciding which exit to take for a bathroom break on the 101 freeway," Bud said. "Go West, old brain, go West."

Almost falling asleep standing up, Bud felt worn out after this heavy philosophical exchange with the friendly female brain whose IQ had already soared higher than his. Mel boasted a new female friend as well, a partner in time, so to speak.

Although his Ouija board thoughts communicated to Bud would be otherworldly and shared, most messages would come from the voice that recently took up part-time residence in Mel's head, a voice calling herself "Syrah," an audible mirage, perhaps, or brainwave that telegraphed the future.

Welcoming this cynical sly devil into his subconscious, Mel even privately talked back to her on occasion when they disagreed over some small point of order. For example, Mel refused Syrah's request that she write a fascist "Dear Abby-type" column in his proposed "Dune Vibes" pamphlet, telling her she was better suited to penning letters to the editor in the neo-Nazi weeklies that sometimes circulated on the beach among vacationing ex-convict Aryan Nation's members from Fresno.

"Sieg heil," Syrah said.

Busying himself shucking clams, getting high and higher, making wine and enjoying life, Mel co-existed with Syrah. He refused to respond to her straight-armed salute. Instead, Mel Moyle flashed a peace sign.

"Tsk tsk," Lee said out loud each time she heard Mel talking with Syrah.

Mel should have taken Lee's advice. Conferring with a hypervigilant brain in a dish is smarter than brainstorming with a Ouija board speaking with a forked serpent's tongue.

DUELING DUMMIES

As soon as the liquor store opened Friday morning Reefer rolled his cart through the aisles until he found a nice bottle of red wine with a cork. Usually finding wine repugnant, Reefer never understood how to properly pull the cork, usually lopping off the top of the bottle at the neck with a hunting knife. Once he drank six bottles of bargain-basement Two-Buck Chuck Charles Shaw Merlot and for the rest of the night spit out glass shards that got stuck in his teeth.

Daddy Fetus drank nothing but whiskey and beer. Aunt Irma drank both, dropping a shot glass full of rye into a German stein full of lager. Everybody in the Weed Eaters' compound smoked weed including Reefer from the time he was about four. Wine appealed to snobs.

But now Reefer carried a beautiful golden corkscrew stuck into the waistband of his blue jeans, a sleek tool carved from oak a brother militia member found at the scene of Daddy Fetus' death, a clue to the as yet unknown killers' identity Reefer assumed to be Mexicans.

Feeling frisky and hip, surrounded by all these new civilized Central Coastal beautiful people, Reefer had decided he needed a bottle of wine if he expected to find a girlfriend. Girlfriends drank wine. So he needed to learn how to remove the cork the way gentlemen did on a Saturday night date. Reefer hadn't heard of twist-off tops for wine bottles so his new corkscrew would do the trick.

Staring the mousy liquor store clerk into cringing embarrassment, he asked to be directed to the wine aisle where he could find one of them "peenose nors" he heard Eeshell describe one day when talking about the kind of wine that might blend best with Hoocha Weed.

If Eeshell liked the pee-nose, he liked the pee-nose. He didn't care if it was a foreign word. Pee-nose sounded French for "the capacity to smell urine" which made Reefer think of the dirty Parisian postcards his daddy stole once from a tourist he mugged at a rest stop and gave Reefer as a gift to celebrate his dropping out of junior high school to go to work in the Weed Eaters' white supremacist militia pot patch.

Standing in the tequila aisle Animal Jr. spotted Reefer wearing his cutoff denim jacket bearing both Crushers' name and insignia stitched across the back, Satan's face with grapes and tangled vines for hair with the ragged edges of a broken wine bottle jammed into a bleeding eye socket.

"That's him," Animal Jr. said. "That's the scum that stole my motorcycle and colors."

Rushing Reefer, Animal Jr. pulled back to punch, but Reefer saw knuckles coming and hit him first, landing a head shot that knocked Animal Jr. through two store aisles, knocking over the Mad Dog Dragon Fruit wine display. Bottles crashed and broke on the floor, gushing sweet alcohol across the already sticky tiled floor. Three Crushers grabbed their leader, helping him stand.

"This here's war, boy," Animal Jr. said.

Reefer accepted the challenge.

"You want to settle this man-to-man, meet me at my house tomorrow, the mansion on the main street in Oceano that looks haunted."

"Get ready to meet your maker, boy!" Animal Jr. said.

Sensing Reefer's lunacy, the out-of-shape Crushers backed off. Let their mouthy president settle this one on his own. If he can't handle some shit-kicker weed head from northern hill country, what good would he be as president of their cowardly club that feared jumping all-on-one-and-one-on-all to crush this lone wolf head case? Animal Sr. would surely have expected his boy to earn his position of leadership. So did the pathetic Crushers who one day hoped to get adopted by a real righteous outlaw California club.

Envisioning the coming shootout, Animal Jr. gave his opponent a choice.

"Guns or knives?"

"Chicken wings," Reefer said off the top of his bong blitzed and scatterbrained head. Because his body clock struck lunchtime, he was starving and eating was the first thing that came to mind. "Man who eats the most wins."

Not knowing how to react to being challenged to a chicken wing eating contest, Animal Jr. said, "Shit, son, I can swallow more wings than my old man could eat crispy cockroaches at Dope's Diner before Dope burned it down for the insurance money."

"High noon then," said Reefer.

And he did mean high.

 # AN INNOCENT MAN

Spinning fast in reverse at the slight soft touch to the back of his neck, Jesús Zarate stopped within a hair of breaking El Maloso's jawbone with a back fist.

"I thought you were dead," Jesús said.

"I thought we won the Mexican-American War, too," said the longtime Santa Maria gang leader who spent a few years as Jesús' cellmate.

"I guess I got to give your car back now," Jesús said.

"No, brother, you keep that. I got another one. I'm buying an airplane next week."

Jesús heard the rumor on the street that El Maloso had died in a gigantic explosion that leveled an abandoned sugar beet silo in the one-time company town of Betteravia near Santa Maria. Gang-bangers had delivered the classic low-rider car to Jesús and Tripper the morning they checked out of the Santa Maria Inn and hadn't mentioned El Maloso's whereabouts. Jesús didn't ask even when they picked up the tab for the short hotel stay as a gesture of respect for the men's deep bond.

"Betteravia's been a ghost town since the '60s," Jesús said to El Maloso. "Why did people think you were there?"

"Guess word got out we kept our dope stored in the silo," said the grinning Chicano who resembled Duncan Renaldo, the actor who played the Cisco Kid on TV reruns he and Jesús used to watch in prison. "We filled that sucker all the way to the top with bales of cheap but good weed. But everybody's growing their own shit since personal possession is legal now. I might have to hit the street on a bicycle and sell hot corn on the cob with mayo and chili powder."

"Hold the mayo," said Jesús. "Who blew up the silo?"

"Not sure," said El Maloso. "Who'd blow up a tower full of dope without trying to unload the shit for a profit even if he thought

I was inside?"

"Any suspects?"

"Everybody wants to be El Chapo, who is an innocent man, I might add," El Maloso said.

"I planned to write columns in Culiacán about corruption, poverty and greed, the real forces of evil that drive young men to the cartels," Jesús said. "Not everybody down there is bad. Not even all the bad ones."

"Change of plan, right?"

"My turncoat Uncle Arturo's men are already here to get me."

"Whoever you are," said El Maloso.

Jesús focused hard on his friend.

"Meaning?"

"You. Are you Jesús Zarate? Or Jesús Malverde? Not to mention that big coyote that lives wherever he lives inside you and only comes out at night."

"Do you think I'm Malverde?"

"Do *you* think you're Malverde?"

Jesús grimaced.

"Go with the flow, bro," said El Maloso. "Don't worry about Brice Springsteam and the C Street Band. We'll take care of them. And El Chapstick."

"I'm all tapped out of violence and chaos," Jesús said.

"You might think you're out," said El Maloso. "We're both still in."

Jesús felt a familiar growl take shape in his throat.

"One more thing, vato," said El Maloso. "You didn't see me. You're not the only one who likes living as a ghost."

EGGHEAD SALAD SANDWICH

WALKING AROUND in circles like a lost dog chasing his tail, Bud went from room to room looking for his best friend and brain-in-a-dish. Normally Lee stayed put in the ceramic casserole dish with painted daisies on the side, secure in her intellect and place.

Until now nobody would ever consider Lee part of the food chain.

Figuring she just up and went for a walk - not having a body, head or legs wouldn't stop her because she was so damn brainy and could likely levitate - Bud headed to the kitchen for a crunchy peanut butter and fresh strawberry sandwich. Juan Gomez, AKA Brice Springsteam, and his four backup singer amigos stood peering into the open refrigerator. Juan clutched a pack of already opened wheat tortillas.

"Hey, homey," he said. "You want something to eat?"

Incredulous, Bud said, "Who let you in my house?"

"Be cool, bro," said Juan. "Reefer told us to make ourselves at home when we came over to interview him about handling security for us at upcoming concerts."

Juan's cousin also named Juan said, "We're looking for leftovers from yesterday, man, when Reefer cooked us up some bad boy tacos de sessos."

Bud struggled with the Spanish pronunciation.

"Take-o's duh say so?" he said.

"Sí, señor," said Juan. "We told him about how much we craved our country's traditional dish of cow's brains sautéed in lard. Reefer said he could fix that 'cause he had a fresh one waiting to go into the frying pan."

"So soft, silky and custard-like," said the other Juan. "Reefer sliced and diced that sucker with chanterelle mushrooms, habanero peppers and onions. There's a little left over in that dish, man."

Rushing to the casserole dish with the daisies painted on the side, Bud recognized Lee's frontal lobe, her pituitary gland and a few pieces of parietal lobe drowning in milky gravy.

"Man, that Reefer sure can cook," said Juan.

Bud fainted.

"Break open an amyl nitrate capsule and wave it under his nose," said the other Juan.

"Save some for me when he comes to," said Juan.

Looking down at Bud the other Juan said, "If only he had a brain."

Snide chortles worse than rabid hyena howls filled the kitchen as ravenous bandito brawn overwhelmed poor Lee's brain. Intellectual prowess meant nothing to this fiendish pack of famished malcontents.

Grabbing the last tortilla in the pack, Juan wiped up gravy from the pan. Brain food no longer meant fish. Brain food now meant brains.

"I feel smarter already," Juan said.

"Me, too," said the other Juan.

WHEN DOLPHINS FROWN

STRONG and happy, Eeshell's normal morning swim turned even more joyous than usual as she took long smooth strokes, cutting through blue-white waves, propelling herself through warm water that refreshed her more than she could remember. Unbeknownst to her, though, the heart of her physical and mental discipline lay just below the water's surface and close enough to taste. Eeshell's battle for her own peace of mind had begun.

Training to fight felt wrong. Eeshell loved peace, worked for peace, expected peace, especially for and from the environment. But nowadays evil too often arose unexpectedly, baring sharpened teeth and jaws to hunt, kill, and destroy. As good as she felt, she sensed an imminent duel with the weird voice she recently sensed in her head.

The voice had introduced herself as Syrah.

Cocky and arrogant, Syrah behaved like a bad girl in high school, mocking and taunting Eeshell to behave recklessly. Bleeding psychic carnage into Eeshell's mind that sometimes made Eeshell cry and worry she was going insane, Syrah poisoned the sense of calm Eeshell craved. As Eeshell glided through the water's warm embrace she wondered if she possessed the courage to successfully confront such bitter malice.

Evil defines inhumanity.

Syrah oozed evil.

Sensing trouble when her dolphin friends appeared and departed hastily, Eeshell remembered what Zita once told her: Beware when dolphins frown. Now she saw the thick gray-white fin moving her way. Protruding a foot from the water, the fin cut a swath through strong current as easily as a sharp blade moving through the caramel flan Zita baked. Turning her head to exert a stronger stroke, Eeshell felt darkness overtake light.

173

La Santa Muerte's face replaced the fiery oval of the sun.

"This is your final test," said the Mexican death saint. "Your performance today determines whether you are strong enough to help those in need."

Breaking the surface with the power of a natural submarine, a 17-foot great white shark arose showing bloodstained teeth. A glowing skull mask replaced the shark's face. Eeshell almost stopped swimming. How do you fight a great white shark and a demon at the same time, a great white shark instilled with a savage split personality? A monstrous great white on the prowl is bad enough. A multiple personality great white sends sadistic shivers up the back of the devil himself.

Syrah no doubt invaded the shark's mind as well.

Diving, Eeshell surprised the shark by swimming beneath its belly. Coming up on the other side, the shark momentarily lost track of Eeshell's whereabouts. Rolling left the great mammal lowered its massive body enough for Eeshell to grab its fin, pull herself up like a bucking bronco rodeo champion and hang on.

Syrah's voice cackled through the air bubbles.

"Ride 'em, cowgirl," said the little devil.

Trying to convince herself the shark fiend had materialized as another horrible figment of her imagination, a hallucinatory panic attack brought on by intense water temperature and hyperventilation due to irregular breathing in rough water, Eeshell persevered.

Maybe La Santa Muerte would allow her to die, judge her as unworthy. Maybe Eeshell would fail the test. Trying to stay calm, Eeshell focused on her breath as the gigantic frenzied fish dove deeper, twisting and turning as if she knew she had a rider on her back, an unwelcome visitor who appeared like an itch you just couldn't reach to scratch.

Curling, spinning, opening and closing her jaws, the shark did her best to shake Eeshell who clutched the fin tighter with both hands. Again changing direction, the shark rose with great speed, allowing Eeshell to catch her breath before the great white dove again, scattering schools of small fish that swam for cover.

Up and down and up and down they went in a seemingly endless nautical roller coaster ride. Eeshell worried she couldn't hang on much longer until she realized she wouldn't have to. Coming fast from the western horizon another gargantuan danger approached. In the distance Eeshell saw the water spout, not the tornado type but the spout of water that erupts from a killer whale's blowhole. Fast closing the distance the great white shark's only predator sped to the rescue.

"Thank you, Orca," Eeshell said.

Syrah screamed, "Thar she blows!"

Eeshell let go of the fin, swimming as fast as she could to escape the impending war between titans. This massive marine mammal, a blood relative cousin to the dolphins Eeshell had befriended, kept coming with all the power of a runaway train. Emerging and swimming excitedly in circles around Eeshell, the two dolphins who had seen Eeshell's predicament and gone for help came through in a potentially deadly pinch.

The dolphins smiled.

One of them winked.

The great white couldn't get away.

Eeshell scanned the sky for La Santa Muerte, but the bony lady had disappeared. Craving peace even in what looked like a soon-to-come battle to the death, Eeshell used the increasing power she felt to command a bloodless resolution to this unnatural natural dilemma. As a princess of the sea she expected nonviolence even from predators, transmitting to beasts the vital life energy the Japanese call ki, the Chinese call chi and Indian mystics call prana. Eeshell called the sacred force her greatest spirit.

Instead of slamming into the great white, the whale abruptly slowed, pulling alongside the smaller creature like an ocean cruise ship docking in a tropical paradise. Just because you can doesn't mean you should. Not every killer whale must kill. Not every great white meat eater must butcher. Wild animals can make peace. The shark backed off, gliding safely to serenity, taking Syrah with her.

Yes, even a great white can harbor a voice in her head, evil in her heart.

Blasting one final gushing geyser, the Orca turned back to the vast seascape, joining her dolphin cousins for a final family dip in their earthly pool before parting. Eeshell swore she saw her sister dolphins blow her a kiss.

Treading water, trying to understand the magnitude of what just occurred, Eeshell allowed the current to carry her to shore where Zita stood holding out a beach towel decorated with images of surfing seagulls wearing Hawaiian shirts and baggie board shorts.

"Did you have a nice swim?" Zita asked.

Within swirling white clouds in a broad blue sky La Santa Muerte's image appeared brighter than usual, wearing a garland of fresh red roses around her neck and a rainbow-colored hood over her skull.

La Santa Muerte blessed Eeshell.

All was well.

For now.

KEEPING SECRETS

AMID A cacophony of sea lion barks from beneath the pier, Tripper and Jesús dug into thick burritos loaded with shrimp, woodland chanterelle mushrooms, and black beans topped with marinated red cabbage and fat green jalapeño peppers that sprayed juice when you bit into them. Pete, who owned "Pete's Pierside," poured icy wine coolers in plastic cups while Angel and Nacho worked the grill as masters of the foodiverse.

"This is my favorite place in the whole world," Tripper said.

Looking out over the Port San Luis Harbor that led to the open sea, Jesús recognized the supernatural appeal in the splendor of gently bobbing boats beneath a crystalline indigo sky. Barking blubbery sea lions helped set the perfectly primitive mood.

"Everything changes," Jesús said. "Sometimes for better. Sometimes for worse."

Tripper's expression soured.

"You sure Aunt Irma and Reefer don't know?"

"They don't have a clue."

"All Reefer talks about is finding who killed his daddy Commander Fetus. Aunt Irma really loves this lovable maniac kid."

"Just like she loved Commander Fetus, his unlovable maniac father."

Tripper's mood fell fast.

"I saw online the detectives have come to a dead end in their investigation."

"You could call it that," Jesús said.

"Yeah, well cops keep murder cases open forever."

"Most homicides go unsolved," he said.

"Commander Fetus and his white supremacist militants started that fight," Tripper said. "We defended ourselves to survive. Even our peace-loving psycho serial killer friend Wally Wilson jumped into action."

"I still can't get a grip on Wally going coastal popping eyeballs with corkscrews," said Jesús.

"That poor berserker boy was sick." Tripper said.

"Sick of chardonnay drinkers," Jesús said. "So our blood-bath, carried out with a little help from your armed and dangerous Northern California radical feminist eco-terrorist women friends, wasn't murder?"

"Pure self-defense," Tripper said. "We knew that ripped rube militia was around when we organized the Mother Earth Patrol. But those bad old boys stayed out of our way."

"Wally's death taught us to sacrifice for peace of mind," said Jesús.

"The search for truth has a strange way of bringing people together," Tripper said.

"So we just keep quiet," Jesús said. "Enter each moment and see where the trip takes us."

"Why do you think people call me Tripper? You want another wine cooler?"

YOU BETTER LISTEN

LA SANTA MUERTE does not repeat herself. So pay attention. I'm talking to you.

Human flesh fashions the purple hood I wear to cover my intentions. My eyes bleed from red corpuscles set deep in hollow sockets of white bone that gleam pure as innocence lost in the torturous pain of solitary confinement. The handle of the scythe I sometimes carry is long enough to slay you wherever you try to hide. The globe I sometimes carry is your tomb.

My skeletal fingers always hold the fate of the world.

You cannot run from me. I am your worst nightmare feeding on your brain cells. You are helpless before me. No one stops my almighty power. Light your candles. Flame ignites my dominance. Light my fire. Pray for forgiveness.

No matter how smart you think you are, your small minds have no idea how adept I have become over centuries of death you brought on through jealousy and ego. Those who respect my energy embody wisdom. You desire safety, health, money, success. You deserve love, good luck, well-being. Some of you crave justice and seek revenge.

I'm listening. Talk to me. Peace and healing remain my preference, but I empathize with your need to get even. I embrace your suffering, your sickness, even your Covid virus. This bony lady hears you.

Holy death will help you in your journey. But first you must ask for my guidance. I invite you to petition my assistance. Please. I decide who breathes, who lives. I decide who gasps for breath and dies. Are you worthy of my touch? In exchange for my protection I expect devotion. Betray me and whither like bad grapes on the vine, shrinking, shriveling, dropping to mix with ancient soil and the sweet mysteries of creation.

Laugh at me. I dare you. Break your promise.

Watch your children and grandchildren one day twist in pain as I inflict misery and claim their lives. I already own their spirits. Do you want them servile and naked, groveling in the foul underworld where my spells turn them into vipers that crawl fetid floors of feces and flame? Go ahead. Laugh. Break your word.

La Santa Muerte always gets her way. La Santa Muerte always gets her wish. La Santa Muerte always wins.

Mother Death eventually claims all her children and takes them home.

Today I offer a sacrifice to teach your breed a lesson and resolve once and for all whether humans deserve to continue their evolution despite doing their worst to kill the planet. You pollute the environment. You endanger majestic animals and other species. You poison the land, water, air and all the bountiful growth that makes Earth the magnificent miracle she is.

So today I choose whom to save, whom to condemn, whom to spare, whom to immolate. Today I choose one special human sacrifice, one whose time has come. Whom shall I select?

Eeshell is my mirror image when I was a young seeker, a great feminist spirit upon whom so much depends. No, the world needs Eeshell. Maybe I should sacrifice more than one to show how easily the good die young. Tripper and Jesús, too?

Whom shall I cast into the abyss? Whom will I choose to join me in the boneyard? The time has come, my children, to name my next gift to our natural order.

Who is ready to die?

 # OUIJA BORED

COMING together at the Oceano house to mark the commune's first batch of what Mel Moyle officially called "Weed Wine Magic," the tribe decided to celebrate.

Bud and Mel's utopian dream of an alternative society provided nice balance for everyone. An impromptu paradise fit each person's personality yet added to the power of the common good. Anti-establishment anarchistic vibes aside, happiness mattered.

At Tripper's urging, since she had experienced communal living with the Mother Earth Patrol family of radical feminist environmental guerrilla fighters, and with a little help from Aunt Irma who coined the term, the newly formed family officially christened their commune "The Cove."

"Let's have a séance," said Tripper.

Sitting cross-legged at the low Japanese living room table, Mel laid eight fingers on his Ouija board planchette, marveling as the birch wood piece moved first to the letter "C," then to the letter "O," on to the letter "O" and then to "L."

"Cool," said Bud.

Excited and already high on weed wine, Tripper clapped her hands like a wired teenage girl at a pajama party sleepover. Jesús sat quietly at the antique dining room table with his mother, looking past the half-open mahogany pocket doors into the other room. Aunt Irma sat on a chaise lounge drinking warm Tecate Mexican beer from a dented can. Eeshell settled into a bean bag chair playing with wax dripping from a flickering strobe candle.

"Everybody get around the dining room table," Tripper said. "C'mon, let's all join hands."

Moving in the spirit of togetherness everyone did as instructed. Within seconds Mel's planchette took off with a mind of its own spelling out "LEE."

Bud fainted.

"Poor Lee," said Aunt Irma. "Rest in pieces."

Flipping over by itself the planchette flew from Mel's hand and lay on the table like an overturned turtle on the beach. Now moving by itself it spelled out "S-Y-R-A-H."

"I know her," Jesús said.

Zita remained quiet, her soft features smooth in the candle-light. All eyes went to Mel who had made it clear he would only speak through the Ouija board but now broke his oath of silence.

"I know her, too," Mel said. "Syrah's my soul sister."

"You're talking," Tripper said.

"I'm bored," Mel said. "Ouija bored."

"Me, too," Syrah mumbled.

Others knew Syrah as well.

Nobody liked her no matter how hard they tried.

HEART TO HEART

IN THE DISTANCE the Sierra Madres east of Santa Maria merged with the San Rafaels, offering sacred mountain energy to Zita. She and Eeshell drove the dirt road from Highway 166 to Peak Mountain, elevation 5,845 feet.

Few people live and work amid the mountain range except for some of the lower northern slopes that slick and greasy corporate profiteers developed for oil and gas production. A single-lane dirt road traverses the mountain. Storms often close the crest best navigated by four-wheel-drive vehicles or motorcycles. That's what Google told Zita when she looked up their destination before the trip, even noting that the endangered California condor inhabits the territory.

A falcon wearing a silver peace sign around its neck accompanied Eeshell and Zita the day they drove to the mountaintop in the commune's VW van. The bird trailed the vehicle, following high in the sky.

"I sense electricity," Zita said.

"I feel it," said Eeshell.

In the back seat new votive candles clanked against each other in a cardboard wine box Zita packed before they left. Jesús Malverde's painted face decorated one side of each candle. A printed prayer decorated the back of each candle.

"Oh Malverde, my Lord!" said the prayer. "Today, as I kneel here before your cross, I ask you for mercy and the healing of my pain. You, who lie beside glory and so close to God, hear the sufferings of this humble sinner. Oh, miraculous Malverde, my Lord, grant me this favor and fill my soul with joy."

"I hiked to Culiacàn's mountains each year for years before I came to the United States," Zita said. "I always lit candles for him."

Now Eeshell recited the prayer Zita taught her as a child.

"I call to you Jesús Malverde," she said. "Please guide and protect me. Open the doors of opportunity by removing obstacles from my path. Give me courage to overcome my problems and defeat my enemies. Bring justice and balance to my life by bestowing your wisdom upon me. With your powers please give me the strength to fight and win my daily battles. I am ready for your winds of change that bring prosperity to my realm. AMEN."

Zita said, "Nowadays even the Internet gives us instruction."

Reading from her phone, Zita said, "He is already in heaven and can intercede for you. In moments of anxiety, you need to hope and believe in something that helps you recover faith and maintain peace in your life."

"Say a personal prayer, Eeshell," Zita said. "What do you want, child? What do you need to succeed in this life, to begin a new life or put to rest your past life?"

"To leave it all behind," Eeshell said. "To resurrect."

Zita continued reading from an ad for the candles she bought for six dollars apiece in a Santa Maria botanica.

"Light the candle with a match or lighter and say a prayer of your choice. You can put the candle out at any time or let it burn to the end. Each time you relight the candle say a prayer to reenergize your goals. You can write your name on the glass of the candle to personalize the prayer. Use a black marker and write your name or another person's name on the candle. After the candle has fully burned down you can throw away the glass."

When they reached the mountain peak the sun had almost disappeared.

"You first," Zita said.

Holding a Scripto pen in her left hand and the candle in her right, Eeshell wrote "Ernesto" and "Chantico," the first names of the man and woman she believed to be her birth parents. Both had died two years earlier when a drunk hit them on the 101 freeway near the Nipomo exit.

"Now you," Eeshell said, holding out the pen to Zita.

Zita wrote, "Jesús Malverde."

"He's already got his name on the candles," Eeshell said.

"Our protector also sometimes needs protection," Zita said.

"I miss Papá and Mamá," Eeshell said.

"Their kindness will always guide you," Zita said. "As will their loyalty you will one day understand."

Grappling with the urge to tell Eeshell the truth about Ernesto, Chantico, and her son, Jesús, Zita knew the time wasn't yet right. Soon, but not now, would she share the secrets Eeshell deserved to know and understand.

Soon, but not now.

Before Zita died, but not now.

Soon.

 # JUSTICE IS SERVED

ANIMAL JR. stood at the center of the circle his club members made around him, nervous but drunk enough to hide his anxiety and delusional enough to believe he would finish the fight as the victor and be carried away on the shoulders of his brothers.

Reefer met his opponent's stare from behind a picnic table piled high with deep-fried wings slathered in red hot chipotle pepper sauce. The aroma wafting off the paper tablecloth smelled like kerosene, burned charcoal and singed hair.

No water, milk, or beer to cool the mouth, just hot, spicy, crispy wings.

With nobody home at the Cove, Reefer's "Crunchy Cage Match" got underway with no unwelcomed witnesses. Stepping to the center of the makeshift chicken wire arena, Animal Jr. rubbed his hands together like a well-trained professional eater. Thick and thin unidentifiable deep-fried morsels sent smoke rising from two heaping serving platters piled two feet high.

"We'll start at the same time," Reefer said. "We finish when one or the other can't eat no more."

Animal Jr. rushed forward, swan diving onto the table and burying his face in the steaming pile of wings. "UMMMMMGGGGH-HHH," he grunted as he started to chew, looked up and snarled, "Look, Ma, no hands."

Not to be outdone, Reefer dug into his wing mountain with both hands. Sauce dripped from his eyebrows as he tore into and gnawed the gristly flesh that didn't taste at all like the wings he ate for lunch when he and Commander Fetus used to drive into town to buy ammunition and comic books back in the good old days.

Okay, so Reefer had to improvise for a discount when he bought these wings from a homeless Army veteran who told him he survived jungle training in the Philippines that got him nowhere in the desert in Iraq except almost killed. So what if the wings filled a burlap bag that needed ice? So what if the wings lacked ample meat?

Neither man expected a free-for-all wing eating brawl to turn into a crippling death match.

Bellyaches started within minutes. About 50 wings in each man felt rumbling vibrate their small intestines just seconds before throbbing in the large intestine led to itching, abnormal redness of the skin, swelling, confusion, nausea, anxiety, altered sense of taste, headache, high blood pressure, low blood pressure, seizure, loss of consciousness, vomiting, kidney failure, irregular heartbeat, and heart failure.

As Animal Jr. writhed and expired he pointed at Reefer and mumbled, "Loser."

As Reefer writhed and expired he pointed at Animal Jr. and mumbled, "No, you."

"You," said Animal Jr. clutching his throat.

"No, you," said Reefer clutching his throat.

When Animal Jr. and Reefer collapsed at the same time and quickly turned blue, Crushers' Vice President Peanut Brittle walked to his leader's body, kneeled and put his ear to Animal Jr.'s chest. Shaking his head he stood, walked to Reefer's blue body and did the same.

Turning to the crowd he said, "I hereby declare this duel a tie. Everybody loses."

The Crushers cheered.

Two club members raised new president Peanut Brittle on their shoulders and joined other Crushers dancing, spitting beer on each other and strutting to their bikes, kicking over the engines and roaring off in a cloud of mesquite barbecue smoke and body odor.

Who would have thought the poor, homeless veteran suffering severe PTSD had snipped off hundreds of bat wings from bats in the cave where he slept and where bat colonies roosted, thinking he could sell the bat parts to a Chinese restaurant for stew, hot pot, soup, or curry? Who knew the landowner where the cave was located regularly sprayed the cave with cyanide-fueled homemade pesticide as a way to get rid of the pallid bats, the state bat?

And who ever expected Animal Jr. and Reefer Johnson to eat dozens of those same poisoned bat wings mistaking them for the yummy chicken wings football fans ate while watching the big game?

This contest was no Super Bowl.

This was the Stupor Bowl.

PLAYING WITH FIRE

FLAMES licked sea-salted misty air with devil tongues of orange fire.

Theosophist believers immediately saw black smoke over the dunes as they exited a meditation service at the sacred Temple of the People in the nearby village of Halcyon. Oceano firefighters shook their heads in frustration knowing they could do nothing to save whatever was burning and already completely engulfed in the dunes.

Mel's shack crackled, collapsed and burned to the ground.

Adam and a dozen middle-aged dune rats stood around the inferno laughing like juvenile delinquents poking the embers with willow sticks they picked up near the beach and popping cans of beer they pulled from the bulging pockets of their Walmart cargo shorts.

"I hope the old bird's inside," Adam said. "Like an overdone holiday turkey."

Drunken motorheads who assembled on the beach earlier that day to offer Adam moral support cackled at the blaze.

"Don't blame the matches," Adam howled, mocking Mel's sad ecological refrain about protecting the coyotes and the great white sharks who shared the land and sea.

Turning away from obvious arson, Adam walked back to his camper, followed by menacing dune buggy troopers carrying pieces of Mel's shack to build a bonfire on the beach and dance in a circle the way ancient Chumash Indians might have danced in their prime.

Watching from afar the coyote family stood with wet noses tuned to danger in the air.

Mel Moyle stood with the coyotes.

So what else is new?

 # SADLANDS

Blowing over the top of her steaming cup of green tea, Zita just listened.

"Reefer's screws were way too loose even for me," Aunt Irma said.

Managing soft empathy under dire circumstances and feeling bad for Aunt Irma, Zita knew Reefer was all the poor woman had left of her so-called nuclear family. And they sure were nuclear. Reaching across the table Zita gently laid her palm on the top of Aunt Irma's hand.

"Reefer was a troubled young man," she said.

"His late dead daddy Commander Fetus, my uncommon law husband, and the Christian white man's militia made him that way," Aunt Irma said.

"Life will be different here," Zita said. "With us."

Aunt Irma perked up.

"Already is," she said. "Did I tell you I'm in love?"

Exchanging quick glances with Zita like card sharks at a poker table, now Eeshell eagerly spoke up.

"Who's the lucky man?"

"Brice Springsteam," said Aunt Irma.

"You mean Bruce?" asked Eeshell.

"My man calls himself Brice so he doesn't get sued when he performs as the Boss," Aunt Irma said.

Giving Aunt Irma the eye, not the evil eye but a discerning eye, Zita frowned.

"You mean that cactus-needle-thin fake cartel bad man from my hometown in Culiacán who says he's up here looking for singing work?"

"That's him," Aunt Irma said.

Eeshell got curious.

"Is he playing anywhere around here?"

"Him and the C Street Band, the C is for Culiacàn, are headlining at Louie Louie's in Santa Maria Saturday after Reefer's funeral," Aunt Irma said. "We can all pile in Bud's bus and drive down to see him."

"Might as well," Zita said. "I'll tell Jesús, Tripper, Bud, and Mel. Poor Mel needs something to take his mind off his loss."

Aunt Irma grimaced.

"Anybody who burns down an old man's house needs to pay," she said.

Zita changed her caring tone to an icy declaration.

"Paybacks are a b...," she said, stopping herself before she completed her sentence.

Regaining her composure, Zita said, "Paybacks are a rich way of evening the score."

 # STASHES TO STASHES

DRESSED in a Confederate flag headband and a red and black checked flannel housedress, Aunt Irma joined other mismatched pall bearers to carry her nephew's hefty remains to his final resting place behind the Cove mansion.

Brice Springsteam paid his amigos five bucks apiece to dig the grave and stand at the edge ready to shovel dirt and cover the wooden coffin Aunt Irma built by herself from lumber she stole from around town. Jesús, Tripper, Bud, Mel, Brice, and Aunt Irma carried the casket and lowered the dead weight into the hole. Instead of laying flowers on the casket, Aunt Irma dropped an ounce of low-test weed on the coffin lid to carry Reefer into the next world—a stash, if you will, for the afterlife.

Once again Reefer had failed, the poor boy going to his grave not knowing who killed his daddy, dropping into the ground like an old transmission tossed into a landfill to decay and end up another corroded hulk laying at the bottom of an earthen pit.

Brice blessed himself scratching his way deeper into Aunt Irma's good graces. This was one devious desperado who knew love has a way of softening even the hardest, meanest heart. Actually, Brice considered his affection "a hungry heart," the way his idol might put it.

Getting so carried away he couldn't help himself, Brice broke into song, warbling a few lyrics from the real Springsteen tune in fractured English as his skinny drunken Mexican buddies sang off-key a cappella backup in Spanish. The impromptu performance worked, getting to Aunt Irma who wiped away a single tear with the edge of her lumberjack smock.

Nobody noticed the re-organized Crushers Motorcycle Club cruise by, the last rider pulling a 4x8 U-Haul cargo trailer in which the remains of Animal Jr. rested wrapped in a tattered Persian rug they found in a Dumpster after their late leader and his nemesis gobbled their way to a draw in a poison bat wing eating contest that would go down in Crusher Club lore as a fight to the finish any hardcore outlaw biker had to love and respect.

At least Animal Jr. got a one-way magic carpet ride to the great by-and-by.

SHORT-TIMER

COUGHING and awakening from a hazy dream, Zita watched two tall shadows hover near the foot of the bed. Whispering with their heads close together, La Santa Muerte and Jesús Malverde stood as grim as a gallows on execution morning.

Reaching for a cigarette on the night table, Zita recoiled when the pack erupted in flames. In a stern voice, La Santa Muerte reminded Zita of her promise.

"You stopped smoking, remember?"

"My time is short, Mother," Zita said. "No one will know."

"I will know," said La Santa Muerte. "You will know."

Leaning into the light of the burning cigarette pack that crackled and curled in the ashtray, Jesús Malverde spoke up.

"How is my great-grandson, Jesús?"

"Better than ever," Zita said. "Married and peaceful."

Zita felt good boasting that her son's famous bloodline on his father's Malverde side provided power to lead rather than follow, unbridled courage to confront the crime that rules both sides of the border. Zita also felt good living as a daughter of La Santa Muerte, her spiritual mother who adopted her as a child and reassured her she would watch over Zita in the absence of her natural mother who died giving birth in a rich Oaxacan field of shining yellow corn.

When Zita married and gave birth to her son, proud to name the baby after her loving husband, she felt the power of two revered family lineages. All these years later her granddaughter Eeshell carried ancestral gifts from both bloodlines offered by Jesús Malverde and La Santa Muerte.

La Santa Muerte asked, "When will you tell her?"

Jesús Malverde asked, "When will you tell him?"

"Soon," said Zita.

JUMPING BEANS

IF YOU LIKE darkness, gloom and unhinged manic-depressive episodes, you'll love Louie Louie's. Bartenders bent and thin as used swizzle sticks swill all-you-can-drink free shots on the job and do the occasional toot of blow in the one-commode men's room where obscene messages spray-painted on the back of the door offer phone numbers to call for a good time and machete cuts cleave the condom machine.

Hard as such pinball behavior might be to comprehend, some Louie Louie's regulars do carry spray paint, machetes, brass knuckles, pepper spray, and other accoutrements of whatever criminal art in which they specialize. Guns, too, the butts of which are sometimes visible in customers' pants or on their hip when, in full delirium tremor, a handful of military combat veterans from various wars and other abuse victims suffering traumatic flashbacks raise their elbows to salute the shredded Old Glory hanging from the ceiling.

The flag once covered the coffin of a Louie Louie's regular and fake Green Beret who sang country music in Portuguese that nobody understood. At his funeral a real former Green Beret A-Team member and alert senior citizen named Green tore the flag off the phony's casket and later hung it from the bar ceiling where he regularly reminded regular customers he should have hung the bogus Special Forces soldier.

The starry banner now dangled above the bar as a steadfast reminder of hard truth. Patrons treated Green Beret Green as a hero hunched over his 40-ounce bottle of Colt 45 beer waiting for a sneak attack and foreign invasion from the Western horizon, never leaving home without his loaded firearm, a vintage .45 Colt legendary lawman Wyatt Earp would have cherished.

Louie Louie himself used an alias to hide his real name which was Raymond (on the run for decades from Buffalo, New York, where he singlehandedly robbed an armored car) who regularly jumped over the bar brandishing a hockey stick to break up barroom brawls especially on music nights.

"This is a really nice place," said Aunt Irma, sipping what the drink menu on the chalk board offered as the evening's special artisan cocktail for two dollars, a "Rotten Apple Martini with Grain Alcohol."

Tripper ordered a double sloe gin fizz, Jesús a shot of "Mad Bull" tequila, Bud a "cranberry juice, hold the cranberries" which the waitress ignored, Mel a water, Zita a can of Tecate, and Eeshell nothing. Leaning close enough to Tripper to smell patchouli oil behind her ear, Eeshell said, "I'm picking up a weird vibe."

Tripper nodded in agreement sending sparkles from the beer lights off the jade earrings Eeshell had given her as a gift. When the door opened to the walk-in closet-sized musicians' dressing room (formerly the office for an outpatient psychiatric patient bail bondsman currently out on bail himself on gang-related assault charges), all four members of the C Street Band shuffled in loaded on La Luna Mezcal and homegrown PCP-laced weed the bouncer sold them. Bringing up the rear show headliner Brice Springsteam himself, resplendent in a rented tuxedo with corn whiskey on his breath, waved to the skimpy audience.

"Over here, sweetie," Aunt Irma said, blowing a kiss.

Brice walked right past her and into the supply closet where he retrieved a long-handled mop which he began holding like a microphone, singing into the handle as he emerged sashaying among the crowd, serenading several women who leered drunkenly, eating up the singer's attention with the gusto of a famished Chihuahua scarfing down a dropped burrito at an illegal bullfight. The C Street Band fell in behind their lead singer, each man practicing the lyrics to different tunes in Spanish and unskilled English, not all of which were Springsteen songs.

That's when Brice Springsteam froze.

Bug-eyed and noticing what he failed to notice before the show, all four members of his band wore bright yellow oversized sombreros. Instead of stylish black leather vests or fashionably colorful silk shirts, each singer modeled a garish red kerchief tied in a knot with the ends drooping to the left and to the right. Each man wore matching white peasant shirts and pants. Each man bounced on the toes of bare feet complete with very long nails that turned to sharp claws right before Brice Springsteam's very eyes. Each man looked exactly like retro cartoon hero Speedy Gonzales! Each man was Speedy Gonzales! Two long thin whiskers protruded from each side of each man's nostrils. Four thin tails trailed them on the sticky barroom floor.

Now belting out the same lyrics they sang, "¡Ándale! ¡Ándale! ¡Arriba! ¡Arriba! Up! Up! Move! Move!"

Brice Springsteam knew somebody drugged him.

Scurrying to escape he tripped over the mop handle, rolling like a beer keg into Louie Louie who slap shot him with his hockey stick into the juke box that automatically kicked into the Mexican national anthem. Most of the undocumented patrons jumped to attention to salute. Green Beret Green who refused to acknowledge anybody's national anthem or nationality except his own, pulled his pistol and fired expert marksman-style into the jukebox with one hand while saluting the Stars and Stripes hanging from the ceiling with the other.

Lightning fast and showing their teeth, C Street Band members turned the tables on Juan Gomez AKA Brice Springsteam the way Speedy always outsmarted Sylvester the cat. Nobody ever expected Speedy to actually hurt El Pussygato, but these mice were out for blood.

Charging the exit and tearing open the front door, Brice Springsteam slammed head-on into El Chapstick on his way into the bar, his jelly belly bouncing the wrecked rocker backrolling into the center of the dance floor. Shining in the hospital-grade fluorescent overhead lights and flickering red and green neon beer signs, the outraged El Chapstick's rubber wrestling mask glistened with sweat that seeped through the eyeholes in the thick rubber head covering. Lumbering forward, El Chapstick picked up Brice Springsteam holding him with outstretched arms over his head as he turned circles on the scuffed floor.

Mexican wrestling fans around the room began clapping in time to the chant, "TIRARLO, TIRARLO!! Throw him, throw him!"

Overcome with the emotion of the moment even Aunt Irma picked up on the chant without knowing what the words meant. Framed in blue cigarette smoke haze she began rooting against her fiancé.

"I never did respect a man who couldn't hold his liquor," she said. "That wrassler is kinda cute, anyway."

With one mighty heave El Chapstick threw his opponent behind the bar where he landed in a basket of live Dungeness crabs, several of which latched onto the exposed skin of his groin on either side of the torn seam of his tuxedo pants that split when El Chapstick spun him around like a Piper Cub propeller. With dinner plate-sized crabs dangling from his crotch, Brice Springsteam got a second wind, a burst of survival energy that sent him dashing for the open door and careening face forward into the bleak recess of the dirt parking lot.

Draining his water glass, Mel slapped himself in the forehead and said, "Oh, shit."

Bud jumped like he sat on a porcupine sleeping on an outhouse toilet seat.

"What, dude, what?"

"I wondered what happened to my gallon of XXXX Hoocha Weed wine," Mel said. "That's the super hooch quadruple power weed wine, the most potent psychedelic Hoocha Weed wine I ever made."

"You don't think Brice Springsteam stole your hooch and drank it, do you?"

Mel pondered the question.

"¡Arriba! ¡Arriba!" he said. "¡Ándale! ¡Ándale!"

COYOTE BUDDHA NATURE

TAKING each step as if he were walking on broken beer bottles he all too often encountered on the beach, Theo the coyote picked his way through still smoldering embers of what once served as Mel's cabin. Human enemies had periodically stopped by the crime scene to throw pieces of driftwood onto the charred wood pile and keep the fire going so they could drink, laugh, and rev the engines of monster machines Theo feared but from which he would never back down.

Quickly spotting the human animal who vied for power over him, the tall skinny man people called Adam who drank from a tall can and held a pistol, Theo growled and bared his teeth. Theo sensed danger.

If nature denies coyotes thought, how did this creature recognize the depth and nuance of such menace in the predatory pattern of this man? Mysterious brain waves puzzle even the best scientists, baffling neurologists and medical specialists who study man and beast which at their root are the same. How could this wild coyote be aware of himself and others, thinking rather than working on pure instinct? Magic breeds among each dune sand grain, materializing in minds open to the pain and pleasure of the occult.

Theo knew.

He just knew.

Zita, Jesús and Eeshell also internalized the intensity of the universe. Mel knew, too. In her own way Aunt Irma captured primal experience and stored specks of cosmic knowledge in her head like baby mice living in a dusty cabin kitchen cupboard. But Jesús, Zita and Eeshell nestled the core reality of human and inhuman experience in individual human portals through which bad energy departs and good energy enters.

Ancient seekers agreed the holy land surrounding Oceano

offered a nexus where potent vibes of nature converged, a blessed place where these three people now exerted influence as conduits for spiritual progress and hope. Atoms give birth to the unknown. Maybe life did manifest from a primal fish sandwich. That's why the faithful believe the Christ child could swim at birth, Mohammed could speak all the languages of the world and Buddha eventually offered both gods peace of mind to embrace romantic differences, extending the deepest most personal Buddha nature to the most untamed cur.

Does a coyote have Buddha nature?

Of course it does.

Primitive senses developed into conscience as Theo felt more human than putrid humans who drove dune buggies, imitated his howl, and lowered evolutionary expectations to the lowest standard.

Sensing four eyes on him from atop another dune, Theo spotted Jesús Zarate and Mel Moyle surveying what was left of Mel's home. With his arm around Mel's thin shoulders, Jesús asked, "What do you want to do, man?"

"I like living at the Cove," Mel said. "But this shack housed my invisible muse."

"We're almost a real family, man," Jesús said.

Theo raised his head and howled, unleashing a long solitary blast that sounded like a bugle call signaling a defiant charge in a cruel, cruel world.

Mel howled back.

WHAT'S HER NAME?

"THOSE guys crossed the border to kill you," said El Chapstick. "Brice Springsteam and the C Street Band are assassins."

Jesús and El Chapstick finally met after going back and forth on the phone over a safe location. El Chapstick won the argument, choosing the Santa Maria Police Department parking lot.

"From that fiasco I saw at Louie Louie's the other night, your big brother looked like he was carrying out a hit on himself," said Jesús.

"I still might kill him," said El Chapstick.

"He might get you first when he finds out you charmed Aunt Irma off her bar stool and stole his girlfriend."

"To make matters worse I can't sleep," El Chapstick said.

"Because you ratted me out to the Culiacàn cartel?"

"No, nightmares."

Jesús listened.

"Every night an evil woman wakes me wailing, cursing, telling me to say her name, say her name."

"So say her name."

"Syrah."

# A LARK IN PEOPLE'S PARK

SECURE living with the others in the rustic mansion on the Oceano hill, Eeshell still sometimes missed her cozy second-floor apartment in Pismo. She truly felt part of this makeshift group housed together in a mishmash of identities and personalities, now including her godmother Zita and the rest of this go-native tribe bursting with hard love and misunderstanding. At this stage of their lives, despite bizarre twists and sharp turns that brought them together, everyone seemed to understand the quest to seek and find some sense of enlightenment.

Eeshell particularly worried about Mel. The sadness she felt for him sometimes bummed her out. But Mel bravely shook off the trauma he experienced when his cabin went up in smoke on the beach, telling everybody about his wondrous past life and time spent in his tiny cabin where he lived out harmless fantasies amid quotes he repeated time and time again.

"Life's a lark in People's Park," he'd say.

One day Eeshell asked for details.

"What's People's Park?"

Mel cracked his rock and roll grin.

"A real place where I used to live in Berkeley, an open space that grows from the open space of the mind where you're always free and can walk whenever and wherever you please."

"Even after somebody burns down your house?"

"Especially after somebody burns down your house," he said.

"Can we take a walk there now?" she asked. "Even though the park's in Berkeley and we're here?"

"Sure enough," he said.

Visionaries from different generations, Mel and Eeshell took off into the recess of their imaginary park, entering the lush field of wonder that offered tranquility and safety, a radiant meadow of solace and gratitude immune to war, hatred and excess.

They weren't even high, except for ample Hoocha Weed residue clogging Mel's system that would never again allow him to pass a urine test no matter how hard he studied. Good citizen Mel no longer drove except for that big unicycle of his mind that spun loaded with lights like a Santa Monica pier Ferris wheel that never stopped turning.

"You have all the answers," Eeshell said. "Do birds live and sing in People's Park?"

"There's a lark," he said, tweeting and chirping the way he imagined a lark to sing in the morning.

Putting on a devilish look more than appropriate for an apprentice witch, Eeshell said, "Like this?" and started to whistle.

"How about this?" said Mel kicking into a flute-like warble that raced up and down the melodic note scale.

Eeshell and Mel whistled a duet until big tears of happiness rolled down their cheeks and they could no longer whistle because they were laughing so hard their faces went numb from happiness.

"You're fun to be with," Eeshell said.

"I'm silly for a reason," he said.

Eeshell grew pensive.

"Silly covers my fears," Mel said. "I'm pretty much afraid of everything."

"I saw you stand up for the fish and the coyotes," Eeshell said.

"Somebody had to do it," he said.

"But you're the one who actually did it."

Mel blushed.

"That was pure bravery," Eeshell said.

"Want to hear another bird call?" Mel asked.

"Sure," she said.

Mel started to squawk and flap his arms.

"What's that one, Mel?"

"A one-eyed, one-horned flying purple people eater," he said.

"Like I told you, Mel," said Eeshell. "You've got spunk."

Again Mel blushed, squawked and flapped his arms.

 # YOU'RE THE JUAN

HARSH reality imposed its will in Juan Gomez's head, pounding with hangover thunder unmatched by any six-pound bronze cannonball fired in anger and retribution during the Mexican-American War.

No more Brice Springsteam. No more C Street Band. No more Aunt Irma.

From now on Juan Gomez would wield wrath as the sickest hitman on either side of the border. The promise of the American Way stole everything from him. Juan would show these gringo thieves a grand finale better than a neighborhood full of Santa Maria celery choppers shooting guns in the air to celebrate the New Year, with no better target than Jesús Zarate AKA Jesús Malverde.

But how could Malverde live and breathe as a human? Only a legend, a figment of Mexican imagination like death saint La Santa Muerte, Malverde existed only in dreams. Knowing the difference between fact and fiction, wicked reality hit hard enough, best exemplified by the recent attempted murderous mice attack on his life with killer rodents resembling the fastest mouse in all Mexico trying to kill him. Why did his cherished cartoon pal Speedy turn on him? Was Juan Gomez finally losing what was left of his sanity? Why did his bandmates turn on him?

Somebody definitely spiked the wine he found at the Oceano mansion when he burglarized the house looking for cash. That decrepit mental patient senior citizen who lived in the dunes and went naked except when he wore striped bell bottom pants to town tried to overdose him. That old nut was possessed by Satan and could see into the future, knowing Juan would break into the crib. That crusty maniac spiked the wine he knew Juan would swipe so Juan would freak out and never freak back in.

That did it.

Juan would kill everybody, burn down the mansion, blow up Louie Louie's and poison the ocean more than all the plastic water bottles could ever do to damage the sea. See what his enemies made him do? Mass mayhem would make his mark in the Mexican cartel world of destruction and profit.

Juan Gomez would become bigger than El Chapo.

Bigger than Bruce Springsteen even!

A woman's squealy voice came out of nowhere.

"Yes, you will, my big hot tamale, you," she said. "Because you're the Juan."

Snapping his head around, scanning the cramped motel room for the unexpected intruder, Juan almost sprained his neck. Waving a bread knife he had been using to spread avocados he stole from trees in Santa Maria, he shouted louder than he had since he was 12 and accidently shot off his little toe while practicing fast draw with his mother's gun back in Culiacàn.

"Who are you?"

Again he yelled.

"Where are you?"

"You are definitely the Juan," the unseen woman said.

In the corner of the moldy room he spotted a transparent hovering figure dressed in a skimpy oversized bikini in a leopard-skin pattern that hung from her frail bones like moth-eaten polyester curtains in a Juarez brothel. Even hungover she looked good to Juan, better than his three ex-wives put together.

"I'm the Juan?"

"My Juan and only," she said.

"Juan what?"

"Juan handsome man."

"The Juan for you?"

"The only Juan for me."

Swollen brain cells spilled from Juan Gomez's ears, oozing good judgment onto his thin shoulders that formed a puddle of love that energized and elated him. Suddenly love-struck and weak, he babbled, "You want to run away to Cancún with Juan Gomez?"

The emaciated spook's voice went sickeningly sweet as a tequila sunrise loaded with extra grenadine syrup.

"Could we have a drunken wedding on the beach? A real big Juan?"

Making kissing sounds, the hovering cadaverous apparition drifted to the floor, landing on pick-up stick spindly legs over which Juan Gomez drooled. Pimply irritated breasts poked like hardboiled starling eggs from her drooping bikini top. Wispy brown hair the color of nicotine stains on a chain-smoking barfly's fingers glistened like yellow barn straw in a woodrat's nest. Far worse than any skin disease, this obscene visage stood as a grotesque image of surrealistic horror, a skanky supernatural hallucination that would appall even an aspiring playboy lounge lizard just released from 20 years in solitary confinement.

Juan Gomez's heart pounded with lust.

As Syrah slinked his way, burrowing deeper into his odious ego, she knew she held him in her clutches—Juan huge accident waiting to happen.

ONE GNARLY DUDE

PONDERING tofu brands at Von's supermarket in Grover Beach, Eeshell tried to decide if she should stop eating organic bean curd. Overly well-meaning so-hip-it-hurts California cultural critics never stopped attacking even healthy alternatives as diseased and destructive to the body and the planet. Eeshell did her best to sort out the soy beans.

The gravelly male voice came over her shoulder too close to her ear for comfort.

"Please excuse me, I'm terribly sorry," Adam said. "Could I pick your brain about a selection?"

Sensing bad vibes shooting off the strapping young man's beard stubble and beery breath, Eeshell sent her mind to her hara, her mental center two inches below her belly button, to help her settle in and stay calm.

"I'm trying to change my diet, eat better," the man said. "I'm training for an Olympic surfing tryout."

"Is surfing now an Olympic event?" Eeshell asked.

"I meant sidewalk surfing, skateboard," he said.

"Gnarly, dude," she said.

"Yeah, shredding," he said.

Wearing untied tan Timberlands without socks, unevenly cutoff blue jeans and a T-shirt emblazoned with the words "I Love Guns, Bacon, and Boobs," he leaned closer.

"You smell nice," he said. "Like cherry soda."

Eeshell sidestepped him, creating distance.

"Like maybe we can go out some time," he said. "Maybe catch a burger?"

"I'm a vegan," Eeshell said.

"Me, too, I meant like a veggie burger."

"You're trying way too hard, man," Eeshell said.

Quick as a rattle snake strike Adam's face contorted.

"Stuck-up bitch," he said.

As she increased her distance Adam reached out to grab her arm but got caught mid-grab, his right wrist turning inward as strong fingers tightened around the outside edge of his hand. Jesús Zarate smiled, leaning in to use fingers on his left hand to bend Adam's arm at the elbow, applying pressure to Adam's forearm as he bowed at the waist like a humble Japanese waiter at the sushi bar.

Adam screamed when hot pain from the basic aikido technique shot through his thin forearm all the way to the shoulder when small bones in his wrist reached the breaking point. Giving a quick twist to Adam's hand, Jesús said, "It's nice to be nice."

Releasing Adam he extended both arms as if looking for a hug. Adam staggered away like a mugged drunk, wordless as he disappeared around the produce aisle holding his arm and rubbing his wrist.

"Nikyo," said Eeshell. "Aikido technique number two."

"I'm impressed," Jesús said.

"I'm a brown belt at the Full Circle dojo across the street," Eeshell said. "And although I appreciate your paternalistic protection, I can take care of myself."

Sensing she perceived insult rather than appreciation, Jesús quickly tried to make amends. From the first time he met Eeshell with his new circle of acquaintances, she struck him as smart and instinctive.

"I'm sorry," Jesús said. "I only responded to teach him a lesson."

Eeshell shook her head.

"I could have done that without touching him," she said. "Words as weapons work wonders."

Nobody knew the value of words as weapons better than writer Jesús Zarate. Watching Eeshell refocus on choosing a block of firm smoked tofu, he sensed how this young woman indeed had a way with words. Wondering where she inherited that gift, where she got that talent, whom she could credit with her awareness and perception, Jesús sensed she must come from good stock. He wondered what type DNA she carried in her soul.

 # MORE DEAR DIARY

Bush-league or not, this sick bunch is coming after me. Five desperate desperados with guns can do damage no matter how inept they are in the process. Somebody's going to get hurt, killed even. Maybe they'll come from different angles one at a time or together at the same time. Maybe I can talk them out of it like Eeshell says by using my words as weapons. I don't think so. If I live, and I plan to, I'll have a good first column for the new magazine Mel plans to publish he's calling "Dune Vibes" in recognition of the original "Dune Forum" magazine the Dunites published so long ago. We'll be the new Dunites, Mel says. But I don't know how long Tripper and I can stick around. I want to go back to Mexico. Get to work. But I can't leave my mother. Maybe I should just settle down, make Hoocha Weed wine with Mel. Write Zen columns about matters of life and death. Tripper can focus on healing the environment and handle weed wine promotion. Mel's the master vintner. Bud's the money-man. Aunt Irma? Now that she's dating El Chapstick and can help turn his life around, she can cook and clean because that's what she said she wants to do *if* she can turn El Chapstick's life around. Eeshell's a mystery. I hate to admit it but she unnerves me. Maybe I'll just drink Hoocha Weed wine every day. See God. Be God.

THE OTHER JUAN

WHILE Juan Gomez went underground with his new imaginary girlfriend he considered better than a free blow-up doll, his first cousin on his mother's side, Juan Ortega, known as the other Juan, took over the piss-poor posse hoping to terminate Jesús Zarate.

"I am now the boss," the other Juan told his three cousins.

A collective gasp went up from the band.

"Oh, man, we're not playing at Louie Louie's again, are we, bro?"

The other Juan glowered.

"Our music days are over," he said. "We're going to become the most feared cartel this side of Tijuana. But we got to get tougher."

Cousin Pancho flexed a mango-sized bicep.

"Like when we was lifting weights in the La Tuna prison at home, man?"

"No, like giving up weed," he said.

Another explosive gasp went off.

"Anything but that," Pancho's twin brother Cisco whimpered. "How can we be a drug cartel without the drugs?"

"Bar-bit-u-ates are my life," drawled Slowpoke Rodriguez whose mother named him after Speedy Gonzales' lazy cartoon cousin.

The other Juan jeered.

"Raise your hands and repeat after me," he said.

Dutifully, the men raised their hands.

"I do attest," said the other Juan.

"I do contest," repeated Pancho who had already smoked three joints before breakfast.

"That I will not use cannabis until Juan Gomez is dead."

All four men had already imbibed and absorbed a variety of cannabis-infused products including root beer, chocolate bars, and body lotion.

Cisco wailed, "Why us, man?"

The other Juan spoke.

"Karma," he said.

# APOCAGEDDON

CANDLELIGHT fluttered.

Mel fidgeted in his lotus position, his legs crossed like a salty beer pretzel, the flaps of his homemade loincloth falling over his bony knees. The Ouija board rested on his lap, his four fingers resting lightly on the heart-shaped wooden planchette Mel called his "cell phone," a connection to his cell-infused biological machine body and the great beyond beyond the beyond.

Bud asked the first question.

"So what's happening, dude?"

Almost instantly the pointer began to move, first to the letter "E," then to the letter "N" and on to the letter "D" before it stopped, as did the clock on the wall that stopped ticking. All eyes focused on the planchette. Bud's voice quivered.

"End of what, man?"

Again the planchette moved, this time to the letter "A."

Bud started hyperventilating.

"A what, man?"

Moving again the pointer drifted to "P," to "O," and then to "C."

Mel started squirming like a wee child wiggling because he had to wee-wee, expressing bewilderment by whining blurred words of confusion.

"A poc of what?"

Mel now spoke in a somber voice, no longer depending on the Ouija board to express deep truth.

"Doom, man, a pock of doom."

Bud walked around in small circles, nervously scratching his head.

"A pock like the apocalypse?"

"Yes, yes," said Mel. "The apocalypse forewarns doom. Armageddon is where it's at. We're where it's at. Armageddon is already here."

Bud blessed himself because he didn't know what else to do and that morning saw the Pope make the sign of the cross on TV.

"What we face is worse," said Mel Moyle. "I'm talking Apocageddon, man."

"I have to pee, man," said Bud.

"I already did," Mel said. "My loincloth's waterproof."

TASTES LIKE CHICKEN

JUST BECAUSE five bottom-feeder bad hombres sneak across the Mexican border shouting "USA, USA" with delusions of peroxide strippers dancing in their heads doesn't mean they can't be deadly.

Especially the other Juan.

Whatever drove the demonic visions Juan Gomez beheld that night at Louie Louie's, the other Juan sensed a final solution to his egotistical power struggle with the leader of the C Street Band. Recognizing Juan Gomez AKA Brice Springsteam posed dictatorial obstacles to success, the other Juan decided to show his homeboys who *really* is the boss.

When his three cousins showed up for "a real Santa Maria Tri-Tip Barbecue dinner" as the other Juan called the feast, they fell all over themselves expressing gratitude for their cousin's hospitality. He had set up a huge grill in the motel camping area that hadn't been used in so long old spider webs festooned the picnic table legs. When the boys arrived sweet aroma of a torso-sized chunk of meat sizzling over a pile of flaming willow branches assaulted their primordial senses, opening flaring nostrils wide as an inch-wide knife fight wound.

"Real Santa Maria barbecue, man," said Pancho.

"That looks like top block tri-tip, man," said Cisco.

"I can see the ribs, man," said Slowpoke Rodriguez. "Save me some of them ribs, man."

Wiping wet crimson squeezins on his apron decorated with a yellow smiley face with a bullet hole trickling blood from a forehead wound, the other Juan seemed distant, deep in thought and content to absent-mindedly turn the metal rod that thoroughly cooked the meat over an open flame.

"More than enough for everybody," he said. "Get ready for some farm fresh Santa Maria-style cooking."

After drinking six Modelo Especial beers each, the men lined up holding paper plates dripping brown sugar sweet pinto bean sauce.

"Ummm-mmmm-ummmm, that smells good," said Slowpoke.

"That's like half a cow, man," said Cisco.

"Moooooooooo," said Pancho as everybody fell out guffawing like their cousin's lame joke was good enough for a Tijuana comedy club.

"Moooo," said Slowpoke.

"Mooo," said Cisco.

Leaning over the grill the other Juan slid what looked like a huge shoulder roast off the spit. Dropping the juicy, dripping, well-done slab covered in charred garlic cloves, peppercorns, lime-flavored smoked chipotle sauce and vinegar onto the cutting board he set up on a nearby picnic table, the other Juan raised a freshly sharpened machete and began to slice.

He got the idea for the last supper-like blowout one night after sharing gummies on the beach with that now dead bundle of pathology Reefer Johnson. Excited as a redneck shooting carp in the river, Reefer went on and on about deer meat ribs and some real crazy talk about cannibals and how he could eat his whole family if the law of the jungle ever called for such extreme measures.

The other Juan spent days planning the feast.

Tacos, he would serve tacos as well as the main course, tasty tacos made from the fallen animal's heart, grilled Tacos de Corazón. No macho man Mexican could turn away from the delicacy of chopped coronary bits mixed with oregano, cinnamon, cumin, hot chocolate powder and ancho chilies.

With greasy plates piled high the three cousins made wet slurping, moaning noises as they dug in and chewed. Slowpoke gnawed on a rib big enough to keep a Great Dane occupied for the afternoon. Cisco came back for seconds. Pancho asked for a doggie bag to take back to his motel room and eat with pickled habanero peppers while he watched the late show zombie movie on TV.

"This meat is so sweet," he said.

Not once did it dawn on the numbskull cousins that the other

Juan wasn't sitting down to eat with them at the picnic table banquet, wasn't joining them to gobble down the grisly sacrifice he would tell them about in the morning, the human sacrifice he used to fortify his cousins with the bravery of Aztec warriors engaging in the holiest of rituals. Scholars acknowledge Aztec Empire human sacrifice killed between 20,000 to 250,000 prisoners each year.

That's a lot of burritos.

Only once did it dawn on Cisco, the smartest of the dumb bunch, that the former leader of the band Juan Gomez AKA Brice Springsteam was nowhere to be found.

The former Juan Gomez wasn't eating, either.

The now deceased "Boss" was eaten.

COYOTE JUSTICE

TENDING the cigarette carton-sized mini Zen garden he kept in his California state prison cell offered Jesús Zarate a sense of solace unmatched at any time in his life.

Simplicity, present-moment awareness, doing time and "just sitting" as the great Buddhist prophet Dogen suggested in a book Jesús once read helped Jesús serve not just the 8-year sentence but also a purpose. Seeing what other inmates missed defined his slowly growing maturity.

If only he had sensed the consequences of teeming pain and outrage before stepping into that nightclub parking lot and killing a man to defend his manhood, mistaking ego for honor. A misguided sense of self could easily lead to confinement of the body and death of the spirit. Lacking discipline to control emotion could bury anyone's true identity.

A simple raked Zen garden helped Jesús improve his focus.

Each Sunday night before going to bed Jesús unwrapped and sucked into nothingness two round butterscotch hard candies he bought by the bag at the prison commissary. Then he cupped in his palm two more wrapped sweet treats manufactured with twisted cellophane ends. Closing his hand and shaking the candies, he rolled them like dice on the rectangular shelf on which he had spread a covering of prison yard dirt he raked with his fingers. Accepting wherever the candy came to rest, he meditated on their singular presence for the rest of the week. The golden butterscotch candies loomed large as boulders in his mind the way smooth rocks rest in a Japanese monastery garden raked diligently each week by a silent Buddhist monk who tends to the space.

Impermanence materialized when Jesús ate the two hard candies and replaced them with another two. Discipline in the sweetest sense helped Jesús clear his mind—dessert amid a desert of despair.

225

One Sunday night before he rolled his butterscotches he wrote these words in his prison diary: "I vow to fight injustice. Walk the Earth as retaliator of conquest past. Conquistadores still exist. I vow to face them. Take back what belongs to my people. I vow to avenge our past."

Jesús' own past often appeared to him as a vision between the bars, a beaten-to-a-pulp visage of fury, his dead victim's pummeled face covered in blood.

The past never disappeared.

One day a Japanese Yakuza killer Jesús met in the exercise yard told him, "If you don't control your emotions, your emotions will control you." The next day the Yakuza, completely in control, cut open his own fleshy belly with a shank and bled to death in ritualistic sacrifice on the shower room floor.

That night Jesús became the coyote.

Stretched out in the darkness of his monastic refuge, Jesús rolled in one smooth motion from his bunk and stood to full height feeling the cool power of hot breath at the back of his throat spreading to warm his body. Feeling the power of an unbridled beast, Jesús dropped to all fours. Unflinching and strong he sniffed the air and listened to night noises on the cell block. Moving swiftly, he stalked beyond the cell door a reckless guard had either left open by mistake or on purpose.

The next morning, awakening to the sound of shouting and guards' boots pounding the metal stairway, Jesús tasted blood. The inmates were screaming about an older prisoner who the week before had raped a younger prisoner behind a stairwell. The older inmate laughed when he finished his vicious assault and boasted for days how he would rape again. Jesús knew the maniac would hurt whomever he could. At the end of the block one of the many killer lifer inmates shrieked and shared the horrid news.

"Homie's got no throat left!" the lifer screamed. "Homie's throat is gone!"

Coyote howls bounced off the walls of Jesús' skull as Jesús' screams echoed off heavy tiled green walls of the behavioral adjustment unit where the system placed men with little hope for rehabilitation, men like Jesús who refused to be broken. Fresh gore on his teeth and hands told him he had killed again.

The dead rapist inmate had bullied, sodomized, and killed in prison. No one could tame his vicious behavior. Did a power even higher than a guard open Jesús' cell door so he could right wrongs, do good things even in the name of blood sacrifice? Did a majestic animal spirit guide his bite as he tore into flesh, ligaments and muscles?

Years later, secure in the comfort of the Oceano commune among a family of kind and gentle friends, the coyote's predatory howls still howled in Jesús' head, blending occasionally with fleeting images of memory. The worst scenes flashed on a mangled outlaw biker dying on a Shell Beach side street where the coyote had appeared again. Had the coyote materialized at other times without Jesús even knowing the beast had charged from the underworld to destroy in the name of righteousness?

Again and again Jesús failed to find peace of mind.

Poor demented Wally Wilson, Jesús' dear friend, had also tried and failed to quench his own homicidal cravings, eventually succeeding only by sacrificing himself for the greater good, pouring gasoline over his head and flicking a lighter to extinguish violent failure the same way Vietnamese martyr monks flared into nothingness to protest an unjust war, as all wars are wrong one way or the other.

Wally died for Jesús' sins. Jesús owed Wally. The world owed Wally.

"Do good things," Wally taught him. "Do good things."

No matter how hard he tried, Jesús worried he might only ever do more harm than good. How could anyone trust let alone love him?

Coyote justice owned Jesús and maybe always would.

SPILL THE WINE

Nestled at the back of his lean-to constructed with a king-sized bed sheet tied to the trunks of two arroyo willow trees and covered in Spanish moss, Mel Moyle cradled the wine jug between his legs. Mel built the lean-to for the many nights he missed the beach so much he couldn't stay away.

Nobody had ever seen Mel cry. Laughter and energy always beamed from his body and mind. No matter how freaky his behavior, joy emanated from his visage so gleefully you could almost see the aura of psychedelic abundance that comforted him and those in his company.

Now a stranger watched tears roll down his gritty cheeks.

Headwinds blew through Mel's nest of white hair, swirling like a supernatural twister making landfall during a turbulent storm. Sleeping outside was taking its toll since marauders burned down his shack. Picked scabs over scratches on his bare legs opened and oozed. Sand fleas nested in his ears, biting whenever he dug wax with his finger. Arthritic knees pounded from long solitary walks on the beach. Red splotchy rash welts itched from wearing a wet loincloth.

Rarely nervous about anything, Mel worried he might spill the wine.

A voice far smoother than any Chamber of Commerce motivational speaker took him by surprise. Standing tall against the backdrop of a raging sea, a rakishly handsome man loomed with confidence over Mel's crumpled form.

"Steady there, young fella."

Mel hugged the wine jug.

"You keep away," he said.

Dressed in green tweed trousers rolled to the calf, a white dress shirt with unlinked French cuffs and a straw boater men wore in the Roaring '20s, the visitor carried his suit coat slung over his shoulder like he was off for a stroll after dinner at San Francisco's Palace Hotel. Yet his hat bore a dog bite on the brim, his pants frayed about the knees and his shirt carried a mustard stain down the front. If you kissed him you would have smelled hot dogs and beer on his breath.

The man extended his hand.

"Gavin Arthur," he said.

Hallucinations came easily and often to Mel Moyle, but America's Twenty-first President Chester Allen Arthur's grandson Chester Allen Arthur III, known as Gavin, was one vision he never expected. Dead more than a half century, the bon vivant descendant of Yankee royalty and founding father of the Dunites appeared as regal as any prince of pleasure looking down on the fretful vagabond.

Mel reached for Gavin's hand. Rising gingerly, gaining his balance and planting his calloused bare feet on what felt like a pasture of honey, Mel stood.

"You're dead," he said. "You'd be what, 122, 23, 24?"

Smirking that irresistible smirk that carried him through madcap years of astrologers, poets, writers, jugglers, dancers, sculptors, drunks, and madmen, through pilgrimages to the dunes by literary legend John Steinbeck, fabled photographer Ansel Adams, guru Meyer Baba, Irish revolutionary and Druidess sprite Ella Young, ultra-hip musician John Cage and visionary journalist Upton Sinclair, Gavin Arthur's motivation and money shepherded his adopted tribe through the '30s, World War II, the Beat Generation brotherhood of Allen Ginsburg, Gary Snyder, Jack Kerouac, and into the hippie lovefest of the 1967 Summer of Love offering a personal bohemian vision of tomorrow every step along the way.

"I have a mission for you, son," he said.

Mel slipped a forefinger through the handle of his green glass wine jug. He grabbed a pillow case he used as a rucksack and the two men walked a crooked dune path through spacious vegetable fields toward Oceano. When they reached the train depot, Gavin raised his arms skyward.

"Welcome home," he said.

It took Mel a few seconds to focus on the cabin he had seen a hundred times, Gavin Arthur's one-time beach shack home and psychic headquarters that stood in the dunes before town officials eventually hauled the by-then long abandoned structure to town where they offered the hut as a simple house to rent. When the local fire department decided to torch the structure as a burn house to train firefighters, a few astute townspeople stressed the structure's historic value and hauled the shack to the Oceano Train Depot on Front Street awaiting rebirth as a unique historical monument to guide mystics and other seekers for generations to come.

Mystics.

Seekers.

Banshee wanderers who call themselves everything but call themselves nothing, bright balls of natural energy dangerous as a close lightning strike and as dark as the deepest black cosmic hole where hypnotic vibrations heal disease and sorrow. All wanderers are not lost as the bumper sticker points out.

"I have two requests," Gavin said. "I am passing you the torch to rekindle and hand off to your successor when your time to depart this existence arrives," he said. "Please accept the love light."

Warmth spread lazy comfort to aching parts of Mel Moyle's aging body.

"I also would be honored if you spend one solitary night of contemplation in my cabin," Gavin said. "Recharge your batteries. Fan your sacred flame. Get back in the game."

When Mel blinked Gavin disappeared in a wisp of perfumed smoke that smelled like Old Spice Cologne. Mel turned the knob to the cabin. The door glided open as he stepped inside. Spread neatly on the floor a cushioned yellow Japanese futon lay beside a blue ceramic vase holding three green bamboo stalks. Looking through the window Mel saw Jupiter and a sharp cheddar slice of moon.

Turning left Mel walked into another snug room packed tight with shelves, some of President Arthur's books, a carved writing desk and Gavin's black heavy metal typewriter that held an un-finished single-paged essay explaining philosophical reasons why a clam has no face and humans, even vegetarians, should accept Neptune's gift from the sea and eat of the holy sacramental bivalve mollusk.

Digging into his pillow case, Mel pulled out ten fresh clams he dug from the beach that morning, their alabaster shells the size of sand dollars, pure white as a flash of awakening in a newborn's consciousness. These soft-bodied invertebrates were making a comeback, the famous Pismo clams fighting extinction and winning in that big wheel of being that offers no beginning and no end with everything connected and nothing permanent, the righteous message Jesus Christ's big brother Buddha offered to the world.

Mel dug his limit that morning. That night he used the fat clams in a fresh pot of Dunite chowder he made for himself in Gavin Arthur's cabin kitchen, boiling and eating all ten sweet fat clams combined with canned milk, carrots, celery and potatoes that fell off a truck at the vegetable exchange, the grower-owned cooperative that fed the nation whether oblivious American consumers knew it or not.

Adding boxed mashed potato flakes he carried in the pillow case to the water-based recipe's already primitive allure, the splendor of real Dunite clam chowder nourished Mel as it had fed Chumash Indians thousands of years ago, paving their way to wisdom with mounds of open empty shells that signified nourishment and enlightenment.

Progress disrespected both Chumash and clams. Now both were back with the successful Chumash gambling casino for better or worse showing the white man how indigenous people of color could get even. Clams would again flourish, maybe one day walking and talking and taking over the world. Mel hoped for clam revolution/evolution to take over the world. Mel trusted clams far more than he trusted people.

Mel looked around the tiny kitchen where Gavin once prepared fantastic pots of thick bubbling chowder for wine and champagne soirees that culminated in loud, fast debates lasting until sunrise and further, even beyond further. Mel sipped weed wine intermittently from the green jug and the Spanish bota bag hanging from his bony bare shoulder. In a voice only a sea lion would love he sang the original Hoocha Weed theme song he expected to use when he and his new partners passed out the wine.

"Hoocha Weed Wine for the people...Get you high for life... Hoocha Weed Wine for the people...Never feel the strife...Hoocha Weed Wine for the people... Purple nectar of the gods...Hoocha Weed Wine for the people...Like two grapes in a pea pod."

Bud would especially dig the ethereal tune even if the lyrics made as much sense as two grapes in a pea pod. Taking another big slug from the tan bota bag, Mel spoke directly to the clams in his full belly.

"We're all in this together," he said. "You're the chowder. I'm the chowder. Be the chowder."

Flexing their muscles, the clams chose to keep quiet.

Gavin Arthur couldn't help himself and reappeared.

"One more thing," he said.

Spinning like the aging Earth on its axis, Mel came face-to-face with the leader of the flashbacks. Sitting in an easy chair with mouse-bitten white stuffing popping from the arms, Gavin sucked on his pipe, the bowl carved into the shape of a pineapple.

"Hey, no smoking," said Mel.

Not one to take criticism or advice, Gavin raised his eyebrows.

"Bud's deservedly dead dad made Zita sick from smoking," Mel said. "She quit so we all quit. No joints, bongs, pipes, smokestacks or anything else that pollutes lungs and the air."

Gavin spit into his pipe bowl, extinguishing the Irish whiskey-flavored tobacco with his thumb.

"Fathers can make terrible mistakes," Gavin said.

"Here," Mel said pulling the bota bag over his head. "Take a hit of this."

Holding the bag at arm's length from his mouth, Gavin directed the ruby-hued flow down the hatch. Lowering the bag after a good three seconds, Gavin swallowed and closed his eyes.

"Ah," he said. "Delicious Dunite delirium."

Grabbing and raising the bag, Mel dribbled weed wine down his chin as he joined the legendary Dunite in a toast to the future.

"Please take a seat," Gavin said. "I've got a confession to make."

ALIEN ABDUCTION

AFTER spending two weeks snorting methamphetamine alone in his pickup camper, Adam Haggard finally flipped. Chalky, chunky homemade meth burned his nostrils, catching at the back of his throat like sour buttermilk phlegm, making him choke as the unhappy hour chemical cocktail burned into already struggling brain cells.

Cooked up back in Bakersfield, the shake-and-bake half-gallon plastic root beer bottle meth blast made Adam and Abbie's vacation all the more eventful (minus her getting mauled and murdered by a mad starving coyote) as they shared bottom feeder status snorting their way to oblivion.

With Abbie gone and almost forgotten Adam concluded all his problems stemmed from the influence of Invisible Negroes from Mars (INFM). He knew they hailed from Mars because he overheard a spaceship full of them talking at the gas station. Knowing they controlled his mind, Adam concluded all by himself that he needed to abduct another enemy alien from another galaxy to swap for his freedom.

No better existential mark existed than Eeshell.

Park rangers expected Adam to resist and make a scene when they asked him to leave his parking space on the beach. Two weeks after the fatal coyote attack that snuffed his wife, Adam's plight simply drew too much attention to the site. Some campers complained he and his unhinged pathology rooted in the thirst for revenge were bumming them out, scaring some of the few mild-mannered dune adventurers who definitely counted in the minority among off-roaders who raced their buggies deep into the sand mountains. Even empathetic bureaucrats at the California Department of Parks and Recreation, who at first took pity on Adam and the loss of his wife, knew he had to go.

So Adam Haggard went, steering the rusted red pickup camper towing his broken-down buggy behind it, slowly making his way off the Oceano strand and driving bleary-eyed with clouds of black exhaust following him the 2.7 miles down into Grover Beach where he parked in a West Grand Avenue supermarket parking lot.

He spotted Eeshell again, the first time since her Bruce Lee boyfriend with the moustache grabbed him and almost broke his wrist. Tagging them both as aliens from another galaxy, Adam knew an illegal when he saw one.

Jews, Chinamen, and Indians were bad enough, but a hot tamale from another planet like Eeshell was the worst. Invisible Negro aliens from Mars living in Bakersfield would happily take her in exchange for Adam's independence. Adam knew their kind, greedy jungle Martians he once battled when he ran out of ammo and came home from the pistol range to see Abigale hip hop dancing in the driveway with their leader who, of course, was the blackest of them all, a pimp trafficking white children back to the angry black planet militant extraterrestrials dyed the color of their skin.

Meth will do that to you.

So will neo-Nazi Bakersfield politics.

Now Adam sat in his cramped camper in the supermarket parking lot after waiting for four days before he saw Eeshell again, spotting his interplanetary bargaining chip pull her dusty VW van into the lot. Using his Budweiser beer can as a microphone he communicated to the mother ship orbiting his psyche. Nobody answered. Adam knew what had gone down.

"The Invisible Negroes from Mars army finally invaded my interstellar space," Adam said. "They finally took over. Negroes from Mars vaporized my mothership commander. This is war."

Eeshell strolled from the store's front door unaware of the erupting intergalactic turmoil. Carrying a small woven hippie bag she used to do her meager grocery shopping, she breathed sweet, fresh California air. Nestled in the bag a container of garlic hummus and a stalk of fresh celery shaped her small treat with which she occasionally babied herself. Nutrition mattered as did her overall health and well-being, habits Zita and her parents helped her develop as a child, behaviors she developed more as she grew into a young woman and set the stage for her ritualistic discipline.

Through the open window Adam said, "Hey."

Already having spotted him, Eeshell smiled and kept on walking.

"I'm talking to you, Little Miss Muff," he said.

Eeshell kept walking.

Holding up the brown and white pet hamster that had belonged to his wife, Adam placed a small baby Glock 43 pistol against the side of the little animal's head. Squirming and twisting beneath the pressure of Adam's thick, grease-stained fingers, the hamster bit into the flesh almost to the bone until it tired of biting and stilled, Adam's finger's blood wetting the matted fur around its neck.

Eeshell stopped walking.

"Please don't hurt the hamster," she said.

"Get in," Adam said.

Eeshell got in.

When Adam pulled from the parking lot, Eeshell said, "I'll only cooperate if you let the hamster go."

"Like stop the truck and throw him out the window?"

"Like pull over there to the pet store and let me take him inside," she said. "They'll care for him. Your wife would want me to do that."

Adam pulled to the curb.

"You have five minutes or I'm coming in shooting," he said.

"What's the little fella's name?"

"Skinny."

When Eeshell came out in less than four minutes, she asked, "Why do you call him Skinny?"

"His name used to be Jimmy, but not long after Abbie split I started calling him Skinny."

"Why?"

"He wouldn't eat," said Adam.

"Hamsters love to eat," Eeshell said.

"Not when you put a gun to his head a few nights a week," Adam said.

Eeshell took a slow deep breath, put her mind at her center, and settled in for a long ride.

"When I'd get bored living alone I used to play Hamster Roulette with Jimmy," Adam said. "Spinning the chamber in my Colt Python, holding the barrel up to his ear and pulling the trigger with his little beady eyes all bugging out and shit. Must have scared him."

Eeshell inhaled consciously.

"You'll be happy to know Jimmy's in good hands now," Eeshell said. "I explained he needed a good home and the store manager fell in love with him right away."

"They're two of the luckiest rats alive," Adam said raising his gun.

Eeshell gave her word to cooperate and despite having the power and ability to take the gun away from Adam or choke him into unconsciousness and even death, she would maintain her belief in nonviolence, peace, and love and maybe get this barbarian help that one day would erase his propensity toward insanity and barbarity. Extending all the gentle energy she could muster, Eeshell spoke in a soft voice.

"So where we going, dude?"

"On a treasure hunt," Adam said. "You're the buried treasure."

BURIED TREASURE

BEFORE Jesús said anything to alarm anybody he checked every room in the big Victorian house, going from the tower to the cellar to the upstairs bedroom suite Aunt Irma now shared with Zita to keep an eye on Zita's deteriorating health, watching out for her and the increasing symptoms of the medical condition doctors diagnosed as lung cancer. Despite telling everyone she stopped smoking, Zita hid a pack of Salem Lights beneath a light orange monkeyflower bush in the garden and snuck two butts behind the cottage late at night and early in the morning. Zita's cough got worse.

Jesús knocked softly on the yellow door to Eeshell's spacious room. Then he knocked again, harder this time. Silence bit him harder than any rattler could. After assembling the other family members Jesús started asking probing questions the way any good out-of-work local news columnist knew how to do.

"Eeshell went to the store to buy peanut butter and celery," said Bud. "Or was it Cheez Whiz and celery?"

Even El Chapstick shook his head, once again feeling inadequate after his macho victory at the fiasco at Louie Louie's. An impressed Aunt Irma had invited him to dinner at the Cove commune's dining room.

"I haven't seen her since she left in the VW van," Zita said, her voice unusually tense.

"I feel a bad vibe coming on," said Aunt Irma.

"We was 'wrasslin aikido in the garden and she said she was getting hungry," said Mel. "She's pretty good for a girl."

Everybody looked at Mel who should have known better than to use the diminutive feminine description rather than the accepted womanly noun. Mel returned the look, sheepish at his mistake.

"She beat me," he said.

Jesús wore that stern look he wore whenever events took a turn for the weird. Tripper read that expressionless expression well. The set jaw could mean wisdom, serious trouble or both.

"Let's split up and go look for her," Tripper said.

As the search party prepared to move out Tripper opened the back door. A Bowie knife bearing a broken imitation pearl handle secured a rolled-up piece of brown butcher paper to the outside center of the door. When the glistening metal blade somehow dislodged itself and the knife dropped with a thud, the paper unrolled on the doorstep.

Drawn in black marker the treasure map showed one big red X that pinpointed the prize as well as a hodgepodge of arrows pointing in every direction. Small primitive drawings, a palm tree, a lagoon complete with ripples from the wind and an avocado, showed the way.

All eyes went to the map except for Mel's who turned on his cracked bare heel and raced to the closet where the family kept the corn flakes. After rooting deep behind the canned red beets and salt free corn he retrieved what he was looking for and placed the adornment on his head. A classic tricorn pirate's hat complete with skull and crossbones adorning the front set the stage for adventure, this time a matter of life and death that unnerved everyone, even Jesús. In a shrill voice loaded with excitement and trepidation, Mel shimmied and swayed and shrieked so loud the fringe on his loincloth shook.

"Aye, mateys," he said with tears welling in his eyes. "Time to dig the treasure."

SAND SLIDE

PAINTED black and made of flimsy light wood, the 70-inch mock coffin sold for $29.80.

Adam had to shop around before he found a box designed for Halloween gags or making vampire porn movies. He had to remember to get himself another one of those claustrophobic corpse crates to impress all the barmaids he knew when he got back to Bakersfield, if he ever made it home to the land of deep-fried intellect, Buck Owens buckaroo roots, re-heeled cowboy boots and oil field pump jack paranoia. For today, though, the wooden body box in the back of the camper would serve one purpose and one purpose only.

At five foot seven, 67 inches tall, Eeshell would fit.

After parking the camper as close to the sand-swept asphalt on the Pier Avenue dunes entrance as he could, Adam hauled the coffin from the back of the vehicle. While park rangers did their best to ignore him, he unhooked the tow bar hitch for the jerry-rigged dune buggy loaded with stolen mismatched parts and used a bungee cord to secure the cramped coffin to the rear of the dilapidated all-terrain machine. Covering the bone box with the bloodstained tarp he last used to cover Abbie's body after the killer coyote attack, Adam leered at Eeshell.

"Take me to your leader, hon," he said.

Broken red veins in Adam's eyes reminded Eeshell of jelly fish tentacles short-circuiting seared brain neurons that rule normal human behavior. Syntax dissolved, gone and burned like crispy marshmallows dangled too long on a campfire stick. Meth-induced mental illness popped through the petrified gray matter in his skull like a string of firecrackers ignited in a barn fire. The maniacal drug of choice among a frantic frazzled few tweakers sent speed-of-sound seduction through the bodies of elite freaks who always wanted more on their journeys to inner and outer space, pulling their brain stems north, south, east and west all at once, the crank cranking overtime. A-Team meth users never stopped cranking.

"Get in," said Adam, patting the filthy, white cracked vinyl buggy passenger seat. "We're taking the scenic route."

Twenty minutes later Adam pulled the neon green buggy with foot-high monster teeth spray-painted across the front grill tight against a sand dune the size of a beachside condo. Giggling like a demented voodoo child, he ran around the back of the quad and pulled out the coffin. Eeshell hadn't seen the shovel until now but knew immediately what he had in mind.

"Dig," he said, throwing the shovel her way.

Lifeguards caution never to dig holes in sand deeper than your knees. Laughing children covering dear old dad stretched out on his back except for his sunburned bald head is great fun, but a deeper hole can collapse and kill, suffocating the strongest human beneath the dead weight of heavy sand.

Three feet down Eeshell stopped digging. Pushing the coffin to the edge with his work boot, Adam nudged the casket into the open grave.

"Get in," he said.

"I said I would cooperate to keep my word," Eeshell said. "I cooperated. I kept my word."

"We're traveling to a new planet," Adam said.

Pulling his gun he pointed to a Filipino family of four surf fishing in the distance. Fixated on the long rods stuck in the wet sand bending in the ocean current, Adam mumbled to himself in his squeaky-tweaky voice, talking into his wrist like he was wearing an unseen walkie-talkie. The brown-skinned boy and girl looked to be twins, about five. Mom and dad dressed in baggy shorts with hoodies pulled tight in the wind. The adults fished there regularly to provide food for themselves and their children. Surviving meant everything.

Eeshell wanted to survive. She also wanted to help Adam, part of her private personal vow to save all sentient beings that sometimes made her feel foolish, like she was hijacking Gautama Buddha's words if he ever really spoke them and calling the mantra her own. Eeshell did want to save the world and if she failed to help Adam, one primitive example of mankind gone astray, what good was she? Is just trying good enough? Eeshell had to try.

Fighting her instincts to close the distance between herself and her abductor, take the gun with the swift aikido technique she regularly practiced at the aikido dojo and break his trigger finger in the process, Eeshell didn't want to hurt Adam.

Eeshell didn't want to hurt anyone.

Kicking off orange Creamsicle flip flops, Eeshell stepped into the box and stretched out. Adam closed the lid. With one shovelful after another he threw sand over the coffin, covering the box and filling the grave. Driving away in a spray of brown sand and a screaming blast from the Spider's engine, Adam felt better than he did when he won a hundred bucks for pulling his second eye tooth with a pair of plyers during customer talent night at the Boobs-A-Lot nude dancing club in Oil City near Bakersfield.

Breathing as slowly and deliberately as she could, Eeshell figured she had an hour or so before she died. She stayed still, trying to remember the man she once saw buried alive on TV and how he survived the way the great magician Harry Houdini did when he, too, went underground. Over the years some tricksters died doing the stunt because of the weight of the sand and the lack of air.

Feeling sleepy, instead of drifting off Eeshell meditated, focusing on each tiny moment of each slow breath, reflecting on the easy movement of her belly the way Indian yoginis must have done during the time of the Buddha. Now she sensed footsteps above. Knowing her friends must be looking for her, she scratched the lid with short fingernails she kept clipped and clean. Hard as it was not to cry out for fear of using the last of her oxygen, she tapped, tapped, tapped on the lid.

No one heard her.

Footsteps disappeared as people searching for her walked right over her crypt. Slowly pulling her T-shirt over her head, Eeshell tied the shirt over her mouth and eyes to keep the sand out when she broke through the lid. Punching hard, she threw a left fist and a right fist, another left, another right and a frantic flurry of short straight snapping punches she had worked on the heavy bag to perfect.

Violence is not the answer until it is, she remembered a wild visiting aikijujutsu teacher at the dojo once telling her. After successfully beating her way through the wooden lid, sand slid from both sides, faster and with more force, beginning to cover her body. Strong enough to sit up she rolled to her knees, pushing up with her hands and well-muscled arms, starting to rise from the dark prison and execution chamber.

Eeshell felt but never heard the tons of shifting sand that brought down the massive adjacent dune. Buried by the building-sized collapse, her mind went murky. Vibrating inky mist thickened before her open eyes filling her consciousness with pounding terror.

Not nearly as tough as she thought she was, Eeshell cast a quick magic spell to connect spiritually with Zita. Maybe Zita could cast a stronger spell that would free Eeshell. No luck. Summoning La Santa Muerte as well, Eeshell begged for the favor of life. She received no response from the very busy angel of death. Hoping Jesús might save her at the last moment, appearing out of nowhere, no one came to the rescue.

Succumbing to soft unlit emptiness, Eeshell lost track of reality. Sensing Cimmerian sleep about to forever envelop her, settling into dark comfort, she prepared for a rayless journey, a somber trip to a lightless destination of total darkness and death.

LIKE A RAINBOW

DOZENS of glossy ravens dark as black bile perch on all sides of the gray stone Maya remains at the southern tip of Isla Mujeres, the sacred "Island of Women" located 12 miles off the coast of Cancún on the Yucatán Peninsula that separates the Gulf of Mexico from the Caribbean Sea.

La Santa Muerte stands alone at the top of the Temple of Ixchel dedicated to the Maya moon goddess who offers happy healing rainbows to humanity despite male Maya gods forbidding the intoxicating multicolored arc of light. Ixchel dismisses their rules. She pays them no heed.

The original Jesús Malverde stands solemnly by La Santa Muerte's side, his blood infusing through the ages each subsequent generation that bears his name, carries his genes and embodies his character.

No one dares call this sacred union between spectral saints a wedding. Think morning and night, light and dark, mercy and wickedness blending in a ghostly interconnected witch's brew.

Raising their arms skyward the couple slowly ascends into billowy clouds close enough to brush. Touching Jesús Malverde's cheek with a bony finger, La Santa Muerte leaves a small cut. Stillness abounds as the couple descends to again stand on the sacred Temple of Ixchel.

Malverde's moustache is black. He wears a black and red satin guayabera shirt. La Santa Muerte's cowl is deep purple. Her sharpened eye teeth glisten.

Again they rise, this time turning into twinkling stars on each side of a full strawberry moon. Malverde's cheek has healed. La Santa Muerte has regenerated smooth young skin on her hands and face. A handsome pair, they watch a plumed snake with purple and green feathers fly in from the east, the snake bird's thickly feathered head shrouded, its eyes gleaming black coals that rival La Santa Muerte's but lose luster when she holds its gaze.

Again they descend, this time to face two jaguars that bound to the top of the steps and sit obediently, one beside Malverde, one beside La Santa Muerte. The satiny animals wear gold collars studded with opals and emeralds. At La Santa Muerte's command the beast by her side goes to Malverde.

"My gift to you," she says.

Directing his beast to her, he says, "My gift to you."

"We are the same," she says.

"No different," he says.

Ixchel appears.

"The same," she says.

Taking their hands in hers, she too becomes part of the covenant. No one can beat these three. Nothing can stop them. Pity those who try. Stepping to the edge of the monolith, Jesús Malverde chooses a conch shell from hundreds of shells, skulls and broken daggers piled on the altar.

Lifting to his lips the shell stained with blood he blows screaming notes of war and softer tones of peace, the sounds reverberating north across the peninsula, past the U.S. Border Patrol crossings into stolen land and deeper into a fearful, pathetic nation where countless migrants beg for help.

Handing the shell to La Santa Muerte, she, too, sounds the alarm that signals their rush to justice that one day will be heeded. Lowering the shell she whispers to her newest, closest ally.

"See the beast in me," she says. "See the beast in you."

Jesús Malverde and La Santa Muerte growl.

Ixchel casts a stunning rainbow across the sky.

JAWS OF LIFE

A FEW MILES up the beach from Eeshell's undiscovered grave, the other Juan used the late Juan Gomez's stolen Visa card to pay for himself and each member of the C Street Band to rent dune buggies for one hour at $259.86 apiece for a one seat Spider XP, fully automatic with no shifting.

"Dude, it's like driving a grocery cart at the beach," said the assistant manager at BLAST OFF Buggy Rentals. "Go, stop, and aim. Gas, brake and steer."

The other Juan asked how fast the buggies go.

"Take you to Hell and back on half-a-tank of gas, Bro," the assistant manager said. "Protected by a relaxed-fit harness seatbelt and indestructible roll bar cage. Breezy peezy, man."

Pancho, the C Street Band maraca player, asked, "How do you say 'breezy peezey' in Spanish, homes?"

The assistant manager said, "We speak English here."

Pancho and Cisco exchanged looks that could kill.

Buckled securely into their Spiders, all four men took off racing their way across skyscraper-sized sand mountains laughing and distracted as they dug into their pockets for fat pre-rolled joints. During the rough ride the team lit joints and lost joints, stopping to look unsuccessfully for the precious pot in the shifting sand without getting slammed by other dune buggies racing towards the same crest like old-fashioned bumper cars at an amusement park. Careening up one side of the sand and down the other they raced helmetless, almost flipping over and rear-ending each other.

Climbing higher and higher they disregarded warning flags where a driver can quickly plunge to broken death over the edge of a high dune, racing 60 miles an hour when a steep drop-off known as a "slip face" appears to take the driver end over end down the steep dune.

Taking the lead like Nazi Major General Erwin Rommel pushing his desert Panzer tank unit further into battle, the other Juan stuck a pre-rolled doobie in his mouth and lit the end, holding the smoke deep in his lungs. Settling into what was left of his brain cells, the mind mist stayed there clouding all reason.

What our peerless leader didn't know is when he whacked Juan Gomez and stole his pre-rolled weed, the weed was the same super Hoocha Weed Juan Gomez had swiped when he stole the infused wine from Mel before embarking on his historic freak-out at Louie Louie's.

Unbeknown to the other Juan that very weed grew as mutant "Bad Bunch" weed, the baddest, most bitter weed of the bunch, the wildest Hoocha Weed that would sink the most seasoned smoker no matter how little a toker toked. This shit was bad, super bad, badly bad. A single hit could easily turn intellect to vapor that douses the twilight forever and ever, amen.

Up and down the hills the other Juan flew, followed by the other three inebriated funsters, screaming and waving straw cowboy hats with one hand like bucking bronco riders while holding onto the steering wheel with the other. Pancho tried unsuccessfully to steer with his huarache-encased feet. The other Juan led his disciples through the dune maze like a trained guide. Cresting a dune he rubbed his eyes with both hands.

Two jaguars stood at the top of a dune, the sleek animals watching the action. Flooring the machine like a frightened fighter pilot engaging the enemy head-on for want of a better plan, the other Juan blew right through what he now believed to be a mirage. Hot breath breathing down his neck lit his fear. Jerking his jaw over his left shoulder he looked into the emerald eyes of a jaguar half the size of the buggy. Jerking his jaw right he looked into the emerald eyes of the second jaguar, another half the size of the buggy, leaving not nearly enough room for him.

The other Juan didn't know what bit him.

Bailing out he hit the sand hard, not yet dead, not yet knowing how white and bloody red his suboccipital muscles shined in sun after each jaguar took a hefty bite from each side of his throat. No longer would he be able to turn his head. No longer would the group of four muscles connect the top of his cervical spine with the base of his skull.

Pancho, Cisco and Slowpoke Rodriguez dutifully followed their leader's unmanned dune buggy over the edge, blasting off into oblivion before realizing five seconds into their descent that the terrain had disappeared from under them and a crash landing soon awaited below. When they hit the roll bars bent like plastic soda straws under the thumb of a steroid-sucking heavyweight powerlifter. Lucky for the three desperadoes, they died on impact, a grisly yet mortal fate better than surviving to face the tearing of their own flesh at the jaws of the jaguars.

When the yellowish-tan jaguars with black spots in rosettes trotted away, the sleek cats nuzzled their necks against three coyote pups that came bounding from their hiding places behind the dunes, tripping, rolling and falling over each other before rising and continuing their charge. The big beasts enjoyed nudging the playful pups before these two powerful felines casually loped into the sunset. The pups' mother and father watched respectfully from the highest hill.

Who says cats and dogs can't get along?

BOPPING WITH THE BEATS

THE NIGHT Vesuvio Cafe opened in 1948 on Columbus Avenue in San Francisco, Gavin Arthur provided a topless grand finale. Wound up tight as a gas chamber restraint on a San Quentin inmate's wrist, the beatnik bon vivant danced on the bar to the devil-may-care beat of a Benzedrine-fueled bongo player.

Poet Allen Ginsburg howled like a wolf in heat, so excited he set a small nest of beard hairs on fire trying to light a cigarette. At least one moth escaped with his life.

"Go, man, go!" screamed outlaw writer god Jack Kerouac.

Godfather to the universe in this family of cosmic maniacs, Neal Cassady beat his forehead on the bar in time to wailing spontaneous bop prosody jazz screaming from an instrumental trio playing at the back of the tightly packed room. Hipster prophets ahead of their time, this generation heralded the beginning of the end and the end of the beginning.

Sally Rose sat alone at the end of the bar looking at Gavin Arthur's bare chest. Shy but having little choice, laughing at the shaking going on above her neatly-clipped black bangs and long locks, Sally snapped her fingers. She shimmied. She shook.

Looking down, Gavin winked.

Gone when she awoke in the morning, leaving his polka-dotted boxer shorts slung over the tasseled lamp in the living room, Sally Rose never saw Gavin Arthur again. Nine months later Thornton Rose shyly entered the world, timid but anxious to learn how to boogie with the shadows dancing on the ceiling above his crib.

Hoping to see Gavin Arthur again Sally took a part-time job serving drinks in Vesuvio's. When City Lights Bookstore opened she took a job as a clerk. One night she met the great social critic comedian Lenny Bruce and at his urging after smoking a joint, a stick of tea as Bruce called the herb, recited a poem in a coffee shop that drew polite applause when Sally presented words in a voice soft as blue velvet.

"A peanut sat on the railroad track," she said. "Waiting for his mudder. Along came a train. Choo choo. Peanut butter."

Poet god Lawrence Ferlinghetti gave Sally Rose a gentle peck on the cheek.

More small nondescript odd jobs followed. She even helped tend bar and work the door at Specs's groovy grand opening in 1968 in North Beach.

In 1969 when "Thorn" turned 21 his self-proclaimed Earth Mother and her darling hippie boy turned up at the Altamont speedway for the big free concert that signaled the official end of the '60s. Between the Hells Angels' attacks on peaceful civilization that resulted in the death of an armed Black man and the stress Sally felt knowing she *did* have sympathy for the devil, her heart weakened even more from a sad year of injected amphetamine and uncertainty. Six months later Sally Rose died in the little apartment she and Thorn shared on Haight Street.

Hustling LSD, panhandling and working the streets the best he could, Thorn hitchhiked to Vancouver, Canada, to live in a city beach commune in Kitsilano as soon as Uncle Sam drafted him to fight in Vietnam. Thorn sold homemade hockey pucks he crafted out of hot glue and beer cans he cut down to size and spray-painted red, white and blue. He didn't sell many so he gave away the surplus to drunks playing in iced-over parking lots in the city or kids on their way to a rink. Coming home to his city by the bay after Jimmy Carter pardoned him and a couple of hundred thousand other re-sisters, Specs's manager hired Thorn to sweep up which he did for many years.

During a particularly bad blotter acid trip during which he watched cartoons nonstop for three days, Thorn decided Bugs Bunny had ordered him to take the bus to Pismo Beach and dig clams until he found enlightenment. When he changed buses in San Luis Obispo he did another hit of acid and walked for hours, missing Pismo and winding up in nearby Oceano.

Thorn quickly heard about the Dunites from a woman he met

at a Japanese strawberry stand, a woman who reminded Thorn of his mother and introduced herself as Mama Osa and told him he should follow his heart, which he did, straight to the sand dunes.

At Mama Osa's urging he changed his name to Mel Moyle. She didn't tell him Moy Mel was the name of the utopian commune Gavin Arthur built in the dunes in the early 1930s. The name means "Pastures of Honey" in Gaelic. When she was alive and living in Oceano long ago, legendary Dunite oracle Ella Young had taught Mama Osa as a child how to speak to trees so Mama Osa was always on the lookout for a kindred spirit. Sensing more nectarous sap running through Mel Moyle's veins than mortal blood, Mama Osa asked Ella's spirit to watch over the holy wanderer who might rejuvenate the Dunite spirit and help pollenate a sparkling new world. In the richness of her eternal life, the Irish fairy godmother wholeheartedly agreed.

Mama Osa had no idea Mel sprung from Gavin's seed. The heavenly avatars in which she believed would tell her when they thought she should know. As these sometimes convoluted sweet mysteries of life convened, Mel did his best to live happily ever after. For the most part he succeeded.

Within a week Mel had built a shack in the sand. Those who knew its whereabouts respected Mel's privacy. Nobody hassled him. People who dug how much metaphysics mattered in Oceano dug Mel Moyle. A humane man who bothered no soul, he eventually came into his own through kindness, good vibes and a desire to live off the land like so many flower children once hoped to do.

With the full bloom of a fresh Seaside Poppy, Mel Moyle blossomed all year round.

When he whispered to the eucalyptus trees, the eucalyptus trees whispered back.

Starry-eyed seer Ella Young approved.

SHAKE, SHAKE, SHAKE

A RAGTAG mix of steroid-sucking, mirror sunglass-wearing, buzz cut, shaved head, musclebound local and county law enforcement officers and other misunderstood first responders gathered at the scene of the multiple dune buggy fatality. Standing and staring at four fresh corpses, the cops compared tattoos, cracked wise-ass remarks and busted each other's chops.

"Follow the leader," said a sergeant.

"Mustsa been some letdown," said a corporal with a straight face.

The sergeant broke up, spitting a just sipped gulp of coffee into the air.

"Probably caught his neck on a hot flywheel that kept spinning and cut through his throat like a buzz saw," said the corporal, pointing to the other Juan's butchered body part.

"Reminds me of that big Crusher Motorcycle Club animal got sliced up in Shell Beach not that long ago," said the sergeant.

"Hamburger helper, man," the corporal said. "Buck knife, box cutter, straight razor, flywheel, what's the difference?"

"Yeah, dirt bags all the same. Outlaw bikers, illegal wetbacks, let 'em kill each other 'til they're not our problem anymore," the sergeant said. "Take our country back."

"White's right, man," said the corporal who normally worked undercover drug buys and stood like a Norse god come to life, combing through sumptuous hair gel on his head. Grooming locks across his forehead he put the greasy black comb under his nose and added a quick Nazi salute.

That's when the sand shifted slightly, tipping both sergeant and disciple off balance causing one to spill what was left of his coffee, the other to stumble like a common drunk. Scared, the sergeant said, "You feel that?"

If the corporal didn't feel the first tremor, he felt the second. Everybody on the Central Coast felt the Earth move. The outhouse-sized guard shack at the West Grand Avenue entrance to the dunes collapsed in the rolling seismic earthquake rippling in shock waves parallel to the beach, stretching from a distant fractured fault line that ran through Pismo and Oceano south into Santa Maria and through the center of Santa Barbara.

In the moments these two useless public servant cops tried to keep their balance above the tremor, a dozen significant cracks appeared in both lanes of the 101 freeway between San Luis Obispo and Orcutt. Feral roosters in Arroyo Grande crowed from tree perches. Gulls scattered from the top of a shabby Avila Beach gazebo facing the ocean. A drunken Fresno vacationer tripped and dropped from the Pismo Pier, requiring rescue from three teenage lifeguards who happened to be smoking a joint and eating fish tacos nearby.

Concrete, tiles and other debris fell from balconies at several dingy Santa Maria motels. Hot tubs upended in Guadalupe. A swimming pool cracked in Nipomo. A Grover Beach surf store actually broke in half, roof and floor separating and collapsing, sending vintage longboards decorating the ceiling crashing into the sunglass case below. A house under construction on a Nipomo mesa hill overlooking the ocean came off the foundation and slid toward the sea. Missile launch facilities shook at Vandenberg Air Force Base and cell bars rattled at the federal prison in Lompoc.

Call it happenstance, theosophic direction or divine intervention, but the good people of the historic utopian community of Halcyon near Oceano felt no movement at all. Already balanced, these good citizens continued their day in the embrace of sages, prophets, unsung saints and avatars they knew watched over them at all times.

Fate protected most buildings and people. Earthquakes are always about the luck of the draw. You just never know. In this case nobody had warning or time to drop, cover and hold on. They just rolled with the quake that registered on a scale of three to eight, minor to great, at 7.0, still a "major" quake, according to the Earthquake Magnitude Class, a significant increase from the last Central Coast quake, the December 22, 2003, San Simeon Earthquake that came in at 6.5 and did little damage to the Central Coast but got everybody's attention.

Empowered by an adrenaline rush accompanying the colossal motion beneath the sand mountain, Eeshell felt as if she were swimming, doing the backstroke in the ocean's warm water in which she always felt safe. Shifting left and right and up and down as if on a roller coaster, she went with the sand that transported her body upward. Seeing an open spot of blue sky, she stretched her arms and stroked left and right, kicking her legs, propelling her body backwards and then upwards, rising from the depths.

Eeshell swam to safety through a sea of sand. Finally able to breathe, kneeling for a moment, she heard gulls cry welcoming her back above ground. Standing awkwardly, she felt the sun's heat on her face blend with rolling beads of sweat. Eeshell felt her heart beat in her throat. Over and over she mindfully inhaled and exhaled fresh clean California air.

Removing her shorts and vintage T-shirt that said "Pete's Pierside," she stepped naked into the water. Wading into the security of the water's friendly embrace, Eeshell bowed at the waist and dove. Swimming easily about 50 yards offshore, she met two dolphins that waited.

Together they dove deeper than usual, surfaced, dove again and swam off into the future.

SYRAH A-GO-GO

POSING with veiny skim milk-colored hands on hips thin as a rusty wire coat hanger, Syrah gyrated in front of the cracked and smudged full-length mirror on the back of Bud's bedroom door.

Jerking, twitching, twerking, wiggling and waggling in bony buttocks-clinging white hot pants and no shirt, she imagined herself dancing in a golden bird cage hanging from the ceiling at Louie Louie's. The men there would buy her drinks because Syrah knew she was hot as a flaming Dr. Pepper boilermaker spilled on a hammered customer's crotch.

As far from human as a soulless specter could get, how could this horrifying voice in some poor prey's head maintain a mind of her own? How could her words banging around in anyone's skull seem so very, very real? EVILE, that's how. Pure EVILE spelled E-V-I-L-E existing at all times without boundary, roosting in a victim's noggin like a carrion vulture waiting to pounce from a tall tree. Gross unadulterated EVILE, Syrah lived as a cross between evil and vile, worse than any mass murdering death row inmate could imagine. Syrah was only an alias, a name she stole from a Santa Maria Valley wine bottle.

EVILE easily infects entire armies. No one can stop EVILE, a maniacal mind-blowing mental condition that unconditionally alters Homo sapiens before they devolve, drop and die. EVILE always works to lay waste to civilization, to crucify salvation. Will Syrah drill into more than one head? YES! Multiple heads at the same time? YES, YES, YES!!!

Syrah could come for anybody.

Syrah might come for you.

BACK TO THE GARDEN

FRUSTRATED and desperate, the search party had refused to give up. When the earthquake struck, Bud, El Chapstick, Aunt Irma, Tripper, Jesús, and Mel sat around the dining room table, all out of ideas about where to next look for Eeshell.

"Please don't laugh at Eeshell," said Mel, hearing Syrah howl like a banshee in his head, hidden away in the deep caverns behind his eyes, hearing her voice in his head and not understanding, at first thinking the laughter came from one of the others sitting at the table.

Pulling the Ouija board from his leather fringe hippie bag and laying it on the dining room table, he positioned the planchette at the bottom line of letters, placing his two forefingers in the middle of the wooden pointer. Two seconds later the heart-shaped piece began to move, spelling out a clue on the clairvoyant message medium that said "G-A-R-D-E-N."

Aunt Irma screamed.

"She's in my cabbage patch out back!"

Eeshell laughed from the doorway.

"More like Hell than the Garden of Eden," she said.

Looking around the table, Eeshell's smile went cold.

"Where's Zita?"

"She doesn't feel well," said Tripper. "She's in her room sleeping."

"Adam kidnapped me," Eeshell said. "Buried me alive in the sand."

Without speaking Jesús crumpled the treasure map, threw the brown butcher paper against the wall, pushed his chair from the table, stood, squared his shoulders and left the room. Never getting used to the unpredictable wired energy of his mood, knowing she'd fail to alter the outcome of his quest even if she tried, Tripper stayed put.

Trying to break the tension, Bud asked, "What did the word GARDEN mean on the Ouija board, Mel?"

"Woodstock, man," he said. "Like the song says, we gotta get back to the garden."

"That's a long drive," Bud said. "All the way to New York."

"Some of them acid-tested Merry Pranksters made it in 1969," Mel said. "We can make it, too."

"Further," said Bud, saying in a reverent tone the name with which the Sixties counterculture witch doctors baptized their bus.

"Even further than that," Mel said.

HOSTAGE

"YOUR BROTHER needs you," said the trembling voice on the cellphone.

Jesús Zarate said, "I'm an only child."

The caller's panicked pitch rose.

"El Maloso needs you, man."

Breathing heavily, the man spoke in clipped, rapid fire sentences.

"Two Sinaloa enforcers snatched him. They're holding him at the Santa Maria Speedway. I promised I'd tell you the cartel wants you."

"Why did you tell them anything?"

"They stole my diamond pinkie ring when they left, man."

The caller began to cry.

"My finger was still attached to the ring," he said.

"Why does the cartel want me?"

"You're Jesús Malverde, right?"

Three long silent seconds passed as Jesús Zarate's saintly transformation concluded.

"Yes," he said. "I *am* Jesús Malverde."

Bristling from his refuge beneath the kingsized brass bed Jesús and Tripper shared in their second-floor two-room suite, Regalo's sensors twitched with energy and the smell of adrenaline he picked up from his master and friend as Jesús spoke on the phone. Infused with supernatural stamina, the scorpion warrior sensed danger. Always up for a rumble, he moved nonchalantly from his corner like a wiry seasoned prizefighter heading to the center of the ring.

"I'll be right there," Jesús said.

Ditto for Regalo, who skittered out the door, down the steps, through the mansion, out the door, up the tire, over the fender and into the open window of the sleek low-rider rod El Maloso gave

Jesús when he and Tripper got back to town.

Police had closed the 101 freeway because of cracks and grid-locked emergency vehicle traffic so Jesús took the scenic route south, past small agricultural businesses and black loamy fields planted with celery and broccoli. The Oceano dunes disappeared behind him as he neared Guadalupe where new dunes appeared.

He remembered jogging in his skirt-like martial arts hakama and practicing aikido rolls on the deserted Guadalupe Beach where he met Wally Wilson, American history's most lovable serial killer. Drinking wine with Wally was fun. Yoga and meditation with Wally felt good.

Yet Wally's fight for self-control deteriorated even as he helped save lives and took lives in the firefight with Commander Fetus and his cracker pot militia that fused them forever in holy brotherhood. The thought made Jesús wonder if he, too, might one day again succumb to the temptation of violence, if he might one day kill again.

Wally set himself on fire to reach nirvana.

Would Jesús do the same?

Reflection crowded his mind, filling his eyes with tears as he drove Black Road toward Santa Maria. Looking up through the top of the dusty windshield he saw the prairie falcon gliding in a wide arc above the car, circling and dipping, climbing and diving, showing off. The glint of a quarter-sized silver medallion in the shape of a peace sign hung from the predator bird's neck.

Blowing the horn Jesús grinned.

"You always have my back, Wally," he said as the bird disappeared into rippled clouds.

A metal gate barred entry to the speedway. El Maloso stood tied to a wooden stake the enforcers planted in the center of the wide dirt track lined with truck tires painted white. More defiant than Joan of Arc, he smirked at his two guards. The goons dressed in matching green alligator skin cowboy boots, burgundy sharkskin suits, black shirts, white ties and wraparound shades stood on each side of their prisoner.

As soon as the men saw Jesús step from his car they held gas cans above El Maloso's head and prepared to pour. Flames would draw attention from the road, but it would be too late to save El Maloso.

High above the tense scene a silent prairie falcon circled. Regalo scurried to the ground, darted across the dirt track, over the top of the biggest gorilla's $3,000 boot and up his black silk knee-high sock, resting just below the bulging skin of his knee. Although El Maloso felt fear, the hardened Los Matadores gang leader refused to flinch, instead taunting fate in the face of his own death.

"Got a light, Jesús?"

"Put down the gas cans and we'll talk," Jesús told the enforcers.

Both men flicked open the tops of gold Zippo lighters and put thick thumbs on the flint wheels. Meaty as a ham hock, the heaviest man's hand began to shake. A sweet calm swept over Jesús who felt the atoms of his body and the genes of his father, grandfather, and great-grandfather merge into a blend of common sense, intellect and defiance. Raw courage helped but brains mattered more than brawn.

"You worry I will kill you both," Jesús said. "Perhaps I *will* order lightning to strike you right now."

If his life depended on it and it did, Jesús had no idea how to call down fire from the heavens. But these men who hailed from rural poverty, despite their current status and prestige among the cartel, trusted in primitive power, devils and superstition. In their simple minds they believed Jesús Malverde capable of anything, a deep belief that gave Jesús the edge.

Pointing to the sky, Jesús said, "I ask for your help La Santa Muerte. Guide me in how these poor men should die."

The men dropped the gas cans.

"La Santa Muerte *and* Jesús Malverde," one man said.

"No way we win this," said the other.

"Be careful, dude," El Maloso said to Jesús. "Ask La Santa Muerte for a favor, you'll owe La Santa Muerte a favor."

"I already do," Jesús said.

Peeking from beneath his potential victim's pant leg, Regalo scurried back to the car, crawled into the window and promptly fell asleep. Again the prairie falcon disappeared. After the would-be executioners untied and freed El Maloso, they stood by helplessly, not knowing what to do or where to go.

"What do we tell our Culiacán bosses, Señor Malverde?"

Taking pity on the hard lives and dire circumstances that brought continuing unwanted violence to their lives, Jesús said, "Tell your bosses I am on their side, the side of equality, fairness, opportunity, and justice against those who hold our people in bondage. Tell them we are the real hostages. Tell them I will help them and their families as I will help yours. Tell them to stop killing each other."

"You speak many words," said the heaviest gunman. "Maybe too many."

"Tell them," Jesús said. "Or *everybody* dies."

By early evening the enforcers had told them. Sinaloa bosses called an unexpected midnight truce throughout Mexico and the United States. Other cartels called off their assassins. Confusion brought peace among some of the illegal drug world's most dangerous killers—for now.

Jesús Malverde had spoken.

 # WOMEN LIKE US

LISTENING closely Tripper held a brown clay tea cup in both hands, blowing across the top to cool the water Zita boiled with vanilla, avocado leaves, oregano and ground rattlesnake she retrieved from a purple cracked leather bag as big as a mango.

"The snake must die peacefully, a natural death that allows her remains to rest," Zita said. "Only then will she allow us to use her power and wisdom."

"Your potion is so sweet," said Tripper.

"The snake likes you," Zita said. "So does my son."

"I hope so," Tripper said.

Sensing Tripper needed assurance, Zita gently placed her cup on the nightstand by her bed.

Summoning courage Tripper closed her eyes.

"What does Jesús like about me?"

"In you my son sees the person he would like to become," said Zita. "You are chosen."

"Did Jesús choose me or did I choose him?"

"Destiny chose you for each other," Zita said.

"Fate?"

"Ixchel," said Zita. "Our Maya moon goddess will help you follow your heart. Men tell us how to look, how to think, how to behave. Yet we all know who we are and what we stand for. Ixchel will help guide you."

Zita easily sensed Tripper's anxiety.

"I once killed a husband who controlled how I lived," Tripper said.

"I know," said Zita.

"Finding peace of mind is difficult," Tripper said.

"Ixchel will help you smooth the rough edges."

"Mine?"

"Jesús needs polish more than you," said Zita. "Machismo is fading but he still needs work."

A wave of sadness flushed Tripper's face as she held back her tears.

"Ixchel will help me?"

"Women like us depend on Ixchel to find ourselves," said Zita. "My mother was Maya. From the Yucatán. She traveled by canoe as a young girl to the tiny island where Ixchel lives where she found strength."

"Does Ixchel need us?"

"As much as we need her," Zita said. "But you will work best with your new daughter, the incarnation of two natural forces - one male, one female - who one day will take over where you, Jesús and I leave off."

"I don't have a daughter," said Tripper.

"The snake likes you," said Zita.

AFTER ALL THESE YEARS

NOT ONE to stay in bed past sunrise but too weak from coughing to get up, Zita watched hours pass on the red numerical digital clock. By noon she once again coughed herself awake, hacking with her chest increasingly tighter and throat so raw the skin burned. Feeling so weak she could hardly lift the water glass to her lips, another spasm rattled what was left of her lung tissue and lifted her inches off the bed.

Zita's coughing stopped abruptly when La Santa Muerte's soft voice whispered in her ear, soothing body and soul better than any store-bought medicine.

"Would you like a glass of wine, señora?"

"I wish for wine with melipona honey," Zita said.

"Ah, honey from the stingless bee," La Santa Muerte said.

"The bee's name in the Mayan language is Xunán-Kab," Zita said. "She only lives in the Yucatán Peninsula."

"That can be arranged," said La Santa Muerte. "I'm starting to like that wacky weedy wine everybody else is drinking."

Both women laughed.

Accepting the long-stemmed glass of sweetened pinot noir, Zita sipped and recalled when La Santa Muerte watched over her as a child maturing into a young woman, protecting Zita from any misfortune or danger that might come her way. Always the savior, La Santa Muerte stayed by Zita's side during hard times. When the "big man with the moustache" stepped in, La Santa Muerte bowed out, until a handful of corrupt police and politicians lynched Zita's husband in the town square.

When La Santa Muerte returned with a vengeance that handful of police and politicians vanished.

"Then you traveled on your own," said La Santa Muerte. "Your journeys always show your courage."

"I depend on your help," Zita said.

Making a cradle of her arms, La Santa Muerte said, "The baby was beautiful."

"Not a baby anymore," Zita said.

"Himself now the big man with the moustache," said La Santa Muerte.

"We have a complicated family tree," said Zita.

La Santa Muerte counted skeletal fingers.

"One, two, three generations of Jesús Malverdes watching over you," she said. "Now the fourth Malverde male awaiting instructions to carry on ancient ways, to uphold his birthright established by the original Jesús Malverde the way his ancestors stood against dishonor and injustice."

"Those men paid with their lives," Zita said. "Today's Jesús Malverde lives."

"Your son refuses to forsake the honor of his genetic roots," said La Santa Muerte. "Even now that he knows his past he believes he has no descendant to whom he can pass the Malverde legacy. He worries the Malverde mission will end with no hero to right society's wrongs on both sides of the border."

"Truth never fails," Zita said.

La Santa Muerte gently placed a skeletal hand on Zita's thin arm.

"How is dear Eeshell?"

Eeshell, with no knowledge of her birthright as sole heir to the Malverde calling, now bonded closer than ever with Zita, the grandmother she thought was her godmother who lived her own secret life as La Santa Muerte's adopted daughter. Eeshell lived each day, each moment, as a faithful adherent to nature. Genealogy, indeed, gets confusing but occult bloodlines answer all questions in the end.

"You must soon introduce Eeshell to her father," said La Santa Muerte.

Sensing Jesús' presence before he appeared in the doorway, La Santa Muerte vanished.

"You should eat something," he said to his mother. "Would you like me to make your favorite shrimp, garlic and cilantro?"

"Please sit with me," said Zita.

Jesús sat on the edge of the bed. Zita drained her glass of wine. Teasing her son she said, "Can you still make the bunny rabbit shadow on the wall I taught you to make when you were a child?"

Holding up two fingers, Jesús made long ears and a head appear on the wall.

"I made the rabbit dance on the cell wall when I was in prison and got homesick," he said. "When I needed a friend."

Zita grew solemn.

"Do you remember the edgy teenager wearing an embroidered peasant blouse, tight white jeans and green snakeskin boots you met at a Voodoo Glow Skulls concert so many years ago?"

Drawing a blank, Jesús shook his head and laughed out loud.

"The Voodoo Glow Skulls? I haven't thought about them in decades."

La Santa Muerte returned to remind him, filling his mind's eye with images from yesteryear.

Embroidered skulls and crossbones decorated the teenage girl's crisp white peasant blouse. Eyeshade glistened green, sparkling with gold glitter. Black hair thick as a mare's mane fell to her waist. She wore a shiny red leather headband and a blue teardrop tattoo on her left cheek and carried a knife in her boot. Salty sweet kisses tasted like caramel Michoacan ice cream.

Rubbing his eyes, Jesús looked at his mother.

"I remember."

Zita spoke with certainty.

"The mother of your daughter."

A cop once told Jesús most people should count to 10 before they act. Jesús was up to 20 when he and Zita sensed another presence in the room. The fresh scent of coconut and pineapple filled the air.

"I'm sorry," Eeshell said. "I can come back."

"No, please, dear one," said Zita. "Come in."

"I can come back," Jesús said.

"Stand and face her," Zita said. "Look at him, Eeshell."

Trusting and obedient, Eeshell turned toward Jesús who stood and met her gaze.

"Take each other's hands," Zita said. "Feel the power of your blood."

When they touched warm current surged through their skin and the sweaty pores of their fingers, sparking elements in their bodies that triggered electrical charges. Atoms commingled and sped through their system as they emitted radioactive particles that stemmed from their common DNA. Neither Jesús nor Eeshell pulled away.

"You share a forever pulse," Zita said.

Eeshell smelled blood and roses.

"Say hello to your father, Jesús," said Zita. "I am your grand-mother, not your godmother."

Jesús stood statue still.

"Why after all these years?"

"The time has come," Zita said.

"If you're my grandmother, who's my godmother?"

Pointing to the fading shadow on the wall, Zita said, "That honor now belongs to her."

Having replaced the finger bunny, a hazy bag of bones drink-ing a glass of wine lifted and drifted to the center of the room and out the door. Another shadow followed, this one visiting from Isla Mujeres, the tiny enchanted island where life began and would con-tinue for all time.

Three soft hours later Zita died.

Fueled by her grandmother's overflowing power and the pure energy of her other guides, Eeshell Malverde lived.

BURNING LOVE

AFTER spending a ragged childhood in Mexico rustling cattle, horses, bulls, and pigs, stealing Jesús' car was easy.

Auto theft always impressed Aunt Irma.

"Oh, my," she said. "How did you start the engine without a key?"

"I use a screwdriver and hammer to eat my eggs and beans in the morning," El Chapstick said. "I'm like a hot car piano tuner."

"You are so cute," Aunt Irma said.

Blushing, El Chapstick jumped from the driver's side, ran around the metallic purple custom-built 1949 Mercury Eight and opened the passenger door. Removing his new white straw cowboy hat embellished with turquoise crystals and crow feathers, he bowed at the waist with a wide sweep of his arm.

Aunt Irma got in the car.

"I like you much better without your wrestler's mask," she said. "You're mucho more handsome since you retired from the ring."

Jumping back in the custom-made ride, El Chapstick gunned the engine and threw the transmission into gear.

"Las Vegas here we come," said Aunt Irma. "I always wanted to get married in the Elvis chapel."

"I'm a hunk-a-hunk of burning love," said El Chapstick.

TOBACCO ROAD

AFTER Arthur von Spittle died an excruciating death from third-degree terminal worm holes, the cigarette company he made famous kept pumping out cancer sticks thanks to the deal he cut with an under-the-radar private equity hedge fund in San Francisco.

Out of sheer traditional conservative responsibility and not a dribble of love, Arthur von Spittle's will named Bud as his eccentric heir, providing enough money for Bud to find himself and others, which, of course, he did. Before he died Arthur von Spittle sold his tobacco company to the shady hedge fund that planned a societal nicotine fit designed to addict vulnerable smokers worldwide.

Hedge fund manager Carnegie VanderGild called the new company Neblina, Spanish for mist or haze. The business expanded to a facility so big the factory occupied a complex that once served as a sugar processing plant outside the Santa Maria city limits. VanderGild oversaw the manufacturing of multiple new brands designed specifically for poor people smokers, mostly new immigrants, especially Latinos living in the inner cities of the United States.

Mayas, Aztecs, and other indigenous people living in pre-Columbian Mesoamerica chewed, inhaled and otherwise used wild tobacco to induce visions, treat pain, and celebrate sport victories on the playing field where winners decapitated losers, and following particularly drunken games, used the conquered players' heads for balls. If the poison plant sometimes providing 10 times the amount of nicotine in modern-day cigarettes was good enough for men who reveled in human sacrifice, it was good enough for VanderGild.

More success than Arthur von Spittle ever imagined lay right around the corner even without weed. VanderGild and the other hedge fund executives disdained cannabis. With an evangelical Christian board of directors, the power elite favored 100 percent pure leaf tobacco products including cigarettes, cigars, vaping, E-cigarettes, and lip pouches because they believed the New England pilgrims justifiably killed all the Indians they could kill to make a profit with their tobacco.

"Smoke 'em if you got 'em" meant smoking (as in wiping out) Indians whenever and wherever you got 'em cornered. Hedge fund board members believed if free smokes were good enough for our boys in World War II, they're good enough for current and future soldiers who need a smoke break when they finish smoking peasants around the world. Board members supported war across the board for that very reason.

With innovative tobaccos the newly incarnated drug brand business plan ramped up what manufacturing visionaries called "cowboy and cowgirl smokes"—raw, rough, and ready cigarettes that appealed to men, women, and wild Western children, who snuck cigarettes behind the barn or at the rodeo where they rode bucking saddled sheep until they puked—the mutton busters, not the mutton.

Not only did Neblina expect to quintuple cigarette production, the hedge fund already bought once-fruitful strawberry fields destined for potential new housing developments with a plan to grow nothing but fresh California tobacco leaf.

Back in the late 1800s Placer County led the state in planting tobacco seeds, turning the state into the new South for smokers and confederates. Indigenous Indians had been growing and smoking tobacco for countless years, so why not desperate illegal fence jumpers quick to embrace the American Dream? With a growing willingness to defy government regulations spreading across America, other new smokers would be easy to addict as well. Maybe the new cigarette company could even offer each new legal and illegal immigrant a coupon for a free carton of smokes.

If Indians of old preferred tobacco over glass beads, and they did, so would today's still vulnerable Indians. Lawyers could easily wrangle deals with tribes and get the new Neblina brand into the gambling casinos where defiant geezers and wheezers enjoyed a smoke while playing slot machines and other gambling games.

An infusion of cash into the Indian lobbying machine would all the more ingratiate the corporate presence into the good graces of the tribes.

Ninety percent of tobacco grown in the U.S. is cultivated in four states: North Carolina, Kentucky, Tennessee, and Virginia. Neblina board members wanted California to take over. Not only would the Big Tobacco South fall, instead of a woke tobacco-free future, company decision-makers expected Neblina to reign supreme. Instead of making life more difficult for children to start smoking or vaping, Neblina high priests vowed to make life one big tobacco tabernacle.

Bud and Mel had already bottled their first 10 cases of Hoocha Weed wine the same week the hedge fund public relations team issued a press release announcing a "brand" new Santa Maria cigarette factory to be built on the grounds of a useless cigarette warehouse the company would implode. The proposed plant would employ 500 people, mostly Mexican-American women, with plans to hire 500 more. Trucks would leave the plant at all hours of the day and night, violating an assortment of local, state, and federal regulations in the process.

Breaking the law came with doing hedge fund business. If you broke the law, an army of lawyers and their dark money backers cut whatever corners they could cut to help defend the scallywags. Unlimited corporate money almost always won. With tax breaks, continuing political influence and access to other powerbrokers, even when the robber barons lost they won.

This hedge fund welcomed litigation that brought any and all publicity that attracted new customers. One soon-to-be-disbarred Chinese-American investor lawyer, notorious for winning tobacco-related jury trials, even named his first-born daughter "Sue Me."

Neblina also quietly bought new land, a secret box canyon in the mountains above Lopez Lake in the Los Padres National Forest near Huff's Hole that offered some mighty fine deer hunting to the few outdoorsmen who knew its location. If the canyon ever caught fire, nobody could get there to put it out. They'd just have to let it burn. So if the cops ever raided, igniting a dozen road flares strategically placed would do the trick.

VanderGild planned to harvest supercharged addictive tobacco in the box canyon, the best high-grade mutated nicotine-laced tobacco science ever chemically altered, a cash crop as enticing and enslaving as any Afghan opium. Third-world smokers would love their newest bad habit. So would the American smoking masses hedge fund executives overwhelmingly considered asses.

Neblina would blow your mind—as well as your heart and lungs.

Nọ BUSINESS AS USUAL

PUTTING their heads together in an empty wine barrel constituted a bigger hurdle than Mel or Bud expected. But that's what it took for vintner partners to figure out quality and quantity. You get a better sniff shoving your head into an oak barrel than sticking your nose into a glass. These two good buddies normally lived pleasant fantasy world lives, but Mel dealt with matters of the day in more practical terms than his apprentice and partner.

Bud rolled with the flow like a wiggly bug stuck in molasses.

"I'm getting real bad vibes, man," Mel said, pulling his head from the barrel. "I'm seeing butterflies fly without wings."

"Oh, no," Bud said. "Monarch creatures from the black lagoon."

"I'm worried about addiction," Mel said.

"You can't get addicted to Hoocha Weed wine, man," Bud said. "Ask the hummingbirds. They just sip and fly, man."

"Not in the heroin sense of addiction you can't get hooked," Mel said. "And nobody's OD'ing and dropping dead like they do on corporate chemical fentanyl. People got enough monkeys jumping around in their heads without them riding on their backs. I'm worried all people will want to do is drink Hoocha Weed wine."

Bud looked forlorn.

"What's wrong with that?"

"We're giving away real magic, man," Mel said.

"For free," Bud said.

"Free as a buzzed hummingbird," Mel said.

"So here's what we do," Bud said. "We give a weed wine test like a driver's test. We say, 'Be careful, dude' before taking that first sip."

"Everybody passes," Mel said. "We don't discriminate."

"And I'll keep paying all the bills, supporting everybody in the comfy commune of the Cove and life goes on until the money runs out," Bud said.

Mel stiffened.

"How much you got?"

"About a hundred million and change."

"That ought to carry us until the end," Mel said.

"When's the end?"

"When it's over," Mel said.

"At the end," Bud said.

"The finish line," Mel said.

Perplexed again, Bud sputtered.

"To whom do we give our magic wine?"

"To people who otherwise can't afford weed and wine," Mel said.

"No snooty wine snobs need apply," said Bud. "Weed Wine Magic for the people."

"Brought to you *by* Dunites *for* Dunites," Mel said.

"*You're* the last living Dunite, Mel."

"As of now I am," Mel said. "We'll swear in each lucky bottle of Weed Wine Magic recipient as a card-carrying Dunite. You don't have to live in the dunes to be a Dunite. Living as a Dunite is a state of mind."

Bud brightened.

"Gavin Arthur said that," he said.

Mel stiffened.

"Who told you?"

"You did."

Bud's thoughts began to bubble.

"So Gavin says all we got to do is believe?"

"If you think it you can do it, even of you can't do it you've done it because thinking it already does it, so do it," Mel said.

Bud's brain bubbles popped.

"So that's why Jesús says the drug cartel in Mexico is calling a truce? Because they believe Jesús Malverde will punish them if they don't listen to him, right?"

"The cartel bosses believe," Mel said. "They believe in the holy and unholy power of Jesús Malverde, the same way people believe in Jesus Christ. These men truly believe. Our savior Jesús Malverde says so."

"I thought his name was Jesús Zarate."

"Not anymore," said Mel. "Dude got born again."

"We born again, too, Mel?"

"Praise the Lord and pass the Weed Wine Magic," Mel said.

"I'm a believer," Bud said.

"That's them monkeys in your head talking again," Mel said.

OLD FRIENDS

PICKING shelled unsalted pistachios one at a time from a bag of roasted nuts, Eeshell waited for Jesús to finish his morning Chinese Qi Gong exercises in the back garden before interrupting. Breathing and stretching, slow methodical movements and sacred sounds that massaged internal organs helped him heal, making his body and mind more fit for existence.

"There's a bird sitting on the steering wheel in the VW van," Eeshell said.

Sure enough, when Jesús and Eeshell got to the parking space behind the house, a bird sat perched on the VW's steering wheel. Cocking his head from side to side, the prairie falcon looked from Eeshell to Jesús and back again.

"Wally misses his bus," Jesús said. "Prairie falcons can't get a driver's license, though, even in California."

Not knowing Wally or the significance of this magnetic moment, Eeshell googled "prairie falcon" on her phone and read aloud from the first definition she found.

"Lovely, medium-sized raptor with a grayish-brown back and a lighter breast mottled with dark streaks and dots. A prairie falcon has a unique facial feature—a thin, dark moustache. Known by several names, including mostachial stripe or malar stripe, the bird's 'moustache' is a line of feathers that extends downward from below its eyes or beak. Not all birds have malar stripes and those that do may have red ones, yellow ones, or most any other color. In prairie falcons the malar stripe is dark brown or black."

Looking up impishly at Jesús, Eeshell said, "That bird reminds me of you."

"We share a lot in common," Jesús said. "More than you know."

Leaning into the open window, he looked hard at the falcon.

"Damn, Wally," he said. "You are starting to look like me."

"Why are you calling him Wally? Do you two know each other? He's looking at you like he knows you," Eeshell said.

"We're old friends," Jesús said. "You look at me like you know me."

"I feel like I've known you all my life," Eeshell said.

"Maybe longer than that," he said.

The bird hopped to the passenger seat and screeched.

"I'm going to need the bus for a few hours," Jesús said.

Eeshell tossed him the keys.

"Where you going?"

"Wally and I are going hunting," he said.

"For what?"

"For Adam."

 # NIPPLE SUCKER

WASP MEANS privilege—White Anglo-Saxon Protestant advantage to the *n*th degree. Private equity billionaire Carnegie VanderGild prevailed as the worst kind of WASP, one who scorned his own kind as weaklings. A predator capitalist so mean he made profit moguls like Elon Musk and Jeff Bezos look like sappy philanthropists when it came to doing business VanderGild chewed up the highest-power corporate WASP nests in America, spitting out board members and employees like bugs caught in the teeth of an outlaw biker racing his Harley cruiser 100 miles an hour on a dare into oncoming rush hour traffic down Highway 1.

Nothing scared or deterred VanderGild from cutting deals with the ease of an employee-of-the-month throat slitter at the chicken factory. After crushing the competition in the '90s Silicon Valley high tech market, he went on a serial killing spending spree building rockets for civilian space travel, experimental solar car prototypes, and artificial intelligence robots suitable for dating, intimate long-term relationships and marriage.

Still, Carnegie VanderGild had no conscience.

None.

Zip.

Zero and then some.

No conscience at all.

When VanderGild took the reins of the new cigarette business, VanderGild already had plans to addict every child in America he could hook. With the help of First Amendment lawyers and crooked politicians who made federal and state laws, he bought countless politicians whose campaign coffers VanderGild helped fill. They all agreed parents who smoked would decide, not government, if their little ones should use nicotine and at what age.

To entice the tykes, colorful images of original cartoon characters would populate comic books, television shows and full-length animated feature films. Modeled after cute and cuddly animals, the unique characters would all smoke cigarettes, encouraging youngsters to buy nicotine-laced candy smokes the way their grandparents did with harmless sugar sticks equipped with a red tip in the 1950s.

Nicotine-laced pacifiers would lead the smallest creepy crawlers from cradle to grave, Carnegie VanderGild's best idea yet. Next up was fruit-flavored nicotine-infused skin lotion for mom so she could soothe chapped breasts after baby tired gnawing on the tips and chomping at the bit for more milk, infusing her newborn with nicotine as soon as the little sucker locked lips around mommy's boob. Forget oysters; the world was Carnegie VanderGild's nipple.

Born in Sunnyvale in the Santa Clara Valley, little Carnegie's sensitive stomach soured early, as he greedily gobbled down fresh apricot, cherry, and prune baby food. Picky and prissy even then, the boy hated the messy mixture that caused him to spit up all over himself and develop a lifelong anxiety disorder.

By 10 years old, after succumbing to his earliest criminal instincts, stealing his dad's cigars and his mom's Pall Malls, he quelled his nerves with nicotine. Thrilled to find that lighting up a pack a day by the time he was 11 soothed his shakes, cigarettes also made him feel cool. Carnegie promised himself he'd grow up to be a real man unlike the educated milquetoast adults who lived on his street.

Cigarettes helped young Carnegie VanderGild come of age and would eventually influence his every move, shaping the new tobacco-addled world he envisioned. At his currently severely obsessed middle age, he still smoked three packs a day. If he smoked, everybody would smoke.

Scientists working his nicotine labs already knew Carnegie VanderGild expected them to find a way to inject nicotine directly into a pregnant woman's womb, perhaps under the guise of fetal vitamins prescribed by bought-and-paid-for physicians on the take, an umbilical cord connection that would fuel fetal smoking impulse long before birth. Unborn monsters like these would grow up to buy Carnegie VanderGild's tobacco products for the rest of their unfulfilled lives.

Santa Maria as a labor pool loomed perfectly on the business horizon. Mexicans and Mexican Americans would work for low wages, buy his various unhealthy products and never raise a stink about poor working conditions especially with discounted cigarettes as part of their employee benefit package. No health insurance, of course, but all the tobacco you could inhale and a free Ranchera music concert in the parking lot each month.

One of his security reconnaissance teams had discovered the secret box canyon in the hills where Carnegie VanderGild could chopper in a work crew to the fields, build a workers' camp and all-climate greenhouses for tobacco scientists to work planting even more instantly addictive mutated tobacco. Law enforcement agents would likely locate his operation, but he'd cross and burn that bridge when he came to it. Until then the new dope business was racing full speed ahead.

Carnegie VanderGild would soon own the Central Coast and the souls of the tobacco suckers who lived there.

Nipples for everybody.

 WE ARE NOT GRAPE JUICE

Wrinkling his nose Bud said, "Too sweet."

"Too skunky," he added, holding his nose.

Appalled and insulted at Bud's formal appraisal of yet another new batch of primo boutique Weed Wine Magic, Mel threatened to fire his assistant.

"You wanna get thrown off the bus? Huh? Do you?"

"C'mon, man," Bud said. "With my advanced MENSA mentality and chemistry background and your Mr. Natural savoir fare, we can tune up this brew and rip the world with a perfect product. Just two heads putting our two heads together. Get it? Get it? You're the Hoochy Hoochy Man!"

"OK," Mel said. "The state requires so-called weed wine producers to make a non-alcohol product. But non-alcoholic wine isn't wine at all. It's grape juice. Our brains may be loaded with zoot-suity fruity stripes, man, but we are not grape juice."

"We are definitely not grape juice," Bud said.

"We are not businessmen, either," Mel said. "The next thing you know we'll be wearing matching gold sport coats like those Century 21 real estate zombies."

Shuddering, Bud raised two forefingers to form the shape of a cross.

"My Weed Wine Magic is va-va-voom," Mel said. "As powerful as an asteroid shower landing on the roof. That's mighty impressive from an astral projection point of view, wouldn't you say?"

Enthralled, Bud paid very close attention.

"Together we find balance," Bud said. "We work in the magic room."

"Our heads are the magic room," Mel said. "We make Weed Wine Magic in the magic room."

"Most weed wine businesses pump about 20 to 40 mg of THC

in every bottle, roughly about 5 to 10 mg per glass, usually either indica or sativa strains," Bud said.

"That strains credulity," Mel said. "Get it, Bud? Strains? Get it, man?"

This stoned exchange went on for one whole week as Mel and Bud tweaked their secret recipe to give wine taster cannabis connoisseurs much better bud booze through science—15 percent alcohol plus a 60 mg hit of THC hybrid blend of sativa, indica and the secret common cannabis core of Hoocha Weed Mel Moyle called the "heart."

"Like the heart of a cabbage, artichoke, palm, celery, and romaine but alive at the core of its interaction with the human reactor, pure human fertilizer loaded with energized plant life," Mel said.

"You're talking too fast, man," Bud said. "I need time to process all those vegetables."

"You need a food processor," Mel said.

Anybody who knew weed and/or wine would swear this Weed Wine Magic world was an oncoming cannabis head-on collision.

Totally wrecked.

A faster blaster.

Even faster than that.

Va-va-va-voom.

HEARTBREAK DO TELL

"I DO," said El Chapstick.

"I don't," said Aunt Irma.

Little El, a small person who defied propriety by proudly calling himself a midget Mexican Elvis Presley impersonator, reached for the gold-plated derringer he carried behind his brick-sized rhinestone-studded belt buckle.

"I *will* blow off your kneecaps if I don't get paid," he said, looking up at El Chapstick.

"You told me Elvis would marry us," said Aunt Irma.

When Little El struck a combat karate pose, the raised collar of his white jumpsuit visibly wilted for lack of starch and regular dry cleaning. When he snapped a front kick into the air, still wet enchilada sauce from lunch flew off his white patent leather boot.

"I expected the real Elvis," Aunt Irma said.

"He's dead."

"Don't you dare talk about my Elvis that way," she said. "You better get me back to California right quick."

"What about our honeymoon at the Heartbreak Motel?"

Snatching the derringer from Little El's pudgy fingers in a move Aunt Irma learned from watching bootlegged Kung Fu movies, she pointed the gun at her jilted lover and said, "March."

Taking prisoners wasn't new for Aunt Irma. Over the years she captured her share of marauding outlaw Northern California pot growers when she served as a commandant in the late Commander Fetus' white man militia, the only woman in that unhinged bunch who, in many ways, was more man than all those bad old boys put together.

"You misled me," she said.

"But honey," El Chapstick said.

"Don't you honey me you butthole, you," Aunt Irma said, violently shoving the gun barrel against her former fiancé's backside, tearing the seam of his rented tuxedo and now probing into dark uncharted territory.

"Please don't shoot me in the behind," El Chapstick said.

Nine hours later, after taking countless wrong turns to locate the state line and winding up only 12 miles from Oceano on the road to Lopez Lake, Aunt Irma said, "I'm pulling over. I have to pee."

The sign along the road said *Black Bear Canyon*. Of the estimated 25,000 to 35,000 Ursus americanus californiensis living in California, one particular black bear family lived in this backwoods fringe of the Los Padres National Forest. A happy female and her two twin cubs the forest rangers called Karen & Company made their den in a small cave near a valley oak grove.

The aging 500-pound bear only wanted to be left alone as she tried to lose some weight after gorging too often on berries, plants, nuts, roots, honey, honeycomb, insects, larvae, carrion, and small mammals which she had given up out of the kindness of her heart. The cinnamon-colored black bear distrusted humans, of course, and did her best to stay out of their way.

Poachers had killed her partner a year ago and her twin daughters already were grizzled delinquents headed for bear reform school and bear state prison if they didn't straighten up and relinquish their grudge to get even for daddy bear's death. Black bears are rarely aggressive toward humans, but these two ignored the genetic message.

When Aunt Irma parked, Karen stood behind a tree watching another man in another car, a brand new expensive Mercedes that pulled up behind Aunt Irma and her captive. Stepping from the sleek luxury automobile, Carnegie VanderGild said to Aunt Irma, "I beg your pardon, but this is private property. This land is my land."

"Oh, yeah?" yelled Aunt Irma before belting out one of her favorite songs from when she sang as a little girl with the church choir, singing even then in a voice that rivaled a rusty chainsaw.

"This land is your land. This land is my land. From California to the New York island! From the redwood forest, to the Gulf Stream waters."

Raising her voice to a warped warble clamor of gnarled octaves, she wrapped up her solo with a note-bending grand finale: "This land was made for you and me!!!!"

Holding up thick hairy wrists bound with gray duct tape, El Chapstick grunted like a wild boar through the piece of tape Aunt Irma slapped across his mouth six hours earlier after tiring of hearing him whine.

"I'm a bounty hunter," Aunt Irma explained. "I always get my man."

"My dear lady," said Carnegie VanderGild who didn't get a chance to finish his sexist sentence.

After enduring a lifetime of misogynistic insults, Aunt Irma, no lady by any polite societal definition, saw the whites of his eyes and opened fire with Little El's derringer, the bullet tearing through the fleshy hanging lobule of VanderGild's left ear. Raw fear propelled her target with the energy of a double-doped Kentucky Derby thoroughbred leaving the starting gate, passing Karen at a sprint. The bear gave him a fair head start before beginning the chase.

With Aunt Irma otherwise occupied, El Chapstick, using sheer brute strength, freed his hands and took off in the other direction. Before she could raise the gun and fire, two pudgy juvenile delinquent bears with ants smeared around their mouths gave chase while making high-pitched laughing sounds that sounded hysterically human. Refusing to let nature run its course, Aunt Irma couldn't hold it any longer and squatted to pee. The woman had spunk all right, one reason Zita liked her from the moment they met.

As he ran El Chapstick hardly noticed the fly that landed on the helix of his right ear, crawled across the fossa, under the antihelical fold and into the ear canal. Nor did Carnegie VanderGild swat, ignoring his fly touching down on his lower antitragus, hopping over to the titragus and then digging and coming to rest at the ear drum.

Both fugitives eventually stuck fingers into their ears, but scratching came too late to save them. Both pregnant flies prepared to lay eggs and settled in for the duration. Both flies spoke to the men in the same voice.

People hear voices in their heads for various reasons. A magic spell, mental illness, an immediate traumatic stress disorder, guilty conscience, a desperate urge for repentance and basic human survival instincts can produce auditory hallucinations. Neither man knew where the voice in his head originated. All each man knew was the voice was real and he should listen. Each man did exactly what the voice told him to do. Each man received a different message, tailored to his individual needs.

Delirious with dread, feverish with terror, perhaps they were just talking to themselves.

Aunt Irma gleefully watched the panicked men run in different directions with playful bears hot on their tails. Opening the Mercedes driver's side door she saw unopened cartons of Neblina cigarettes strewn across the front seat. Aunt Irma used one of the new gold Zippo-type lighters bearing the Neblina brand name piled in a cardboard box, samples for distributors and future Neblina distribution managers, to light the visor above the steering wheel. Within minutes the car blazed like a winter solstice bonfire at a nude wizards' convention.

"Run, run," the voice said to El Chapstick.

"Faster, faster," the same voice said to Carnegie VanderGild.

El Chapstick whined louder than ever through the duct tape.

"Who are you?"

"Call me Syrah," said the voice. "You can trust me."

Aunt Irma pulled away from the chaotic scene in the big low-rider car El Chapstick stole from Jesús, who would surely forgive her once she explained how El Chapstick buffaloed her. Tripper once told her she really dug Elvis too, so she would definitely understand why Aunt Irma got so upset.

"Time to head home to the Cove," Aunt Irma said to herself. "I like living with those weird weed winos."

 # THE STRUGGLE CONTINUES

SUNRISE in the dunes always welcomed Eeshell to the raw western edge of America. After a long meditative walk to the ocean rim from her new home in the gingerbread-trimmed Victorian mansion to the ocean's edge, she stood for a moment to contemplate all she learned in the past few months.

After uncovering previously hidden truths and facing her deepest fears and roots, Eeshell felt fresher than ever. Despite the turmoil and chaos, she realized the innermost meaning of her life - to do good things, right wrongs when she could. The words came to her in a dream just the night before, words that hung around her heart like a cherished birthday locket dangling from a teenager's neck.

"It's nice to be nice."

Wearing a black one-piece bathing suit to keep from drawing the attention of early morning fishers, she stepped into the water and swam with strong, smooth strokes to the point where she last frolicked with her dolphin friends. Again they waited, greeting her with squeaks and gentle nudges, the same loving mammals that helped Zita on her long-ago swim to freedom.

Diving, Eeshell saw the sea from within. When she surfaced the world awaited. Finally knowing the truth she glided through the world as neither fish nor mermaid nor lost soul visitor from another galaxy, sensing connection not separation between herself and existence.

Sweet La Santa Muerte would guide her the way she had guided Zita. Drawing from the power of the ancients, good would always replace evil. Balancing the previously all-male rule of the Malverdes with feminist womanhood would be challenging. Yet, equalizing one species under the moon and the sun, indivisible, with liberty and justice for all who seek timeless liberation was not beyond Eeshell's reach.

When Eeshell got home her father greeted her at the door.

"Neither of us knew," she said.

"We were growing, you and I," Jesús said.

Eeshell wouldn't let go.

"Why did grandma keep the secret from us?"

"My mother wanted us to become our own people, mature enough to one day deal with each other."

"So she believed we're now both ready for anything."

"Are we?"

"Are you and Tripper really going to stay in Isla Mujeres?"

"If it's good enough for Ixchel, it's good enough for us."

"Can I come?"

Rarely uncertain, Jesús bit his lower lip. Sensing his concern Eeshell walked to his side and kissed him on the cheek.

"I'm just playing," she said. "I like it here. This is a good place for me. I feel infinite energy rising from those dunes. Grandma said cosmic radiance bubbles up from certain parts of the Earth. This is one of them."

"You're one of them, too," Jesús said.

"One of what?"

"One of the Dunites," Jesús said. "We all are. We're all part of the Dunite rebirth."

"I feel electric," Eshell said.

"Me, too," Jesús said. "We'll be back to visit. You planning to help Mel and Bud with the free Weed Wine Magic distribution? That's what everybody agreed to call the product, right? Weed Wine Magic?"

"I'm driving the bus," Eeshell said. "A real magic bus."

"Sounds good," Jesús said.

"The best part is it's all free," Eeshell said. "Bud has more money than he knows what to do with. Spoils from a dirty tobacco war. "

"Will you keep making jade jewelry?"

"Giving my necklaces away as gifts, too," Eeshell said. "Free is the operative word here."

"You know when I'm gone you're the last of the Malverdes?"

"With La Santa Muerte, Ixchel, and grandma as backup," Eeshell said.

"You think you're up to the job?"

"I come from good stock."

Feeling awkward as a proud father on the night of a quinceañera, Jesús fumbled for the right words.

"I love you," he said.

"That sounds weird coming from you," Eeshell said. "Guess I'll just have to get used to it."

"We're getting good getting used to weird," Jesús said.

"Nobody's weirder than Syrah," Eeshell said. "She tried to get into my head, but I talked her out."

"She never tried to get into mine," Jesús said.

"Mel's Ouija board says she's gone, that Syrah was just evil incarnate," Eeshell said.

"The struggle continues," Jesús said. "That witchy woman sure got around."

"Kindness frees our minds," Eeshell said.

"One nation under Dunites," said Jesús Malverde.

"Right on, dude," said Eeshell Malverde. "I mean Dad."

DEADWOOD IN THE FOREST

AFTER a week of pounding rains unlike any other downpour in the modern history of Central Coastal California, birdwatchers found two bodies washed up in a parking lot on the east side of Lopez Lake near Mallard Cove. Picked clean by condors nobody came forward to identify the rotted remains, although police agreed Carnegie VanderGild's missing person report could be shelved as a closed case.

If any good news existed in their demise, each body served as a maternity ward for the pregnant mother flies that landed in their ears. Each mother laid about 150 eggs. In the ensuing week they laid six more batches. All those baby flies were still living little fly lives when the shocked birdwatchers found the corpses.

Pathologists agreed the men died from broken bones and exposure to extreme elements of cold and torrential wind so strong boulders rolled over their limp bodies. A mudslide sent both corpses careening down a hill that caused lacerations. Sticks of various sizes stuck in orifices of various sizes. Nobody claimed either body.

The hedge fund investors disavowed Carnegie VanderGild, stating in a terse press release that as manager he had surreptitiously commandeered control of their money. The fund would demand that his estate pay back the theft. Future county, state, and federal court battles would ensue. Newspaper reports would detail divisive lawsuits, complete with juicy personal details, including relationships with husbands and wives of various Santa Maria public officials and Elks Club members. Social media would blast the lawyers, investors and consumer smokers themselves.

Tripper led a protest march through Santa Maria to demand closure of all local VanderGild-related cigarette factories, warehouses, and outlet stores, paid job training for the mostly local Latinx women who worked in these businesses and a permanent ban on smoking of any kind in California. Fighting a losing battle wasn't new to her. Tripper always won even when she lost. Fighting injustice is winning even when you're losing.

What no one would ever know is El Chapstick had survived the initial bear chase by climbing and sitting in an oak tree until he fell asleep. Carnegie VanderGild had done the same.

A voice in their heads awakened them.

The voice told them to jump.

 ¡OLÉ!

HOLDING a driftwood stick in each hand high above her head, Tripper imitated a bullfighter preparing to plunge the brightly colored harpoons called banderillas into a bull's neck. Her graceful movements rivaled anything you'd see in the 40,000 person capacity Mexico City bull ring packed for every fight. Lowering both arms at the same time, Tripper imitated sticking the sharp barbs that stay in the neck of the bull for the remainder of the bullfight. The steel spears anger and slow the bull before he dies.

"That was practice," Tripper said. "In real life they'll go deep into the flesh of El Matador's ass."

A spellbound Eeshell watched from her cross-legged seat in the sand.

"How deep?"

"Not enough to kill him but enough to make my point that bullfighting is cruel and must be banned throughout Mexico."

"¡Olé!" said Eeshell. "But you're not moving to where they fight bulls in Mexico. You're going to Isla Mujeres."

"We can thank Maya moon goddess Ixchel for guiding me to her island of and for women," Tripper said. "Mostly we can thank Zita's Maya roots."

"Yeah, cool. Dad says I can come visit." Eeshell said. "Me and my jade."

"Your jade?"

"Maya jewelry dates back 5,000 years," Eeshell said. "Mayas were master jewelers who valued jade as the ultimate symbol."

"Symbol of what?"

"Eternal love," Eeshel said.

"Maybe you'll stay," Tripper said.

"Maybe I will," Eeshell said.

"We can help the sea turtles," Tripper said. "Did your dad show you the poem he wrote about the sea turtles?"

"No way," Eeshell said.

"I memorized it," Tripper said. "Listen."

Closing her eyes and keeping them shut until she finished, she recited, "You couldn't see them at first, but they were out there, bobbing helmeted heads, riding the tide, ancient surfers from faraway lands a thousand miles away. Swimming toward edgy earth to accept Ixchel's help in choosing a mate, connecting in cosmic unity, giving birth to new life that awakened in sifting sand before crawling slowly with baby turtle steps back to the sea."

"He really wrote that?"

"A poet who's beginning to know it," Tripper said.

"He couldn't do it without you," Eeshell said.

"Or you," Tripper said. "You realize I'm your stepmother now."

"I'm glad you are," Eeshell said, lowering her eyes to watch tiny sand hopper beach fleas scamper across her toes. "Do you think people will ever stop hurting and killing each other?"

"No," said Tripper.

"What can we do to make the world better?"

"Be kind," Tripper said. "But be smart. Help when we can. Don't buy into the bullshit."

Spinning with the ease of a seasoned matador performing a Veronica, Tripper planted both spears in the sand and walked to the water's edge.

"Let's go for a swim," she said.

"Look who's waiting for us," Eeshell said.

About 100 yards offshore a small gathering of green sea turtles waited in the rising and falling water.

"They must like my dad's poem," Eeshell said.

WHERE NIRVANA HAPPENS

BACK in her room at the Cove that afternoon Eeshell locked the door and kneeled before the La Santa Muerte shrine she had created on an end table she bought at a Halcyon yard sale. Spotless and neat, all the offerings she placed on the table carried unique symbolic meaning.

A Zippo lighter-sized jade likeness of Ixchel she recently carved into the face of a stone sat in one corner. Four empty washed and polished halves of two Pismo Clam shells as big as tea saucers sat in the other corner. A rubbery bundle of wild white sage she picked in the mountains and tied with a red string lay on the altar. A purple statue of La Santa Muerte stood at the center of the table Eeshell had covered with a purple velvet scarf.

Bowing her head Eeshell asked for help.

"You, who dispense justice and equality, please give me a sign you will strengthen my resolve to live as the best Malverde ever," Eeshell said.

Zita's long-time-coming confession confused and emboldened Eeshell. Yet, she worried she couldn't handle the responsibility and expectations of living up to the Malverde legacy.

Within seconds she felt a gentle wind tickle the back of her neck. Standing and turning in a smooth motion, Eeshell skipped like an excited child to the open window. Peculiar dark clouds had parted. A wide full rainbow arched north to south over what locals called the Irish Hills, glowing mostly purple amid radiant bowed variegation of psychedelic melded color.

Eeshell wondered if she had fallen into a trance. Was she seeing life clearly for the first time with her psychic third eye? Closing her eyes she saw, even felt, brilliant flashes that reminded her of trippy light shows Mel Moyle told her about seeing when he hung out with wise pranksters and happy Deadheads during early con-

303

certs at the Fillmore West Ballroom.

That's when Eeshell saw the fairy, a tiny winged sprite sitting on La Santa Muerte's shoulder. The fairy called out "Eeshell" in a Gaelic Irish brogue. This fairy was no Hollywood cartoon Tinkerbell. This fairy was as real as the Irish fairies Mel Moyle talked about, marveling how the queen of the Dunites chose him with whom to talk regularly as she checked in with freaky long-haired, bell-bottomed, tie-dyed Irish fairies who lived and partied till eternity in the dunes. Mel boasted of his own proud Irish descent and the honor bestowed upon him by an Irish queen named Ella who helped him through rough times.

Now feeling close to Ella although they had never met, Eeshell asked for Ella's help the way she once asked Zita to show her the way. Women helping women, especially since she now carried the sacred burden passed down from the men in her family. In the search for truth good *can* triumph over evil. Still, guarantees only exist in minds of naïve daydreamers. Truth often surfaces in the dark with teeth. The truth often hurts. Anxious and afraid, Eeshell wasn't ready for the epiphany that hit her with the mind-bending jolt of a 650-volt electric eel strike.

The Dunite spirit and the Maya spirit is the same spirit, the nexus where nirvana prevails. No separation existed between her and Maya moon goddess Ixchel after whom she was named. No difference existed between Zita's mother's Maya bloodline, Ella, La Santa Muerte and Eeshell. All shared the same female will. All stood against injustice. All searched for truth.

With them by her side Eeshell couldn't fail.

"Couldn't?" asked the nice little fairy who read Eeshell's mind.

"Wouldn't," replied Eeshell.

"Want to dance?" asked the little far-out fairy.

"Of course," Eeshell said, rushing to put on a CD, her already out-of-date way to play music. Although she usually kept her preference to herself, Mexican electronic dance music energized the hidden subconscious self she worked so hard to polish. Techno beats arose from ancient rhythms, jungle drums and the sound of monkeys laughing in trees. Eeshell's soul music provided a living connection to her past, present, and future. Feeling wildly animated, celestially spirited, Eeshell couldn't help herself.

Although she would remain living on the Central Coast for now, in her mind she felt drawn to Isla Mujeres where she vowed to one day visit. Hot sun and pure white sand glistened in sweat and tequila, bathing the island of women in the sweet mysteries of life, a transmigration of Mesoamerican tribal vibes that boogied into the future.

Eeshell and her new tiny fairy friend danced and danced.

Then they danced some more.

 # BONGO BEACH PARTY

Racing hell-bent from one end of Guadalupe Beach to the other, the dune buggy bucked like a bronco stabbed with an electric cattle prod, kicking up sand, sliding into foamy waves, and spinning in circles until thick bald rubber tires finally freed the groaning machine.

Alive and screaming the engine matched Adam's roars. Within the past 24 hours Adam snorted, shot, swallowed and smoked a combination of drugs that included cocaine, methamphetamine, oxycodone, PCP-laced pot, crack, Pabst beer, and Ex-Lax maximum strength stimulant laxative that propelled him ready to rock with the exuberance of a blitzed high school marching band playing a raucous off-key Star-Spangled Banner.

After parking in the vacant macadam lot Jesús slid from the driver's side of his car and walked to the beach. Smoothing creases in the folds of his skirt-like hakama, the samurai dress of ancient Japanese warriors, he bounced on the sand cushion beneath his bare feet. Soft and newly-washed, his white gi top smelled of strawberry/apple scented soap.

Guadalupe Beach was where he first met Wally Wilson, his deadly friend from a dangerous time who journeyed as far into himself as he could before exploding into flames that destroyed the uncontrolled violence that defined his melancholy life.

Dressed for aikido practice instead of a bar fight, Jesús focused on slowing his pulse and relying on muscle memory that kicked in from that night long ago when he, too, lost control and killed a man in a nightclub parking lot. Dressed now for a spiritual encounter rather than a brawl, he ambled toward the buggy with smooth confidence and dignity.

Adam braked as soon as he spotted the lean imposing figure approach. Pointing and hooting, he beat his hands on the steering wheel. Spit dribbled from his mouth. Cords in his neck strained against peeling sunburned skin as he repeated the same maniacal mantra over and over again.

"Man in a dress, man in a dress."

A prairie falcon circled high in the sky.

"Peace, man," Jesús said. "Relax."

"Look who it is," Adam said. "Steven Sea Gull."

"You need help, brother," Jesús said. "Let me help you."

Jumping from the dune buggy, Adam waved a corroded steel pipe wrench he held in his left hand.

"I got something to help you," he said.

Raising his hands in a nonviolent gesture that also provides his first line of defense, giving him distance from which to move when the time comes, Jesús spoke in a tone smooth as one of Eeshell's polished stones.

"We're not all that different," he said, noticing the tattoo inked into Adam's chest where the crooked red and blue Pabst Blue Ribbon emblem of a 16 ounce 6-pack glistened in Adam's dirty sweat.

"I ain't you," said Adam. "You're one of them."

"One of who?"

"The Mexican Martian Mafia," Adam said.

Unhinged, Adam foamed at the mouth. Brandishing the rusty pipe wrench, he lurched toward Jesús who saw the pistol grip protruding from the snakeskin holster Adam wore hanging low on his hip like a saloon-soused Wild West gunfighter reeling in a spaghetti western movie.

When Adam swung Jesús stepped in, entering the chaos, welcoming the attack as a gift, catching the haymaker right with his left hand that easily slid down his attacker's arm to a wrist thick as a worn hangman's rope. Redirecting the weight of the wrench and Adam's forward motion, he applied a right handhold above his left wrist to create a tight double grip. Raising and stepping under Adam's arm, Jesús lifted his shoulder, turned his body to the right and extended both arms.

Controlling Adam's balance, he held Adam's outstretched arm and wrist in his hands the way a samurai holds the tsuka or handle of a traditional katana sword. Jesús considered cutting in one swift downward motion, snapping Adam's arm at the elbow and shoulder. The aikijujutsu combat technique called shihonagi is designed for self-defense and survival on the battlefield, a death-giving force.

Instead of a fatal cut Jesús gently lowered Adam to the sand the way iconic aikido founder O'Sensei polished the technique into a life-giving sword and the way of peace and harmony.

Swiftly reaching to Adam's hip Jesús drew the gun from the holster, throwing the deadly weapon far into the wet sand. Restraining Adam was easy as pouring strong saké for a friend at a Japanese cherry blossom festival.

The bird continued to circle. Climbing higher and higher, the falcon veered left, banked and abruptly changed direction, diving and picking up speed with talons outstretched and headed for Adam's upturned face, the sharp hooks headed for Adam's eyes.

After having tripped a few times in the past on acid and organic purple mescaline, Jesús tried to clear his head of this delusional mirage. How could gold corkscrew-shaped talons tip the ends of the bird's legs as the predator descended in a rush of death from above?

Wally once reveled in popping despicable chardonnay drinkers' eyeballs with a corkscrew, the tool Santa Barbara wine snobs embraced until they forever lost sight of their good life. Wally once ran amok in the vineyards of the Central Coast. Wally would know Adam couldn't even spell chardonnay. Yet Wally seemed to still want revenge.

Psychedelic images can vary as sour chemicals in the brain hotwire, mix, mingle and play tricks on dancing cells. When Jesús tripped he saw what he wanted to see or what the spirits moved him to see. Undulating walls melted into flower power orange elevator lights flashing lucky numbers of the high-rise floors before you reached the stairway to heaven. That actually once happened to Jesús as he sat on a motel elevator floor shooing people away from the doors as they opened floor after floor.

Had somebody dosed Jesús without his knowledge? Was Jesús watching Adam's future unfold in the sky? Would Wally kill again, using his trademark means of gouging out the eyeballs of yet another victim Wally personally sentenced to death? Did Wally's final pure enlightenment wash away like crushed body parts beneath the gush of a high-powered fire hose at the scene of a fatal car accident? Would this reincarnated Wally Wilson again offer vicious retribution to the world he once so easily doled out like pineapple chunks at a vintner's picnic? Would love still elude Wally as he nestled in the soft bosom of the cosmos?

Swirling clouds gathered like an ice cream cone tornado in the darkening sky above Jesús' head. Pressure from thick humid air gripped his skull fast as a tightening vice in a high school wood shop. Electric music blasted in his ears, classic California surf songs with bongos pounding out a foreboding beat. Wally's favorite loony tunes! Sixties songs Wally loved that laid down the deadly soundtrack of his demise,

"No, Wally, no," Jesús growled through fangs pushing through bleeding gums.

Dropping to his knees he found comfort in strength he shared with a male jaguar preparing to pounce on wide paws with splayed hunter's claws. On all fours now the spirit animal that mirrored his true self, the jaguar—not the coyote that killed the killer in prison and the Crushers Motorcycle Club president in Shell Beach—now protected Adam's unconscious six foot body sprawled on the earth.

Frenzied and dazed, Jesús closed his bright animal eyes that flashed reddish golden yellow in the sun. Preparing to take the falcon's hit, he braced for searing pain from the pointy twisted corkscrew nails ripping flesh from his shoulders as he tried to save Adam's life.

Wally softly landed on Jesús' back, pecking gently, kissing his friend on the neck.

Behind a nearby mountainous dune, a five-member traditional coyote family watched the tragedy unfold. Silent predators witnessing other living, breathing beasts negotiate existential coincidence and uncertainty, they began to howl.

Raging clouds dissipated as Jesús pushed off Adam's body and stood brushing sand from his hakama. Feeling human again, he spread his fingers and looked at his hands, relieved to see wet sand, not blood, beneath his fingernails. Adam's eyes flared wide as new dimes flattened by a freight train as he began to convulse from the accumulation of fentanyl and other poison in his system, his tortured heart winding down like a toy race car run off the rails.

Dead.

Opening wide wings the falcon lifted off Jesús' back as smoothly as it had landed. Conscience dictates predation. Instinct guides choice. Animals evolve.

Watching the bird climb Jesús wept.

Finally able to resist the savage temptation of violence, the now peaceful prairie falcon carried Wally Wilson's born-again spirit over the sea. Beneath his wings he watched traffic, people walking the dog beach and boats bobbing in the harbor. Before landing near Reefer's grave behind the big communal house in Oceano, the prairie falcon momentarily hovered in the wind, reaching to clasp his talons around the handle of the gold corkscrew engraved with the words "AVILA BEACH" Mel Moyle had respectfully placed on the mound of dirt.

Lifting off again the big bird climbed over Port San Luis Harbor. Two miles out he purposely dropped the corkscrew, watching the glinting metal turn over and over on its way to an unexplored stop in the sea. Enjoying the ride, Wally Wilson kept flying, raising his face to meet cool mist in the air and warmth rising from the ground.

Disappearing into the bright horizon, no one on the ground noticed the fleeting glimmer cast off the small silver peace sign held by a cheap thin chain dangling from the falcon's neck.

# ISLA MUJERES MAGIC

TAKING our time getting to Cancún makes sense. El cheapo lodging on the way, roadside food stand corn tortillas filled with ripe grilled vegetables, iced cold beer, and fresh blue tequila sound too good to be true.

"I hate Cancún," I say.

"Me, too," says Tripper.

That's why we'll sell the retro low-rider car when we get there to the first homie we find who will jump at the chance to own a sweet Chicano carriage. Then we jump on the ferry a half hour across the Caribbean and land on Isla Mujeres.

Again I read the last note my mother wrote to me.

"Scatter my ashes from the Punta Sur cliffside, the southernmost tip of the Island of Women. The time has come to connect with my mother's ancestors who await me in this sacred place."

Zita said Tripper and I should forever remain with her on this small island off the coast of the Yucatán Peninsula. Zita never realized her dream of visiting. Now she'll stay forever helping Ixchel rule our universe.

"I'm in," Tripper says. "No more rocket launcher attacks."

Regalo breathes a sigh of relief. Guarding me takes his full-time attention. A bodyguard scorpion simply doesn't have time for a girlfriend. He and the fierce female lizard he met said their respectful goodbyes over a last romantic meal of mice and beans. Add Tripper to Regalo's security duty and no time exists for a mixed marriage between crawling species. I have been talking to Regalo, though, about introducing him to a nice black tarantula.

Until we reach our destination Regalo will look after Zita's ashen cremains contained in the small jewelry box Eeshell carved from driftwood and topped with a half-dollar-sized piece of polished lavender Big Sur grape jade. Zita cherished that box in which she stored her favorite Maya-style red glass ceremonial necklace complete with animal charms including fish, birds, rabbits and other creatures, a gift her mother gave her when Zita was young.

Eeshell will now wear the necklace.

Me?

I'm not promising anybody anything but a small storefront aikido dojo in the center of town where I can teach the art of peace and harmony, non-fighting rather than war. Tripper can raise as much hell as possible fighting for the Earth and the animals of the planet—peacefully, of course.

At least that's Tripper's plan. Combat-tested radical feminist guerrilla eco-warriors usually keep armed resistance as an option. Tripper promises to give peace a chance. That's all I can ask from her, myself, or anybody else committed to standing against injustice in the face of what look like insurmountable odds.

I'm told most Mexican cartel leaders, even those united against Sinaloa, respect the Malverde legend. Sinaloa bosses watch out for Isla Mujeres and Cancún to protect the tourist trade. In the event of trouble I'll do my best to mediate. I expect no favors.

Some believe I am the physical embodiment of my blood ancestor Jesús Malverde.

Some don't believe.

Most heed the power of the legend.

Deniers usually keep their thoughts to themselves. Those who show faith, even some members of my enemies' families, aspire to walk the path of the outlaw patron saint. These men and women do not treat disrespect kindly. Word's already circulating that Tripper carries La Santa Muerte's personal blessing, a partnership no cartel dares challenge. Jesús Malverde and La Santa Muerte make an unheard of and unbeatable team.

Tripper points to the new tattoo inked in burnished brownish orange with black spots that runs from the inside of my elbow to my wrist, a prowling jaguar among a rosette pattern of yellow dots so vividly cut and colored the lines undulate when I move my arm.

"What's with the big cat?"

"My new animal spirit."

"No more coyote?"

"The coyote reflects the past."

"You give him a name?"

"He's a she. The Maya called her Bahlam. My mother is of maternal Maya descent, remember?"

"A jaguar and not a coyote?"

"If I'm tempted to dismiss my past, the jaguar will remind me of my hidden self," I say. "Bahlam means 'he who kills with one blow.' "

"You and the coyote have grown," Tripper says.

"Survivors always do," I say.

"I can dig that," Tripper says. "I read jaguars see into the future. Intuitive and decisive, they move between worlds, between night and day, between light and dark."

"Just like us," I say.

"Just like us," Tripper says.

# EVOLUTION REVOLUTION

Syrah's whisper carried on Dunite fairies' wings.

"Wally," she said. "Wally, it's me."

Sailing through milky clouds, the startled prairie falcon heard Syrah's hypnotic murmur and expected the worst. Closing both eyes in anticipation of her attack, he held his breath.

"I love you, Wally," Syrah said in a tender voice.

The bird's beating heart quickened at the surprise thought of devotion. Syrah died long ago, releasing her vicious hold on Wally's mind in the afterlife of a physical renewal that changed him from human to falcon. Wally died as well, reincarnated to soar alone above the savage society that once coldly rejected his existence.

How could Syrah be reborn, this time to embody true love as a mate? Could Wally, a former psychedelic serial killer, finally share a trusting and sanctified relationship with a transformed demon who loved him as much as he loved her?

To take seriously such psychobabble is insane.

Madness lacks a mind.

Tell yourself birds don't fall in love the next time you see a nuzzling couple of tender turtle doves and hear them coo. How about a matching pair of crimson cardinals building a nest together, teaching a frazzled fledgling to fly and spending the rest of their lives together? Can't you feel the sanguine moods of men and women possessed by evil as they look for true love to rescue them from hatred?

Of course you can.

Wally and Syrah's crystalline conscience, now aware and alive with unlimited mercy, savors nature's potential in a vast unlimited sky. If greed and loathing, hostility and revenge one day falter, a heartening wave of goodness just might wash our world.

Maybe this faithful couple's one-time acute reflections of lunacy will again incarnate, this time shifting into an evolution revolution. Imagine a wide arching rainbow, a bright candy-colored symbol of lustrous life, a splashy crescent spectrum magically appearing even at night lit in dazzling moonlight as a supernatural beacon for the blazing cosmos promising Earth another fresh and beautiful chance.

Wish for it.

Go ahead.

Wish.

The End

Email Steve at
stephencorbett01@comcast.net
or through his website at
theoutlawcorbett.com

www.ingramcontent.com/pod-product-compliance
Lightning Source LLC
Chambersburg PA
CBHW072107020726
47501CB00003B/740